Barenaked Jane

Also by Deanna Lee:

Undressing Mercy

Barenaked Jane

DEANNA LEE

APHRODISIA

KENSINGTON BOOKS

http://www.kensingtonbooks.com

For Erica and Annette whose patience, amazing wit, support, and friendship got me through more than one day while writing this book.

In memory of Rita K. Musgrave who blessed me with a great friend and the world with three beautiful children before her passing. May we all be so lucky in love and in life.

1

Life doesn't play fair. In fact, it cheats, lies, and steals its way through a person without a single thought to the consequences of its actions. Since I know this, I really shouldn't have been surprised to find myself in my situation. Flat on my back, beneath a strange man.

Since he probably outweighed me by at least a hundred pounds, struggling would've been a waste of energy. How many minutes had passed since I'd heard something outside my office and had gone to investigate? I should've stayed hidden after I'd called the police. Instead, I'd stalked out of my office, determined to give the intruder a piece of my mind and maybe kick his ass in the process. I'm really not a stupid woman, honest.

The man had fended me off effortlessly and tossed me on the floor as if I weighed nothing. Every minute of my training at the police academy in Georgia and hours of kickboxing lessons had proved useless in a matter of seconds. The man, whomever he was, hadn't hurt me more than it was necessary to subdue me, and he was putting off an air of shocked frustration.

He was built well, firm muscle and sleek warm body pressed

all over me. It had been, for a few seconds, sort of exciting. Then, since I'm normal, panic set in. Being underneath a man was one of the most vulnerable situations a woman could be in. I was exposed to all manner of physical insults. As yet, he'd done nothing but hold me down and growl with frustration.

"If you promise not to hit me, I believe that we can both get up without causing each other further harm." His voice was soft in my ear. I thought for a second that his lips had brushed against my earlobe.

I took a deep breath and turned my head abruptly away from the sound of his voice. The pitch-black room offered me not a single advantage. I glanced toward the flashlight he'd had; it lay a few feet from us pointed, of course, in the opposite direction.

"I'm going to punch you in the face as hard as I can." And I was. My fingers balled into a tight fist just thinking about it.

"Lady, you're trying my patience." He lifted his head away from mine and sighed.

Trying his patience? He was holding me down on the floor and *I* was the one being aggravating? "The last man that spent this much time on top of me was at least *trying* to make me happy." I bucked upward against him and hissed in frustration.

The man stilled completely and then to my utter amazement started to laugh. "Jane?"

His use of my name shocked me into being still for a few long seconds. Who the hell was he and why did he feel comfortable enough in his knowledge of me to use my first name? "Get the hell off of me." I jerked at my hands and tried to push him off me. It was like trying to move a wall.

"Promise not to hit me," he demanded, his voice soft with amusement now.

"Like hell I will. You break into my workplace, sneak around like a thief, and then hold me down on the floor . . . and you honestly expect me not to hit you?" I was going to hit him and enjoy it.

"I'm not sneaking around like a thief. If I'd been sneaking around you wouldn't have known I was here," he responded, his voice tinged with disappointment and something that sounded a little like embarrassment.

"But you did break in." Why the hell was I arguing with a thief? "How dare you break in here! This gallery is a nonprofit organization and all of its proceeds go to the Holman Foundation. I can't believe anyone would be so low as to steal from a charity." Jerking against him again, I gasped and winced when my hip protested. A sharp pain dug through my hip, down the thigh muscle all the way to the knee. "You're hurting me."

"No, you're hurting yourself," he snapped. "And for the record, I've never stolen a single thing in my life."

"Not one thing?" I didn't believe him for a second. Everyone has stolen something.

"Never."

"Office supplies from work?"

"No."

"Candy when you were five?"

"No."

No one beats me at this game. "A pen from a bank?"

"I . . . bloody hell, woman. Pens from banks don't count."

"Did you pay for it?"

"No."

"Was there a sign that said 'Please take our pens you thief'?"

"No," he ground out through clenched teeth.

"Then don't tell anyone that horrible lie again. You *have* stolen something," I responded, smug.

"I am not a criminal."

"You broke into this building," I reminded, aware that I was probably very close to pushing him too far.

"Yes. It's my job." He lifted off me and pulled me roughly into a sitting position. "You're Jane Tilwell. You have brown hair with blonde highlights that is cut way too short for a woman, blue eyes, and you're the assistant director of this gallery."

"Too short?"

"That's what I said."

"You don't like the highlights?" I frowned. My hair stylist had caught me in a weak moment.

"I liked your natural color better."

"Well, who the hell cares what you think?" I jerked at one hand and was surprised when I broke free. I slapped him across the face and would've done it again if he hadn't grabbed my arm. "Let me go."

He pulled me forward abruptly to keep me still and demanded, "Don't you want to know who I am?"

"No. I want you to get your ass off me." I used my arms to shove at his chest, but it did no good. "Get off me."

"We wouldn't be in this position if you hadn't attacked me."

"I was defending myself." Well, not true. I had attacked him, but I was defending the gallery, and that meant a lot to me even if it had been a stupid thing to do.

"You were risking your life over a thing." He jerked at my arms a little as if to shake me. "A thing. A few scribbles on a piece of canvas that only have meaning because rich snobs think they do. My five-year-old cousin could've painted that crap for all anyone knows. You're just lucky that I'm not a criminal."

"Don't you dare lecture me! You don't know a damn thing about me or how important this place is to me. You've no right whatsoever telling me what is and is not worth fighting for." I jerked back but didn't break free of his grip. "You're also holding me hostage. From my point of view, you're passing from illegal entry with intent to commit grand larceny into felony kidnapping."

He got to his feet abruptly and pulled me to my feet in a single breathless second. "I've never hit a woman in my life, but if you even think about kneeing me I'm going to knock you out."

"I wouldn't kick you in the crotch."

"That's a relief to know."

"As far as I know, your cock could be the only thing you've got going for you." I pulled free of his hold and would have punched him if he hadn't backed away. Almost immediately, I missed the heat of his body. That was irritating. I had no business thinking about a criminal that way. "Turn the fucking lights on."

"Nice language."

"I can say a lot worse, asshole." And I probably would. The man had knocked my world off kilter in more ways than one, and I had a lot to say about that.

In the dark, and now from a few feet instead of inches, I could barely keep track of his movements until he picked up the flashlight. I watched the beam of light run across the wall to the left of him until he encountered the light switch.

I blinked against the light as he flipped it on before settling my gaze on him for the very first time. And his dick wasn't the only thing he had going for him. He looked like sin. Rich, chocolate sin. He was at least six feet, and the dark jeans he wore hugged against a trim, tight waist.

I looked over his face, taking in the smooth lines, full but masculine lips, and the slight slant at the corner of his eyes. He was beautiful and it was irritating. What man needed a face like an angel?

The man was insanely attractive, but even good-looking men can be psychos. I backed up a few steps from him and surveyed my surroundings.

We were in the middle of the second floor where Shamus Montgomery's latest collection was being displayed. There wasn't a single thing in the room I could pick up and use for a weapon, except for his flashlight. I glanced toward it; he held it tight in his hand.

"Don't even think about it."

I met his gaze and took another step back. "What are you doing in here if you don't plan to steal anything?"

"I'm doing my job, as I've already explained."

I could've laughed. "Who the hell has a job that involves breaking into art galleries?"

"Mercy Rothell hired me to test the security of the gallery. My name, Ms. Tilwell, is Mathias Montgomery," he said, delivering his news with an understated arrogance that was so irritating and yes, attractive, that I could barely stand to look at him.

Mathias Montgomery.

Great. Just great. Of all the would-be thieves that I had to go attack it just had to be the older brother of my boss's future husband. It was one of those moments when I wished the floor would open up and swallow me whole. How many times had Mercy discussed the security of the building with me in recent weeks? Too many to count, as it had become her favorite subject after she'd become director.

Since James Brooks had put her off repeatedly, she'd been plotting drastic measures. I hadn't thought it would include a mock break-in. Well, she'd certainly found a way to get his attention.

"I didn't realize you'd already made the move to Boston." I grimaced at the weakness I heard in my words.

He pointed one finger at me. "You just can't go around—"

"Don't lecture me. I'm a grown-ass woman, and if I wanted to be lectured by a man who *thinks* he knows what's good for me I'd have stayed in Savannah under my brother's thumb. Besides, I thought you were a thief." Getting my back up about something made me feel better. I straightened my shoulders and glared at him.

"Why? Because all black men are criminals?" he demanded, his tone just a hair from being petulant.

"No, you jackass, because you were skulking around an art gallery dressed in dark clothes with a flashlight." I crossed my arms over my breasts, disappointed that I would resort to such a defensive gesture, and glared. "What? Do you think all southerners are racist?"

"Of course not."

I tilted my head and looked him over. He really was quite pretty, for an asshole. "I called the police."

"Great."

"It's your own damn fault." I turned on my heel and walked away. "You'd better be able to produce identification, Mr. Montgomery, or I'm going to see you handcuffed and charged with criminal trespassing, attempted burglary, and assault."

"Lady, you assaulted me!"

"That's not the way I'm going to tell it." I stalked toward the stairs that led up to the administrative floor.

He'd certainly proved that the gallery's security was bad. Beyond bad, which put me on edge. I'd honestly never worried about my safety in the gallery. We have six guards during the day and one at night. I turned abruptly and glared at him. "What did you do to Wendell?"

"He's not here."

"Excuse me?" I tucked my hands behind my back to keep from putting them on my hips. How dramatic would that have looked?

"Your so-called security guard left the parking lot more than twenty minutes ago and hasn't been back. I've been watching this place for a week, and he's done the same thing every night." He glared at me as if it were my fault. "You're just lucky it was me casing this place and not someone with more sinister motives."

"Great." I winced at the sound of sirens. It had taken nearly fifteen minutes for a police response. "Well, I guess I can be fortunate you aren't a criminal."

"You'd best call Mercy and the owner."

Yes, indeed. I was never, ever going to live this down. Miserable, I went up the stairs and headed toward my office. I turned at the stairs and looked toward him. "You'd better not go anywhere."

"I wouldn't dream of it."

"So, let me get this straight."

By this time, I had both hands covering my face. It was the third time I'd had to repeat what had happened, and this time it was for James Brooks—the owner of the gallery and the only man in recent memory that intimidated me. I hated that I had disappointed him.

"You're working late, *again*. At some point, you realize that there is a stranger in the building. Instead of tripping the alarm, calling the police, and locking your door—you call the police and then set out to apprehend him on your own."

"I acted without thinking." But admitting that I did something stupid wasn't exactly my strong suit, and I knew that I didn't sound nearly as contrite as he would have liked.

"You certainly did."

I dropped my hands and met his gaze. "It was a mistake."

He glared, but I could tell he was far more disappointed and worried than angry. "It certainly was."

"Mr. Brooks . . ."

"Don't 'Mr. Brooks' me, Jane. You could've gotten yourself killed."

"But I didn't."

"That's really beside the point." He stood from the chair he'd been sitting in like a king and glared pointedly at me. "This place is important to me and it was important to my mother. She dedicated her life to it, and I do in turn to honor her memory. Having said that, I'll say this. Nothing in this place is more valuable to me than the lives of the people who work for me. If this were to ever happen again I would expect you to hide and wait for help. Do you understand?"

"Perfectly."

"Good." He sighed. "Now, Mercy is going to come in here and pamper you like women do. I'm going to get a drink because you've scared ten years off my life."

"I'm not weak."

"No. You aren't." He leaned against the side of my desk, reached out, and tilted my face up until our gazes met. "You're also quite priceless to me, Ms. Tilwell. Remember that."

I sat back in my chair and watched him walk out of my office into the bull pen. He'd knocked the wind out of my sails. "Damn it."

"What a dirty mouth you have."

I looked up and offered my friend and boss, Mercy Rothell, a smile. "Hey."

"So, GI Jane, I'd lecture you if I didn't know James had already done it." She glanced out into the bull pen where he was talking with Mathias Montgomery. "You also gave him quite a scare."

"It was a stupid thing to do." I held up my hands in a sign of defeat and then relaxed back in my chair.

"Granted." She sat down in the chair that James had abandoned. "So, just how long did the two of you tumble around on the floor?"

I flushed and then bit down on my lip. "Mercy."

"What? So you weren't sprawled underneath him for several minutes?"

"You make it sound tawdry."

"I was just hoping."

"I thought he was a criminal."

"A pretty fine criminal, I'd say." She grinned. "The good thing is that James is so rattled that he's agreed to upgrade the security in the building and get us a new security firm contract."

"I wasn't sprawled."

"Sure sounded like you were." Mercy laughed when I glared at her.

I glanced out toward the men. "He *is* pretty."

"I've come to think all the Montgomery men are."

"Why didn't you tell me he was here?" Well, that sounded childish. I hated being whiny; it totally conflicted with my internal image of myself.

"I didn't know. If he'd told us he was coming to do it tonight, we might have altered how we do things. An honest assessment of the business was important to determine our security needs."

An honest assessment. "In retrospect, he's not a very good burglar. He made enough noise to wake the dead."

She laughed. "That can hardly be a detraction."

"When you and Shame talked about him, neither of you mentioned how arrogant he is."

Mercy grinned. "I sort of like arrogant men. He spent four years in the army and six in the FBI before he went into the private security sector, so maybe there is an aura about him. As if he knows how capable he is." She stood. "Now, I'm going to go home and crawl into my bed. I'll see you on Monday."

At least I had the weekend to recover. I glanced out toward the bull pen just in time to see James wave good-bye. "Hey, I'll walk out with you."

Mercy laughed. "Actually, I think your *burglar* isn't quite finished with you."

I watched, exasperated, as she greeted her future brother-in-law with affection and swished away. They'd left me alone with him. It was obvious that I needed to choose friends and employers more carefully in the future.

Careful not to look in his direction, I picked up my purse and headed toward my office door. He was standing just outside of it and let me get just about a foot past him before he took my arm and brought me around to face him.

"Mr. Montgomery, I assure you that I've been manhandled about all I can handle this evening." I looked pointedly at his hand and then met his gaze. "I think it might be best if you gave me some space."

He released my arm. "I owe you an apology. I'm not normally so rough with women."

"I *was* trying to hit you in the head." I ran my fingers through my hair and then met his gaze. "Is my hair really too short?"

"Shamus seems to think so." He touched my chin gently and tilted my head. "But it suits your face."

I took a step back; his touch was pleasant and far too distracting for my peace of mind. "I should be going."

"Let me walk you to your car."

"I can take care of myself." I lifted my chin and met his gaze with all the determination I could muster. Just because he'd tossed me around like I weighed five pounds and made it abundantly clear that I was no match for him didn't mean that I was going to admit to any kind of weakness.

"I know."

I glared at him briefly. "Are you being condescending?"

"No, I'm not. I outweigh you and I put up more of a fight than you anticipated. I'm actually quite sure you could have taken down someone else. I spent too much time with a badge to have slow reflexes." He moved toward me and paused when I straightened. "I've really put you on edge, haven't I?"

"It's not every day that a man takes me down, pins me to the floor, and straddles me without even breathing hard." I crossed my arms over my breasts. "I'm not some pansy girl, you know."

"I know."

"I've taken kickboxing lessons for five years."

"Yes, and trust me I'll feel the repercussions of those classes for a few days." His hand drifted to his left side.

"I parked in the parking garage down the street." I went to the coatrack located near the top of the stairs and grabbed my coat. My fingers curled into the wool briefly, and then I pulled it on.

I wasn't weak and I shouldn't have been relieved that he was going to walk me to my car. All of that aside, I was relieved. As far as I knew, he wasn't the only criminal watching the place and monitoring my habits. How long had I been so lax about my own personal security? Why hadn't I noticed Mathias watching the gallery?

I hadn't been a cop for more than six years, yet I'd been more attentive to my surroundings before I was a cop than I could account for now. My job had softened me up in a lot of ways, I knew that. Not being exposed every day to the criminal element had a way of blunting the violence of the world to the average person, and it had done it to me.

For a long time I missed being a cop, but over the years, that feeling had drifted away and left me with a strange sense of relief. Relief that I could go to work every day and not really worry all that much about dying. And that relief had made me stupid and unobservant.

2

_____

I opened my car door and tossed my purse inside. "Thanks."

"No problem." He glanced around the garage and then shoved his hands into the pockets of his coat. "I guess I don't need to tell you that this isn't the safest place to park."

"No, I'm aware of it. I've complained a few times." I shrugged. "The city won't care until someone important gets jacked up in here."

"Politics aren't pretty."

"I know. I try to stay away from them as much as possible." I crossed my arms over my breasts and looked down at my shoes. "I suppose that Mr. Brooks will be hiring your firm?"

"I'll be allowed to submit a bid," he admitted ruefully. "I didn't expect anything different, honestly. I know enough about James Brooks to know that even when he's pushed into a situation he'll make a careful and considered decision."

I laughed. "Well, he's also a very frugal man when it comes to the Holman Foundation."

"I'll keep that in mind."

He reached out and touched my face with the tips of his fingers. I wanted to back away from his hand but found myself leaning into him. Craving a man's touch was foreign to me, and for a few seconds I considered letting it continue. I shivered at the thought and moved away from his hand. "Summer was too short."

"Yes." Mathias nodded. "There is something about you."

"Oh yeah?"

"Yeah, something that has had me all twisted up inside. I've been this way since I saw you for the first time." He shrugged and looked away from me. "It would help if you weren't so damn beautiful."

"I should wish myself ugly solely for your comfort?" I asked, amused by his tone.

"It wouldn't be for just me. I can't be the only man you do this to." He lifted his hand as if to touch me again and then dropped it. "I honestly didn't know you were still in the building."

"I know." I flushed a little; the memory of us struggling on the floor burst forward, and desire slid into my body like an old friend. I couldn't even remember the last time I'd been turned on by the mere presence of a man.

Mathias Montgomery was a stranger, yet in a lot of ways he wasn't. Because of his brother, Shamus, I knew a lot about him and what he wanted for his life. I knew how much time he'd spent in the military and how much he'd changed when he'd finally come home. But hearing about the man and having him stand right in front of me was an entirely different situation.

The idea of him had been attractive. A strong, ambitious man with long-range plans for his life and a deep love for his family. But the idea paled in comparison to the living, breathing man. I wanted this man despite myself and every rule I strived to live by. I didn't need a complication like Mathias Montgomery. Didn't need it one bit, but I knew it wouldn't stop me from indulging in things I had no business getting involved in.

He moved then, closer, and I braced myself. "You've already been on top of me once this evening, Mr. Montgomery."

"And?"

"I'm just saying . . ." I gasped against his mouth and melted against him.

His tongue pushed against my lips and into my mouth in a rush of sensation that had me grasping his shoulders and pulling him tight to me. He tasted amazing, and each stroke of his tongue against mine sent a river of lust rushing through me. I moaned against his mouth as his hands slid down my back to cup my ass. Even through several layers of clothes, the bite of his fingers excited me.

I hooked one leg around his and snuggled into his body as close as possible. He responded immediately, pressing me against the car and lifting me upward slightly so he could press his cock against me. I shuddered at the contact of that hard flesh, even through all of our clothes, and when he lifted me farther, I wrapped both of my legs around his waist.

I jerked my mouth from his and let my head fall back as his lips drifted down my neck. For a few seconds, I let myself get lost in those soft, amazing kisses. Then I forced myself to release him.

He gave me room to put my feet on the ground and sighed. "If I'm going to manhandle a woman, that's the kind I prefer."

I laughed and sucked in a deep breath. "I agree. But you realize that it was a mistake."

Mathias laughed softly and backed away from me. "Then I plan on making some really horrible decisions about you."

"Oh yeah?" I watched him take another few steps back. "What's that supposed to mean?"

"It means, Ms. Tilwell, that the next time I'm on top of you I'll be doing a hell of a lot more than *trying* to please you."

Silence has never been my friend, but I retreated behind it as he laughed and then strolled away. I was in way over my head.

He'd flipped on my hot switch without even really touching me and then he just walked away. Not that I'd really expected him to whip it out and fuck me up against the car.

But, really, a man ought to know when he's created a situation that requires further attention, and I suppose he did. I really could hardly wait for the next time he found himself on top of me.

Sliding behind the wheel of my car, I started lecturing myself. Getting involved with a man like him was against my only rule. Never fuck a man I'll be required to see outside of the bedroom. Violating this rule caused all kinds of problems, and I was old enough to know better.

Yet I also knew that I was going to fuck him the first chance I got. Hard, mean, and truly as deviant as I could muster fucking was exactly what Mathias Montgomery had to look forward to.

I woke with a start, my shoulder stinging like the wound was fresh instead of the neatly healed scar it was. I sat up carefully as the pain drifted away. The dreams were always the same, always painful.

Shoving the covers back, I pulled my damp T-shirt over my head. I hadn't dreamed about the night I'd been shot in nearly five years. I dropped my hand from my shoulder, aware that I'd been rubbing it, and left my bedroom. My apartment was small but neat and minimal.

Clutter has been my mortal enemy since grade school. Neat and orderly represented control, and that's something that every woman needs. My childhood had been full to the brim with clutter, mostly my mother's. She'd kept everything, and it took months of careful planning to remove most of the crap from the house after she was gone. At first, my father had been militant about keeping things just as she had left them. I guess he'd stopped caring when he'd finally realized that she wasn't coming back.

It was then that I'd learned that my brothers had hated the junk as much as I did. I can hardly describe how relieving it had been to throw out years and years' worth of magazines. As an adult, I knew that we dealt with our mother's abandonment by cleansing the house of her. It was just too bad cleaning out our minds hadn't been so easy. All three of us had abandonment issues, and none of us have ever come close to getting married. I had serious doubts that either of my brothers would ever marry.

I pulled a soda from the refrigerator, popped the tab, and drank half of it standing in my kitchen. Caffeine was a mistake, especially at three in the morning, but it tasted good. Of course, pouring a couple fingers of rum in it would've been nice too.

Clad only in my panties, I walked to the hallway and stopped in front of the floor-length mirror there. With a grimace, I turned on the light and stared at myself. My eyes immediately went to the puckered flesh of my scars. One on my shoulder, another on my hip, and then the last one on my thigh. Being shot in the line of duty had ended my career in law enforcement. It had also changed me in ways I'd never thought possible.

I glanced over my breasts and then the rest of my body. I worked out but ate like a pig. I'd never really been able to gain weight or grow tits. I was probably in line for more attitude when breasts were being given out in heaven. I turned out the hall light. Staring at myself in the mirror was the kind of activity that would lead to a mental disorder of some kind.

By the time I reached the bedroom, I'd concluded that my mood and my bad dream were all his fault. If he hadn't gotten me all worked up I wouldn't have dreamed about the shooting. Mathias Montgomery had to be removed from my mind, but it wasn't my mind that he'd really infiltrated . . . it was my body. I'd been attracted to him before he said his name. When I'd thought he was a criminal. Me, the daughter of a cop, attracted to a criminal. My father would roll over in his grave.

But he was no criminal. I tipped up my soda and downed

the rest. Thinking about him was not good for me . . . at the rate I was going I'd go back to bed and have obsessive sexual dreams about him.

Mathias "sex on a stick" Montgomery was going to be a permanent fixture in my life, and it was very important that I put him in the right place in my mind. Professionally, I couldn't afford to lose focus. My position at Holman Gallery was new, too new to mess with. I had a finite amount of time to cement myself as the assistant director of the gallery. When Mercy Rothell had taken over the directorship of the gallery in August and slid me into her place, the opportunity took my breath away. I'd known it was coming for months, and when it happened it still knocked me off kilter a little.

Disgruntled, I went to my bedroom and pulled on workout clothes. If I wasn't going to sleep, I might as well get some time in on the treadmill. My apartment building had one of the best in-house gyms in Boston. In fact, I'd chosen the building because of the gym.

My hip was sore from my tumble with Mathias, but since it was more my fault than his, I couldn't hold it against him. I pulled off my sweat-damped T-shirt and dropped it on the floor beside my shorts. Four miles on the treadmill and I was still wound tight with emotion.

When I'd first moved to Boston, I'd hoped that the change of scenery would help clear my mind and push my past firmly behind me. It hadn't. In fact, if anything, being so far from my two brothers had only intensified the desperate feeling that I'd carried around with me since I'd been shot. I could still feel the hot pavement underneath me when I thought about that day.

I don't remember how long I lay there on that road. I do remember my brother, Stan, combing road tar from my hair in the hospital. The patient and thoughtful look on his face lingered with me even six years later. I'd been a cop in Savannah,

Georgia, for less than two years when a traffic stop turned into my worst nightmare.

Wes, the middle child of our family, had told me repeatedly that I shouldn't have been out on the street to begin with. That had only made me want it more. How many times in our lives had I strived so hard to prove him wrong? I'd proved that day that I could take care of myself; the price, however, had been a horrible one to pay.

My partner lay dead on the road because we'd both under-estimated a seemingly mild-mannered history teacher. The altercation we'd had earlier in the day with the man hadn't led us to believe he would be dangerous. To this day, I still had no clear reason why the man had come out of his car firing at us, and I never would. Because the same day I'd been shot in the line of duty, I took a life.

I briefly planted my hands flat against the wall under the showerhead before I reached down and turned the water on. Too hot, but it helped. I sighed softly when my muscles started to relax under the stinging spray. Having my day start before the sun even came up wasn't the ideal Saturday; in fact, it wasn't ideal for any day.

I left the shower and started to grab a towel to dry off, and my doorbell rang. Disgusted, I went into my bedroom, grabbed a T-shirt that would cover my ass, and pulled it over my head as I headed toward the door. The bell sounded again as I entered the small foyer of my apartment. The only thing worse than an ass-crack-of-dawn visitor was an *impatient* ass-crack-of-dawn visitor.

One peek out the peephole told me that the visitor was far more than just impatient. I jerked off the chain and undid all four of the bolt locks as quickly as I could. Throwing open the door, I glared at Mathias Montgomery.

"So, do you make a habit of skulking around in the night?" I leaned against the door and inspected him. He'd come to my door; I figured I could look at him like a fresh blueberry pastry if I wanted to.

"It's at least six o'clock in the morning." He glanced me over and swore under his breath. "Do you make a habit of answering your door practically naked?"

"I'm not naked."

"No. You're soaking wet in a T-shirt. Which in any man's book is actually better than being naked."

I took a step back as he moved forward and actually jumped when he shoved the door shut. "I didn't invite you in, Mr. Montgomery."

"Yeah, and it was rude of you."

"Rude of me?"

"Yes. Rude. You stand naked in a doorway and then don't have the decency to invite me in." His gaze dropped down slowly until he reached my feet and then he focused on my face. "Don't call me Mr. Montgomery."

"I decide who I'm on a first-name basis with, not you." I ran my fingers through my hair and motioned to him. "What was so important that you couldn't wait until Monday? Some people might spend their weekends working, but me, I like to lounge about my apartment half naked and do nothing that resembles work."

"I doubt that. I've seen how much time you put into your job. But that's besides the point; I'm not here to discuss the gallery." His gaze drifted downward briefly and then he focused on my face.

"Then why are you here?" I glared at him and crossed my arms over my breasts as he turned and twisted one of the bolt locks. "I normally lock people out, not in."

"I'm going to be an exception," he responded.

He was working on being several things, none of them pleasant. I didn't want or need some arrogant alpha-male type dripping testosterone all over my apartment. But he was just too tempting to throw out. "Just who the hell do you think you are?"

"I'm a man who was up all damn night because of you." He moved forward, every step predatory and calculated.

I couldn't even remember the last time a man had actually excited me so much without even touching me. It was easy to think back on those few moments in the parking garage, his mouth on mine . . . staking claim and invading in one breathless instant.

"Because of me?" I gasped a little when my back met with the wall. The blasted man actually had me running. I don't run. I never have. "How's that my problem?"

"It's my problem, and I've come over here to rectify it."

"I don't like or appreciate this kind of behavior. If I wanted a chest-beating Neanderthal in my life, I would have stayed in Georgia and married one of my brother's friends." I pushed my finger in the middle of his chest, and he backed up a few steps. "Some women might find this take-charge attitude of yours charming and attractive, but I don't."

"Is that so?" he asked, his voice taking on a silky quality that made me want to run for cover.

"Yeah. I ought to kick you out of my apartment." I think we both knew that wasn't going to happen. "How'd you get my address?" I raised one eyebrow and waited.

"My brother is very indiscreet at four in the morning."

"I'm gonna kick his ass."

"If you have any energy left when I'm finished with you, I'll drive you over to his studio."

"Finished with me?" I asked, and hoped that he didn't hear the thrill of excitement that zipped through my voice. As it was, I could barely stand waiting on him to get started.

"Yeah." He placed both hands above my head on the wall and met my gaze. "I have this theory about us."

"And what would that be?"

"I think if we spend the next two days fucking ourselves silly, by Monday morning we'll be over whatever this is between us." He reached out and touched my face. His fingers trailed along my jaw. "What do you think?"

It was the most unbelievable thing I'd heard in my entire life. In fact, as his fingers moved down my throat and his gaze dropped down to my breasts, I realized that I had every intention of totally exploring his theory. Though a part of me knew that on Monday morning I'd be thoroughly fucked but nowhere near getting over whatever he was doing to me.

"I think you are very sure of yourself."

"I am."

"And blunt."

"Yes." His fingers moved from my neck and down between my breasts.

"I don't like arrogant alpha males." I gasped a little as his thumb brushed across one rigid nipple. "Most women don't. We just like to read about them in romance novels."

"So you said. Is that what you really think?"

"You're arrogant." Though he did have that smooth, tailored look of the average metrosexual male, there was something rough about him that didn't jive with that, and that rough, unknown quality had me so very curious.

"No. I mean that you don't find arrogant men attractive." He cupped my breast and rubbed the nipple back and forth through the all-too-thin material of my T-shirt. "You want me."

"You're an attractive man, and I'm not immune to that." My body was humming like my favorite vibrator, and I figured he knew it.

He smiled briefly and lifted his hand from my breast. "Tell me to leave."

I wasn't going to tell him to leave and he damn well knew it. I pressed my thighs together and held firm against the wall as I watched his face. He was amazing, and I wanted to wrap myself around him and not let go for days. "Tell me what you're thinking."

He laughed softly, his dark brown eyes lit with amusement. "I'm thinking that my theory about this weekend could be slightly flawed."

"Oh really?"

"Yeah, but I'm willing to take the risk."

"Why?" I asked, though I wasn't sure I wanted to know his answer. Especially since I was nowhere near figuring out why I was so willing to take the risk of getting sexually involved with a man I barely knew and would be required to interact with on a business level in the very near future.

"Because you've got me all twisted and confused."

"And you think that fucking me would solve that?" Hell, I didn't care what it solved. I wanted him, and everything else be damned.

"I think that fucking you repeatedly as often as I'm capable for the next two days would go a long way toward solving my problem."

I was barely clothed and burning up. My nipples were tight and already aching as if he'd had his mouth on them. I pressed my lips together as I considered what I knew was coming. Sex is good. Sex, in fact, could be the best part of being alive. There had never been a time in my life when I'd denied myself, and I figured I was nowhere near starting such an atrocious habit.

"Invite me into your bed." He leaned in and brushed his lips over mine. I leaned briefly into him, unwilling to end the soft and alluring contact of his mouth on mine. "I need you to say it."

"Why?" I tilted my head and looked over his face, looking for anything that would make his motives more clear.

"Because I need to know I'm playing this game with a

woman. You're not a shy little virgin with a head full of candlelit rooms and sheets covered in rose petals." He moved in closer. "Are you one of those women who needs that?"

"No. I'm not. I don't need empty promises and lies."

"I know." He cupped my face with both hands and kissed me again. "Just looking at you makes me hard."

Every woman has a breaking point, and that is mine. "It just so happens that I have a place designed to take care of that problem."

"Tell me about it."

I laughed and slipped underneath his arm. With a smile, I reached out and offered him my hand. His fingers slid against my palm, and I tugged gently. "It's hot and wet and tight."

"Tight?"

"Yeah." We moved down the hall toward my bedroom. I glanced over my shoulder as I walked into my bedroom, and suddenly I felt like prey. His gaze was consuming me, and he looked like a tiger ready to pounce. "I do those exercises."

"If you expect me to be even remotely gentle with you, you'll shut up now," he murmured through clenched teeth.

I let go of his hand, turned around, and pulled my T-shirt over my head. "What makes you think I want you to be gentle?"

I slid onto the bed and watched as he pulled his shirt over his head and pushed off his shoes at the same time. My mouth literally watered at the sight of him. He was beautifully cut and sculpted . . . like he spent ten hours a day working out. I watched him pull his belt away and then work his jeans around an impressive erection.

My thighs clamped together of their own volition when he finally freed his cock. He was probably close to nine inches long, but it was his width that gave me pause. I thought with some seriousness that I wouldn't be able to wrap my hand completely around it. I absolutely couldn't wait to try.

He pulled several condoms out of his jeans pocket, dropped them on the dresser, and rested one knee on the bed. "Last chance."

I spread my legs and leaned back on my hands. "Come here."

He moved completely onto the bed and then between my legs. I watched him pause as if he weren't quite sure what he wanted to do, then he leaned down and placed the softest kiss I've ever known between my breasts. I gasped softly and let my head fall back as his mouth drifted to one breast.

I sucked in a breath and stiffened my arms to keep from falling completely back on the bed as he pulled my aching nipple into his mouth with firm, determined lips. His teeth brushed against me, and I arched upward. I needed more. Wanted more, and I really didn't know how to say it. I wasn't even sure what I wanted more of.

He released my nipple and covered my mouth with his in a rush of movement that left me breathless. I wrapped my arms around him as he lowered me to the bed. The warm heat of his body against mine felt perfect. Mathias pressed his cock against my labia and rocked gently against my wet flesh. The friction was delicious, just as amazing as his mouth on mine.

I slid my tongue between his lips, and he groaned against the intrusion. I loved the sound of it and wrapped my legs around his waist. He lifted his mouth from mine and met my gaze as he continued to rub his cock against my clit. The silky wet movement was just enough to be both soothing and frustrating at the same time.

My legs fell from his hips as he lifted away and then moved down. "Don't tease."

He laughed softly, spread my legs wider with firm hands, and lowered his head to my pussy. His tongue teased at my folds briefly before he brushed over my clit. I arched deeply up off the bed and fisted my hands into the blanket beneath me.

Helpless against the pressure of his tongue, I relaxed on the bed as much as I could and shuddered against each tantalizing stroke. He pressed his tongue against my entrance and then slid in. The shallow penetration forced me to lift my hips upward against his mouth.

"Mathias?"

He lifted his head and glanced me over before he turned his head and kissed the inside of my thigh. "Yes?"

"Your cock isn't the only thing you've got going for you," I explained weakly, suddenly at a loss for anything real to say.

Every graze of his skin against mine sent a rush of excitement over me. The feeling was addictive and so very seductive.

He sat back on his heels and reached for a condom. "Looking at you makes me hurt."

I watched in silence as he freed a condom and rolled it into place. Restless, I moved my hands across my nipples and then downward over my rib cage. Since he was watching me intently, I spread my legs wider and slid one hand down to cover my pussy. My fingers slid over my clit just once before he grabbed my hand and lifted it away.

"Trust me. I won't leave you hanging." He brought my hand to his mouth and kissed the palm before he released it.

Laughing softly, I relaxed on the bed and let him have his way. He pushed the blunt tip of his cock against my entrance, and I lifted my hips against him. As wet as I was, my body still protested the penetration. One hand drifted down my leg to my knee, then he lifted my leg up against his hip.

"Easy." He kissed my lips softly as he came to rest on top of me. "Relax."

I nodded abruptly and tried to relax against the intrusion of his cock. "I want this."

"Trust me. I won't hurt you."

I arched against him as he pushed deeper into me. "So said the man hung like a horse."

He laughed, and the gentle sound of it was a relief. "Am I hurting you?"

"No." I touched his face. "I guess I do need you to be gentle."

"I want to be everything you need."

How do men know what to say? My heart started to pound harder when he retreated and pushed into me again. I relaxed against him completely. I gasped as he slid deeply into me.

He stopped and rested his forehead against mine. "Perfect."

It was indeed perfect. I wrapped my legs around his waist and threaded my fingers with his when his hands sought mine. "Yes."

Mathias moaned against my mouth as we started to move. The thick push of his cock into my body was divine and better than I could've hoped for. My fingers tightened in his as our movement became frenzied. I dropped my legs from his waist and braced my feet against the mattress as his body slapped against mine.

"Damn." He pressed his mouth against mine briefly and slowed his pace. "Slow down, Jane, I'm not ready for this to end."

"I need it hard." I strained against his body, physically demanding more. "Harder. Fuck me."

He released my hands and placed his hands on either side of my head. I moaned against his lips and rubbed one hand over his head to pull him closer still. His tongue slid into my mouth, mimicking the action of his cock until the pleasure of having him inside me was overwhelming. Mathias slid his hand between us and pressed his thumb against my throbbing clit. The pressure of it was enough to rush orgasm to the surface. I stiffened beneath him and came so hard that my vision darkened briefly.

"Yes." He kissed my mouth softly as I relaxed beneath him and slid deeply into me and arched against me as he found his own release.

I clenched my muscles around his cock again and again as he continued to move. Mathias shuddered and buried his face against the side of my neck. Abruptly, he lifted off of me and sat back on his heels. He was still for a few seconds, and then he slid from the bed and disappeared into the bathroom.

I rolled over onto my stomach and buried my face in the bed. The sun was bright in the window, there was a naked man in my bathroom, and I'd just been fucked nearly stupid. So maybe getting up at the ass-crack of dawn really isn't such a bad thing.

A hand drifted up my leg, across my ass, and then upward to trace my spine. He hesitated and then his fingers drifted over the neatly healed scar on my shoulder. I turned my face to look at him as he laid down beside me. His gentle exploration stirred something inside me that I wasn't really prepared to deal with.

"I was a cop."

"I know." He touched the scar again. "I looked you up on the Internet when I got home last night."

"I'm on the Internet?" I frowned.

"Well, yeah. I expected to find you listed on the gallery's Web site. Nice bio there, by the way. I also found some articles about a young patrol cop gunned down on a highway in Savannah."

"Did you read the details?"

"The press painted you as a survivor. A woman too pretty to be a cop who witnessed the murder of her partner and took a bullet herself. One witness said that you pulled your gun and fired within seconds of being shot. You called for help and stayed conscious long enough on the scene to report to your commanding officer, a man who just happened to share your last name."

"My brother. Both of my brothers are cops, and my father was also. None of them wanted me in patrol. They thought I'd ride a desk and be safe."

"Did you leave police work because of them?"

"No. For a long time I wasn't all that sure what had happened that day. It seemed to blur and change every time I thought about it. The nurses and the doctors in the hospital were so careful with me—everyone was careful. It made me crazy at first; I couldn't figure out why they were all treating me like I was a hero."

"Until you saw the news and realized that every news station in the state was running the footage from the camera of your patrol car."

I grimaced. "You saw that too?"

"Yes. The Internet is surprisingly helpful these days."

"The Internet is the single biggest threat to privacy in this country." I cleared my throat. "I just couldn't be a cop anymore. Not the kind of cop I wanted to be when I'd first joined the force."

"I understand." He touched my hair and sighed. "I think I might have a bit of a crush on you."

"Wow." I rolled over to my back and pursed my lips. "I don't think that's ever been said to me."

"I don't believe that."

I turned and looked at him. "Why not?"

"You didn't have a ton of little boys in junior high sending you notes telling you how pretty you were and to check *yes* if you liked them back?"

"No. I was too much of a tomboy in school to get those kinds of notes. My father raised me and my brothers basically on his own, so I didn't have much of a female influence until I went to college." Thinking about my father hurt, so after a few seconds I pushed all of that back and smiled. "After college, I dedicated myself to my career."

"Why did you become a police officer?"

"I liked order and justice. I wanted to contribute to society in a meaningful way, and I thought a badge was the way to do it." And giving up that badge had been extraordinarily hard. Talking about my past was unsettling, but I felt compelled to answer his questions honestly.

"You don't like talking about this."

"Why do you say that?" I looked at him and saw the shrewd amusement in his eyes. "Okay, fine, I don't."

He reached out for me and pulled me close with an easy strength that caused excitement and concern. In the back of my mind, I couldn't help but remember the first time we'd touched— just hours before. His hands hard on my arms, pressing me into the floor. Those same hands that now trailed gently down my back as he shifted me completely on top of him.

"I scared you last night." Mathias pushed his fingers into my hair and met my gaze without hesitation. "I regret that a lot."

"You said you'd been watching the gallery for a week."

"I got there late last night, long after closing, and your car wasn't in the parking lot."

I sat up and snuggled my ass against his groin. The rapidly hardening flesh I found there was not a disappointment. "You watched me all week."

"You're the last to leave." He slid his hands up my legs to my waist and then upward over my rib cage. "So, yes, I watched you all week. Your routine was just as important as the guard's. A body in the building can trip the alarm, which would throw off the results of my endeavor."

I tried to think back if there had been days when I'd looked like crap but couldn't remember. I normally have at least one day during the week when my hair won't do what I say or I run my pantyhose before I even get in the building. It never failed.

"Were you really going to take something from the gallery?"

"I had permission from Mercy to remove a small painting from Level 1 in the north wing. I even brought a case for it so I'd be able to transport it safely."

"Very forward thinking of you."

"I'm a planner." He sat up and pressed me against his chest. "I didn't plan on you."

"Then or now?" I asked softly as his hands trailed down my back. The soft fleeting touch on skin that I never knew could be so sensitive made my breath catch briefly.

"Either, both. To be truthful, I don't think I could've planned enough for you."

I wrapped my arms around his neck as he pulled me closer and tried to remember that it was just sex. Emotionless sex. That's all it could be. I didn't have room for more. But that was becoming very hard to keep in my mind. Being wrapped up in his arms, all of his warmth seeping into my body, had me practically stupid.

"You know, I don't normally have sex with a man just because I find him attractive."

"I know." His hands cupped my ass and he moved me until his cock could slide between my labia. "I'm a lucky man."

"Yes." I let my head fall back as I moved against the silky skin of his cock. "I'm ready for more."

"I know you are."

My fingers tightened on his shoulders as he lowered his head and sucked my nipple into his mouth. It was odd how comfortable I was in his arms, with his mouth on me. I didn't feel too skinny or boyish. I've never needed a man to feel like a woman, yet it was amazing to find a man who did make me feel female and soft. He rolled us with careful hands until I was flat on my back.

I sucked in a breath when he lifted his mouth and sought out my neglected breast without pausing, and I curled my hand against the back of his head and moved my legs against his. His cock was trapped between our bodies, pressed against my thigh, reminding me of how empty I was. I spread my legs and pressed my feet against the mattress. "Fuck me."

"Don't worry. I will." His tongue darted out briefly and

flicked my nipple as he lifted his head. "You're mine until Monday morning."

I watched him slide downward through half-closed eyes. "Is that what I agreed to?"

"Yes."

"I don't get with possessive crap like that."

He laughed and dipped his tongue briefly into my belly button before moving down farther. Without any warning, he pushed his tongue into me again. I jerked against him briefly before forcing my body to still.

He used his thumb to separate my labia to find my clit. I shuddered against the calloused flesh and nearly swallowed my tongue when he started to rub my clit in tiny little circles. The man was turning me into an idiot with just his thumb. I rocked against the intense and centered pleasure of it briefly and then stilled as he pressed his tongue once more against my entrance. My flesh gave way to his invasion immediately.

My hands clamped onto my aching breasts as I moved to the tight rhythm he was creating with his tongue and thumb. I used my fingers to pinch my nipples until they hurt; the stimulation was overwhelming, but I was past caring. I felt it building, and I surrendered to orgasm as soon as it would let me.

He licked upward until he met my throbbing clit and grazed it gently with his teeth before he raised up, slid both hands under my ass to lift me, and pushed his cock into me slowly to the hilt. I was weak with pleasure and the need for more.

Mathias gently rested some of his weight on me and started to move inside me while I wrapped around him. It was so easy to give in to him and the hot, needy pleasure he created. What was it about this man?

He pulled from me abruptly. "Fuck."

"Yeah, you were doing a great job." I sat up and glared at him, disgruntled.

Laughing, he ran his hand down the side of my face. "You're a challenge, that's for certain."

I watched him grab a condom from the nightstand. "Oh."

He rolled the condom on with ease, and I reached out to him. Pulling him down with me, I spread my legs to cradle him as he slid into me. It felt so right, so perfect, having him pushing inside me, becoming a part of me. The man was taking me over and I reveled in it.

3

Sitting on my closed toilet behind a locked door is not my style. I haven't done that since I was in college. In fact, I think I might have done it only once even in college. Hiding after sex was not mature or worldly. I'm a modern woman with self-confidence, strength, and dignity. So I had no reason to hide, yet I was.

I didn't feel so damn modern and worldly. At least not as worldly as a woman who had just fucked a near stranger twice should feel. I'd actually forgotten to make sure there was a condom. I'd never, ever in my life gone that *naked* with a man. Birth control wasn't an issue, but I hadn't given the first thought to STDs. I hadn't even bothered to ask him about his past.

He could've lied, of course, but modern women asked those questions. Neither one of us had asked. We'd just jumped on each other like animals in heat. Self-lecture aside, I didn't feel guilty about the actual event. Still, there had been few times in my life when I'd made such a decision without a lot of thinking.

My body still tingled with the pleasure of him. I stood up

and glanced around my bathroom. It needed to be revamped, especially if I was going to take to spending a lot of time in it. I went to the vanity and picked up a brush. My hair, which I kept about about four inches all over my head, was standing on end. I tamed it the best I could, washed my hands, and braced myself for the naked man in my bed.

The naked, hung like a horse, beautiful man who had turned my tidy little world upside down in a matter of hours. It was clear that I would have to send Mathias packing soon. I unlocked and opened the door. He was sprawled on the bed staring at the ceiling. After a few seconds, he turned his head and looked at me. Send him packing? *Maybe* on Monday morning.

"Food?"

"Shower. Food. More of you."

I laughed softly. "Sounds like you've got your afternoon agenda all planned out."

"I'm a planner." He stood from the bed and glanced around at his abandoned clothes. "I'm going to have to go down to my car."

"So, condoms weren't the only things you brought with you?" I went to my closet and pulled out a robe to put on.

"No." He grinned and pulled on his jeans. "Clothes and the rest of the box of condoms are in the car."

I looked toward the nightstand and saw only two condoms remaining. "Well then, you go get our supplies and I'll figure out something for lunch."

He walked to me, his shirt dangling in his hand. "I'm wondering if you'll let me back in."

"It's not Monday."

He touched my face and leaned down to kiss me. I met his mouth way too eagerly and groaned against him as he pulled me in. Finally, he lifted his head and sighed. "Monday is going to suck a little."

Yes, it was. I walked him to the door and then went into my

kitchen to consider my options. I shopped for one and had for years. I was in no way prepared to deal with a guest, mostly because I didn't have guests. Not ever. I had a "dick on the side," but I always went to him and never spent the night. Now I've got a freaking man in my apartment, and my modern-woman lifestyle didn't mesh with cooking for a man. Damn it.

A cursory check of my cabinets yielded nothing more than a slight concern over my daily vitamin intake. I really needed to start eating better. Living on fast food and bagels wasn't a good lifestyle choice. Of course, I knew I was fixated on the food question so that I wouldn't have to dwell too much on the sex question. It wasn't like me to fuck a stranger, which was why I always kept a man on the side. That way I wouldn't have to resort to a one-night stand when I needed sex.

Yet there was a man on his way back to my apartment who had spent the better part of the morning inside me and I barely knew him. Most of what I knew I'd learned from his brother, Shamus, and those things weren't all that intimate.

Did I want intimate details? I was beginning to think perhaps I did, and that was not a cool thing in the least. It would be easier to get rid of the man if I didn't involve myself in his life. Easier? The thought made me laugh. Already it was clear that there would be nothing easy about Mathias Montgomery, and maybe that was part of the attraction. He certainly was not the kind of man that I could pigeonhole and keep in a certain part of my life.

I went back to the door when he knocked and let him in. "I don't have anything to cook." My frown quickly turned to a glare as I watched him laugh. "It's not funny."

"Jane."

"What?"

"That's nothing to frown over." He motioned toward the bedroom. "Let me shower and we can consider our ordering-in options."

"You don't mind?"

"Of course not."

I watched him disappear into the bedroom. After a few seconds, I followed along behind him, shrugging off my robe as I went. When I entered the bathroom, I found him already in the shower, and his stuff was sitting on my vanity next to my toothpaste. Since looking at his "boy" stuff mingling with my "girl" stuff made me kind of giddy, I joined him in the shower and tried to forget my stupid girlie thoughts.

Mathias looked amazing wet. I moved my hands up and over his back before he turned and pulled me under the water. The level of intimacy startled me. In fact, I couldn't remember ever allowing someone so close. He was in my shower, using my soap, and in my life. Where would this take me?

I stretched underneath his hands and turned my head so that I could watch him. The scented oil I'd pulled from the bathroom had saturated the room with a soft lavender mixed with musk. I'd bought the oil during a weak moment in a salon a few weeks back when Mercy had talked me into spending a Saturday being tortured in the name of beauty.

"Turn over."

I rolled onto my back and sighed. "I haven't had a massage like this in years."

"You need to relax more often." He leaned down and brushed a soft kiss across my lips before he grabbed the bottle and drizzled a thin line of oil down between my breasts to my belly button. "The first time I saw you on Monday afternoon you were leaving the gallery. Hands full, talking on your cell phone, and dragging along a briefcase on wheels. I had profiles on everyone at the gallery, so I knew who you were. I couldn't, however, figure out why you were working yourself to death."

"I'm in a new position."

"One that you wouldn't be in if you hadn't already impressed the hell out of a lot of people." He slid astride my hips, his erect cock brushing against my stomach as he did. "I see calculation in your eyes now. As if you're planning something."

I laughed. The only thing that was really on my mind was an unusual urge to suck his cock. To be honest, sucking a man's cock had never been high up on my list of things I love to do. "I'm totally relaxed."

"Hmmm, so you say." He spread the oil over my breasts and then down my rib cage. "I have a feeling that you rarely allow your mind to relax."

He was making me stupid. I couldn't imagine he thought I was even capable of having a coherent thought while he gently rubbed oil into my breasts. I jerked against his fingers as he rolled my nipples gently between his fingers.

I reached out and wrapped one hand around his cock. My fingertips barely touched. Using my thumb, I rubbed across the head until he started to move against my hand.

"Jane."

I met his gaze then and slowly released his cock. He looked feral. "You've been teasing me for nearly an hour. There is just so much a woman can be expected to take."

He released my nipples and reached for a condom. "Roll over."

I moved between his thighs, rubbing against him with every motion as I rolled over. Mathias ran his hands down my back and over my ass. He moved back briefly to free my legs, and I spread them wide as his cock brushed between my thighs. I arched briefly as the head of his cock slid up between my labia and over my clit. Unable to keep from jerking, I rocked against the contact and moaned in frustration when he pulled away.

"Fuck me."

His fingers tightened on my hips and he pushed his cock against the entrance of my pussy and slid in hard. I cried out as slick, nearly painful pleasure washed over me. I curled my fists into the sheets underneath us and lowered my head as he started to thrust repeatedly.

I gloried at the hard, repeated invasion of his flesh, the slap of his body against mine, and the elemental feelings that were being pushed to the surface. Losing sight of my civilized nature didn't scare me; in fact, if anything, it was exciting. I turned my head, and my gaze snapped to the double mirrors that adorned my closet.

The sun streaming across the bed highlighted the differences in us beautifully. His dark skin and my paleness startled and aroused me. It had never occurred to me how erotic it would be. Mathias turned his head and met my gaze in the mirror. If he was startled that I was watching us fuck, he didn't show it.

He slid one hand under me and pressed against my clit as he slowed the stroke of his cock into me. The walls of my pussy clung to him and pulsed with a deep, nearly unbearable pleasure. Orgasm rushed over me and I collapsed against the bed. Abruptly, he pulled from me and turned me over.

I pressed my feet against the mattress as he positioned himself to re-enter. I gasped a little at the sharp pleasure of being filled by him. Pulling him down and wrapping myself around him seemed the only thing to do. He buried his face against the side of my neck and pressed hard into me as he came.

He shook against me and moaned softly. I loved the sound of him. The knowledge that he found pleasure in me made me feel like the most amazing woman ever created. I couldn't remember ever getting so much satisfaction out of pleasing someone else. After a minute, he pulled from me and rolled onto his back.

"You're amazing."

I rubbed my stomach and nodded. "You too."

"I'm not done with you."

I sure as hell wasn't done with him either. I'd never known a man like him, and I doubted I would again. He was a more than amazingly gifted lover. Why was I so drawn to him? He certainly had strength and a great deal of personal dignity, which I appreciated.

But he was also the kind of man I'd steadfastly avoided all of my adult life. Aggressive alpha males are too much to control for any length of time. And I figured he was also something of a womanizer. To be honest, I like to be the only *player* in my relationships. How many women had he left along the way? Was there a woman in his past whom he loved enough to return to, given the chance?

"Penny for your thoughts."

I laughed softly and rolled to my side. I figured if he knew what I'd really been thinking about he might have run for the hills. "How did you lose your virginity?"

"Well." He turned his head and looked at me. "I was nineteen and my high school girlfriend gave me one hell of a going-away present."

"This was after boot camp?"

"Yeah. I'd been trying to nail that girl for two years."

"Great term."

"Yeah, well." He shrugged. "She's married now with about four kids."

I shuddered a little. "Four kids?"

"Total nightmare." He frowned and sighed. "I mean, don't get me wrong, I like kids. I'm just glad that I didn't have them with her. It's funny how we can think someone is perfect at the time and look back at them later and wonder what the hell we were thinking."

Laughing, I nodded. "My high school boyfriend turned out to be gay."

"Ouch."

"I think I knew." But having that truth bandied about the known world had been thoroughly humiliating. At eighteen, the news had been devastating. But now that I was older, I didn't take it so personally.

"So when did you lose your virginity?"

"Twenty-two. It was about six months after the shooting; the guy was a friend of the family. Something was missing from my life; I thought it was a man."

"It wasn't."

"No." I shook my head. "It was me. I was missing. All that time I'd spent mourning my partner and my own career served only to highlight that I was wasting the time I had. The next day I went out and started shopping around for a college I could afford. My brothers helped when they could, and now here I am."

It sounded a lot more simple than it actually had been. The decision to leave law enforcement behind had broken my heart. I couldn't even count how many times I'd gone to the phone to call my brothers and ask to come home. Boston had been a hard move for me. Being so far from the family I had left and knowing that I would never get back the one thing I'd always wanted.

"Must have been difficult getting into the college scene after being a cop."

I laughed. "Yeah, needless to say I didn't fit in with those kids. In fact, I really didn't even understand them half the time. By that time I'd already seen so much and lived to tell."

"Why art?"

"Because it's beautiful and intriguing. I find it fascinating that there is so much of ourselves put into the art that we as a species create. It's amazing that even at our most primitive we were drawn to express ourselves. We see it repeatedly all over the world."

"And that beauty drew you into the art world."

"Yes. I want to believe that everyone has that kind of creativity and beauty in them. Those that can't express it well, like me, can enjoy the work of others." I cleared my throat. "At first I thought about going into teaching. The man I killed had been a teacher for nearly twenty years. I wanted to give back some of what I had taken."

"You didn't make that man come out of that car with a gun."

"No." I shook my head. "But if we'd arrested him the first time . . . maybe things would've been different. His behavior was erratic enough that we could have had him evaluated at a hospital or something." My fingers tightened into a fist.

"I read the files, Jane. I know you and your partner were both cleared of wrongdoing in both incidents that day."

My gaze snapped to his. "You read the files?"

"I still have friends in the bureau. It only took a few calls to get copies of the official reports."

Disgruntled, I wondered why neither of my brothers had called to tell me that the FBI had pulled the case files on the shooting. They'd never hesitated in the past to keep me informed of information requests. Since I'd worked in several galleries over the years, my personal records with the Savannah PD had been requested more than once.

"Clark didn't want to deal with the paperwork of an arrest." My fingers tightened against my palms. Even saying that much had hurt. "That's why we gave Leonard Daily a pass on the disorderly conduct. We told him to go home and cool off."

"That isn't in the report."

"No." I shook my head. "It isn't. We both made that mistake and there was no way to get it into the report without making my partner look like a lazy cop, and I couldn't have that. I would have taken all the blame if I could have."

"So tell me about it."

I sat up and grabbed a pillow from the head of the bed. "Okay. We'd been on duty about three hours when there was a call from a grocery story in our area. There was a man in the parking lot having hell's own fit and raging at another customer. They hadn't come to blows or anything by the time we got there. We separated them and sent them both home. We stupidly assumed they were strangers."

"And the guy raising hell was the one you pulled over later."

"No." I shook my head. "We pulled Henry Jakes over about four hours later for running a stop sign of all things. He'd been on the receiving end of the verbal abuse at the grocery store. I wanted to take them both in and get everyone calmed down. Clark didn't, and as always I gave in to him."

"Henry Jakes went home, got his gun, and went after the man he'd argued with at the grocery store."

"Yes, at least I've always assumed so. We should have taken one or both of them into custody, and because I didn't go with my gut two men died that day."

"They weren't strangers."

"No. There had been two previous physical altercations between them. Apparently, both of them had boys on the same Little League baseball team. Leonard Daily was an abusive loudmouth. Jakes and he had both gotten thrown out of a game over the weekend because Jakes told Daily to shut up and they ended up in a shoving match." Two grown men who couldn't let a bunch of little kids play a game like it was a game had caused so much death. I pressed my lips together briefly and then finally met his gaze. "His wife apologized to me. In the hospital after I came out of surgery. She was standing there beside my brother, her face puffy from crying. I think I knew the moment I saw her who she was. She told me that her husband was a good man. A good man who had been pushed around once too often. It wasn't an excuse for him; what he'd done was wrong . . . but that was what he'd been. Then she apologized to me."

"Must have been a hard moment."

"Yes." I nodded. "I killed her husband and she's telling me

she's sorry for what happened. It was insane. I think a part of me would have preferred her screaming and yelling."

"And your brother didn't press you for details?"

"The whole damned department knew what happened. Savannah is really a small town that way. They all knew what kind of cop Clark was. No matter what I did, I couldn't change that. I never committed it to paper and I never will. I won't have a piece of paper in a file telling anyone that my partner, my dead partner, was a lazy cop. Or that I was a weak one for giving in to him."

"He was the senior officer?"

"Yes."

"Following his lead doesn't make you weak, Jane. You were still quite green. Frankly, you should have never been placed with a cop like him. He certainly wasn't a good role model for you to observe."

"Clark was a good man." I glared at him as if he might deny it.

"And not all good men need a badge and a gun."

I couldn't argue with that. "Okay."

"We all have things we'd do differently if we had the chance. Dwelling on the past solves nothing. For all you know, Henry Jakes could have gone home and gotten his gun regardless of what you did that morning."

"Maybe." I sighed and hugged the pillow tighter. "I've never said this out loud to anyone. I mean, even at the review hearing I just kept my mouth shut and answered the questions they had. But offered nothing additional. It was like we were all edging around the truth."

"You can trust me."

I knew that and it made me very nervous. After clearing my throat, I took a deep breath and nodded. "In the end, I knew I had to be true to myself, so I didn't get a degree in education.

Art gives me something that was missing before, something that I didn't even know wasn't there."

"I see."

"And it might not have value to you . . . but it does for others. Art can stir the soul and heart if you let it." I waved my hand around in defeat. Discussing art with him would probably always be really frustrating.

"I understand the value of beauty." He reached out and ran his finger along my jawline. "I also understand that there is no *thing* worth your life. I've seen plenty of death, and I know you've seen your share."

"Yes."

He cupped the back of my head with his hand and pulled me toward him. I sighed against his mouth as he kissed me. The danger of losing myself in this man was suddenly so real that I was overwhelmed. I pulled free and lay back against the headboard. Since hiding in the bathroom was not an option, I retreated to silence and tried to figure out why I was letting Mathias Montgomery turn me inside out.

I normally dumped men before they even came close to making me like them. What was wrong with just sex? Nothing. Not one damn thing had been wrong with it before. I glanced briefly at him and forced myself to remain still. All I really wanted to do was jump on him and beg for more. More of everything. "Want some water?"

"Please."

I left the bed and walked naked into the kitchen. I snagged two bottles from the fridge and leaned against the counter. There were a lot of hours between me and Monday morning. Those hours seemed too short and too long all in the same moment. My body still hummed with pleasure, and I was torn between wanting it to end and wanting to never see it end.

Indecision isn't something that I'm comfortable with, but

I've never been above ignoring a problem. I took the bottled water back to the bedroom and found him resting against the headboard of the bed with the television on.

"I have some DVDs in the living room."

He picked up the remote and turned it off. "I didn't know how long you'd be gone."

I handed him one of the bottles and sat down on the bed. "Oh really?"

"Yeah, you looked like you were ready to run."

"I don't run from men." And if I did, I sure as hell wouldn't admit it to the one sitting in front of me.

"No." He laughed. "Not even ones that might be criminals."

"Fuck you."

"You just did." He tipped the bottle back and drank deeply. "Very well, I might add."

"I'm good at everything I do or I don't do it." I lifted my chin.

"Is that so?"

"It is."

He put his bottle down on the nightstand on his side of the bed and looked me over. "I like being naked with you."

"Yeah?" I liked being naked with him too. Beyond the sexual energy, something else lingered. Something comfortable and familiar.

"It's interesting. I don't think I've ever really thought about being naked with a woman outside of a sexual encounter."

"We've had several of those this morning," I murmured.

He was very close to expressing something that would make me uncomfortable and I knew it. The fact that we were so at ease with one another had me pondering fate and the like. The last thing I needed was for him to be pondering it too.

"But it's different. It's a level of comfortable that's rather foreign to me. I mean, I wasn't raised to be ashamed of my body, so I don't have any hang-ups in that area."

"Well, you have nothing to be ashamed of."

"Good genes." He reached out and tugged me from my place so that I rested next to him. "We fit well."

I glanced downward before I could help myself. "Yes."

He laughed. "Well, yes, in that way too—but I meant that it's comfortable to hold you. Some women can't get relaxed enough to be comfortable."

I rested my head on his chest and looked around my room, bright with the sun. Yet again, I was struck by my circumstances. Had I really just met him hours before? It seemed like so much longer than that. "We need to talk about the gallery."

"We can discuss the gallery on Monday. I have to submit a bid to Brooks by the afternoon. There will be plenty of time for you to brush me off and pretend for the world that you didn't spend the whole weekend fucking me."

Since that was exactly what I had already planned to do, I could hardly get mad at him for voicing it. Though hearing him say it did make it sound cruel and heartless. "I have a reputation with the gallery to consider. There are plenty of places that need mending because of my foolishness last night. I can't very well prove that I'm reliable and trustworthy if it's well known that I spent the weekend having freaky sex with a stranger."

"We're going to have freaky sex?"

"Yeah, I figured we might."

"Want me to spank you?"

I jerked my gaze to him and laughed softly at the grin he shot me. "I actually had a guy that wanted to do that to me."

"Did you let him?"

"Hell no. But I did offer to beat the shit out of him."

"Very generous of you." He rolled to his side and propped his head on his hand. "Have you ever been in love?"

"No. At least I don't think so. I had crushes when I was younger. I remember being desperate to see this boy in the fifth grade. He didn't even know I existed. What about you?" Directing the question his way gave me a few seconds to consider how much his simple question had hurt. Even Clark, to whom I'd been insanely attracted, hadn't inspired anything beyond an unknown sexual thing.

"I thought so once. But then I realized that it was just lust, and lust fades."

"Yes." Just like his attraction to me. There would be a day in the future when he would look at me and his blood wouldn't quicken. He wouldn't have the urge to take off my clothes and bury his cock in me.

"But I believe in love. I know that there is someone out there that will always have my attention and thoughts."

"Okay. What kind of woman will she be?"

"When I was younger I dated a series of women that were exactly the same, but now that I'm older I find that I'm over that. Now I look for things beyond the physical in the women I get involved with. I appreciate beauty, as I've already said. But these days I have to be able to talk to a woman or I don't waste my time on her. What about you?"

"I promised myself when I was twenty-five that I would never marry a man who didn't eat pussy. He also has to have a really big dick." I grinned when he laughed. "Sex is important."

"Yes, it is. So beyond your sexual needs, what other things should this man have?"

"I don't know." Shrugging, I wondered why I'd lied to him. I had a list dedicated to the perfect man. I knew exactly what I was looking for. Maybe I didn't want to ruin the mood.

I leaned back in my bathtub and blew at the bubbles covering me. He lounged at the other end. "You're going to smell all girlie after this."

"There was a time when that would've been horrifying. But somewhere along the way I realized that an excellent way of getting a woman naked was asking to bathe with her."

"You already had me naked."

"I did, indeed, but I figured you needed a soak in a warm bath."

I certainly couldn't argue with that. Pleasantly sore probably described me very well. His hand ran down my leg, soap sliding along with it. "So this bathing thing works for you?"

"Yes, it has in the past. It's intimate, and women dig that."

Laughing, I shook my head. "You're such a player."

"Look at it this way, no man will ever be able to manage you again. I'll tell you all my secrets if you tell me yours."

"Oh yeah?" I asked, amused. I figured there wasn't much a man could get past me anyway.

"Yep."

"Like what?"

"What's your tell? How do you tell a man that you want to have sex with him?"

"It depends on the man. If I've been dating him a while I'll just ask him to take me to his place. If he's a new guy . . . and I'm rather impatient for him to make a move, well, I might just ask him outright for sex."

"See, women have it so easy."

"No way."

"Yes way. Women always know when they are going to get laid."

I paused and considered his words. "Okay, that may be true. But that's only because men are so easy. A breeze can make you guys hard." Reaching out, I took my poofy and rubbed it between my hands. "There is a double standard. I take a lover . . . maybe several lovers in the same year, I'm a slut. You do the same thing and you're just being a man."

"Which means that all men are sluts and people are just so

used to it that it isn't worth saying." He grinned and leaned back on his end of the tub.

Well, I couldn't argue with that. I shifted my foot and slid it across his chest and teased his nipple with my toe. It hardened under my attention. "So, what else do you do to seduce a woman?"

"I treat every woman like she's special and the only woman I need."

"Lord, that probably gets you laid all the time."

"Every woman is smart, amazing, and so sexy that no man can resist her."

I laughed out loud. "You're impossible."

"It works." He snagged my foot and massaged it briskly with both hands. "What works for you?"

"As you know, women don't have to do a lot of work when it comes to men and sex. You guys are easy as hell. But I find letting a man think that he's in charge goes a long way." I glanced at him and had to laugh at the speculation on his face. "But I'm not very good at playing the damsel in distress."

"No, I don't imagine that you are." He tilted his head. "Come here."

I slid to my knees and scooted across to him, straddling his thighs as I did. "And sometimes I even follow instructions."

I gasped a little as he pulled me forward. Water sloshed between and over us as I settled on his thighs. I reached down between us and wrapped both my hands around his cock. I loved the silky feel of his skin and the way he shifted under me as I stroked him. In the past, I'd taken some satisfaction in pleasing my sexual partner, but I'd never been so compelled to pleasure a man like I was with Mathias. I wet my lips at the thought and met his gaze. As if he knew what I had on my mind, he moved against my hands.

"I do enjoy a woman who can pretend to be obedient when it suits her." He cleared his throat and then groaned softly.

"Later on will you put on that pin-striped suit you wore to work on Tuesday?"

"Why?" I tilted my head as I rubbed my thumb across the head of his cock again and again.

"Because it made you look sexy and powerful. And all day Tuesday I wanted to take you into a dark room and fuck you up against the wall." He cleared his throat and closed his eyes. "Are you trying to kill me?"

"As far as I know no man ever really died of an orgasm."

His hands clamped onto my hips. "About that suit?"

"I'll have you know that it would be disgraceful to fuck in a two-thousand dollar suit." But I was going to put it on the first chance I got and we both knew it.

"Disgraceful and hot." He lifted his hands from my hips and cupped the back of my head. "Give me your mouth."

Who could deny such a demand? I moaned against the press of his lips and slid my tongue inside to taste him. I sat back abruptly and pulled my mouth from his. "We need to get out of this tub."

He laughed. "Why?"

I glanced at him briefly as I stood and exited the tub. "Do you know how many accidents happen in bathrooms every year?" Grabbing a towel from the counter, I glanced back at him just once before going into the bedroom. "Besides, I want to suck your cock."

Every little moment I spent with him had started to hurt a little. How many hours had we known each other? He would be gone on Monday. Not gone from my life, but gone from this small space we'd given ourselves. There wasn't room for more . . . was there?

I dropped the towel into a basket near the bathroom door and then left the bedroom. I hadn't spent so much time naked in recent memory, but I knew putting on clothes would've been a waste of time. I grabbed some juice from the refrigerator and poured half a glass. I reached for another glass when he came in, a towel wrapped around his waist.

"Thanks."

"You need to keep your strength." I handed him the glass and put the juice away. "What do you want for dinner?"

"How about we put some clothes on, find some out-of-the-way place with bad service and good food?"

"It just so happens that I know such a place. Best pasta in town, family-owned business, and all the waitresses are family members who hate their jobs." I walked over to him and slid my fingers into the front of the towel. "But at the moment I just want more of you."

He set down his empty glass and reached out for me as I pulled at the towel and it fell away. "That I can do."

His lips brushed against mine briefly and he picked me up. A modern, liberated woman isn't supposed to be giddy about a man carrying her around. Yet I swung my feet a little and grinned as Mathias took me back to bed. I ought to have my head examined.

I sat back on the bed as he put me down and raised an eyebrow when he went down on his knees. "My, this looks exciting."

He laughed and motioned me forward. "Move a little closer."

I moved to the edge of the bed and jumped a little when he lifted my legs to his shoulders. "You could be perfect."

He nuzzled his mouth against my labia and then boldly slipped his tongue in to tease at my clit. My arms weakened and I laid back on the bed, stunned. No man had made me feel so weak and so powerful in my entire life. I bucked against his skillful tongue with every breath I took, and I came within seconds. Being in a constant state of arousal surely had its advantages.

I sat up as he stood, grabbed a condom, and pulled it from its packaging.

"No." I reached out for the condom. "Not yet." He stilled in front of me as I tossed the condom on the bed and ran my hands up his thighs. "I want you in my mouth."

"Yes, you mentioned that earlier," he whispered softly.

I grinned and glanced up briefly at him as I started to stroke his cock with one hand. He was watching me intently, his hands fisted against his thighs. I sucked the head of his cock into my mouth, and he took a deep breath. Cupping his balls with my free hand, I whipped my tongue around the head and then slid him in until he pressed against the back of my throat.

"Christ."

I felt one hand drift over my head and then lift away. He groaned softly when I pulled off him and then sucked him back in as far as I could. The way his body was tensed told me that he wouldn't let me suck him for very long. Using my tongue, I played and sucked at the head intently. Tasting and taking in pre-come that flowed freely from him, I'd never felt more powerful and female in my life.

He touched my head and pulled free. "Get on your knees."

Handing him the condom, I rolled to my knees, my clit still pulsing with the orgasm he'd given me. He gripped my hips tightly as he pushed against my entrance. My flesh gave way as he pressed, and I buried my face briefly in the bed beneath me. He filled me again and again, each thrust brisk and deep. It was perfect. He was perfect.

"Yes. Yes." I continued to rock back against him, pulling him in as deeply as I could with every movement.

He ran his hands down my back again and again as we slapped against each other. I wanted as much as he could give and more. I braced against the bed as I edged closer and closer to another orgasm. He slid one hand underneath me and started to rub my clit.

Tears sprung to my eyes as I gave into him and the pleasure he gave so effortlessly. He pulled me tightly against his hips and rocked in a jerking movement as he came.

4

The restaurant was crowded, loud, and overstimulating by anyone's scale, but it was amazingly easy to tune all of that out. He made me feel like I was the only one in the room, and considering my appearance that was a pretty mean feat on his part. No makeup, jeans, and a T-shirt that had been new about ten years before had been my attire of choice when I'd gotten dressed. It had occurred to me that I'd dressed down to sort of scare him off. He hadn't blinked an eye when I'd come out of the bedroom.

"This place is all that you promised." His tone was dry as he looked around.

I laughed. "The first time I was here I took it personally. Now I just realize they hate everyone equally." I reached out and plucked a small loaf of bread from the basket between us. "But the food is to die for."

"This is an odd time to ask such a question considering how we spent the day, but is there a man in your life?" He swished his straw around in the water glass in front of him, and I didn't believe for a minute that the question was as casual as he'd made it sound.

"You're right. It's an odd time to ask." I tore a piece of bread from the loaf and put the loaf back in the basket. "There isn't anyone I'm serious about. I date, of course, but I'm commitment-phobic."

"How about a 2 A.M. friend?"

"Of course." I inclined my head. "It's funny how we all refer to the backup sex partner in different ways. I knew a girl in college who called him a friend-friend and another simply called him BUD."

"Backup dick." He shook his head. "I used to believe that women didn't think about sex the way men do."

"Well, in some ways we do and in others we don't. I think that both men and women deal with sex differently. There are plenty of people who treat it like a hobby, while others invest themselves emotionally into every encounter." I certainly preferred to think of sex as a hobby, but I had a feeling that he wouldn't enjoy hearing about that particular habit of mine.

I'd been shifting sex around in my mind since before I'd even had it. As a younger woman, sex was a revered physical act that had to involve love and commitment. Then, in college, I'd turned it into a game. Playing with sex and the men I had it with had been something of a sport for me. I'd been careful if free with my body, but I'd rarely ever given my heart a say in the matter. Falling in love, even then, had been too risky.

"It is better with some level emotion. It doesn't have to be love, but if there is interest there . . . interest beyond the physical." He shrugged. "So tell me about your backup dick."

"Why?" His curiosity was surprising. Most men don't like to hear about men that used to be in your life, much less a man that is actually still in your life.

"I'm just interested in the kind of man you normally spend time with."

"He's a lawyer."

"That's telling."

I laughed. "Well, yeah, he is sort of lawyerly. Arrogant and something of a shark when it comes to the law. He's a corporate attorney."

"When does he make partner?"

"It's in his five-year plan."

"Blond, blue eyes, and he can trace his family tree back to the Mayflower." He plucked up the bread and tore off a piece for himself.

I frowned. Charlie Wallace was everything he'd said and then some. "Is there something wrong with that?"

"No. Of course not."

I didn't believe it. He thought it was all kinds of wrong. Charles Dixon Wallace III was the Mary Poppins of men, practically perfect in every way. The oldest son of an old Boston family and a rising star in a large law firm, and he could fuck for hours. But Charlie certainly couldn't compare to Mathias.

"So he thinks you're serious about him."

I glanced up and found him staring at me. He didn't look upset or even all that interested. Was he playing a game with me? The thought irritated me. "We've been honest with each other. Now isn't the time to engage in something serious."

"Sounds interesting."

It sounded just horrible and impersonal. Was I really allowing myself to have a relationship like the one I'd just described?

I dropped my keys and pushed the button on my answering machine as Mathias locked the door and took our leftovers into the kitchen. There were two new messages.

"Hey, just thought I'd check and see how my favorite commando is doing." Mercy laughed at her own little joke, and I couldn't help but grin. "I'm going out to Lisa's tomorrow to help her with some man-bashing bitching. Let me know if you are interested. I'll pick ya up."

"Man-bashing bitching?"

I glanced at Mathias as the message ended and shrugged. "Lisa has a horrible ex-husband."

"And you guys schedule time to bitch about him?"

I nodded. "Yeah, we do."

"Hey there, Janie-girl." My gaze jerked back to the answering machine as Charlie's voice filled up my foyer. "Just wanted to remind you of the benefit dinner you promised to attend with me. It's this Friday at 7:00 P.M., black tie, and promises to be amazingly ass-numbing. My mother wanted me to remind you that you agreed to have lunch with her on Wednesday at the country club. God knows why you'd allow yourself to be tortured like that. Anyways, give me a call."

I blew air through my lips and crossed my arms over my breasts.

"That sounds rather serious to me."

"His mother showed up unannounced at his apartment about a month ago. After about five phone calls I had no choice but to agree to lunch with her." I frowned at him. "Why am I explaining myself to you?"

"I haven't a clue, Janie-girl."

"Don't call me that. I hate it." I walked past him into the living room.

The intrusion of Charlie had totally ruined my mood, and it reminded me that I was having a completely empty relationship with a man. Charlie was everything I'd always wanted, but as I stood there listening to his message I realized that I would have to break it off with him.

I threw myself down in my favorite chair and stared at the floor in front of me as Mathias followed. Lifting my gaze, I watched him sit down on the couch and stare at me. "What?"

"You look put out."

"It's just that . . ." I waved my hand toward the foyer and the answering machine. "I don't want to talk about it."

"Would you like me to leave?"

Frowning, I stared at him for a few seconds and then shook my head. "No, not at all actually."

"You feel guilty about fucking me."

"Charlie and I don't have an exclusive relationship. So who I fuck is none of his business. We go out sometimes, but that's rare. Mostly I just use him for sex."

"I have my doubts that he would agree with that assessment."

Mostly, I just use him for sex. The statement lingered in my mind and made me feel sick. First that it was true and second that I'd admitted it without a second thought. "We aren't serious."

"No, but I have a feeling he's going to start pushing for something more than what you currently give him."

The thought made me itch. I did feel guilty and horrible, but not for the reason that Mathias thought. I'd been sleeping with Charlie for nearly a year and I knew next to nothing about him beyond his family pedigree and his career choice. I didn't even know what his favorite food was or what he'd wanted to be when he was growing up. Things that I had learned about Mathias in a matter of hours.

"Yeah, I agree."

"You need to make a choice about that, Jane. It's not cool to let the man dangle like that." He was frowning at me, which sort of ticked me off.

"I never made the man promises. Not a single one."

"Yeah, but then you give in and make plans to have lunch with his mother."

"Fuck." I crossed my arms over my breasts and sighed. "She wouldn't even know I existed if she didn't insist on intruding on her son's life whenever she feels like it."

"You're dating a mama's boy." He laughed softly and relaxed in his chair as if he'd just come to the conclusion that Charlie was zero competition for him.

"I'm not dating him." But, Christ, he *was* a mama's boy. Fuck. Fuck. And double fuck.

I glanced up as Mathias stood and walked to me. Every step he took was predatory and thrilling to watch.

"Okay, we're finished talking about him."

Gasping, I clutched his shoulders as he picked me up from the chair and walked off toward the bedroom. "Hey, you're manhandling me again."

"This is my weekend, and until Monday morning—you are my Jane." He tossed me on the bed.

I propped myself on my elbows as he plucked up my left foot and pulled my shoe off. "I belong to no man."

He chuckled softly as he pulled off my right shoe and looked me over. "Wanna bet?"

"I warned you about that arrogant alpha-male crap." When he pulled at the legs of my jeans, I unbuckled them and lifted my hips. "I'm not some empy-headed twit that likes to feel *owned*."

He tossed my jeans aside and curled his hand into the front of the barely there panties I'd put on. "Don't frown at me, woman, you'll ruin my concentration."

I laughed and gasped when he jerked at my panties and they tore away. "Hey, those were new!"

"I'll buy you some more." He tossed the tattered silk aside as I pulled my T-shirt over my head.

I watched through half-closed eyes as he undressed. Sleek muscle moved under dark skin, and by the time he was crawling up between my legs I'd totally forgotten why I'd been frowning at him in the first place. He rolled a condom on and spread my legs with gentle hands. Warm, smooth skin brushed against my own as he covered me with his body and his lips drifted across mine.

Wrapping my legs around his slim waist was the most natural thing I'd ever done; the hard press of his cock against the damp flesh of my pussy was just what I needed. He rocked against me gently as he settled his mouth on mine and slipped his tongue into my mouth. I moaned at the gentle invasion and I tightened my hold on him.

How in the hell was I going to function around him after this weekend?

He pushed the blunt tip of his erection against my entrance and paused when I tensed. My insides were slightly swollen from our earlier encounters. I sighed in frustration when he pulled away and lifted his mouth from mine. Mathias moved down my body and placed several soft kisses on my belly, on the slightly puckered scar on my thigh, before he kissed my labia.

The tip of his tongue brushed over my clit again and again as he pressed two fingers into me and curled them upward against my G-spot. I cried out and pressed my lips together firmly to keep from doing it again. The dual stimulation was too much, too fast. I fisted my hands into the sheets and pressed my feet against the mattress as I thrust upward against his mouth. He didn't disappoint; his tongue quickened on my clit and I shattered with orgasm.

I wrapped around him completely as he moved upward and pressed his cock into me without pause. My body gave way to his invasion, and I buried my face in his neck as he started to move. No man had ever made me feel so weak and so vulnerable, yet in the same instance I felt powerful. He groaned softly when I found the strength to move with him. There it was, the power over his pleasure. No man had ever given me that, or at least he'd never let me know it.

He jerked and shook against me as I tightened my legs around his waist. My clit throbbed furiously between my labia, my own orgasm still echoing in my heated flesh. Mathias stiffened against me, and my name slipped past his lips as he came.

* * *

I reached out in the darkness and picked up my cell phone. I flipped it open as I sat up. "Jane Tilwell."

"It's me, Mercy."

Glancing toward the clock, I frowned. "What's wrong?" She'd never called me in the middle of the night before. It was barely 3:00 A.M. "Are you all right?"

"It's Lisa. Someone tried to break into her house. She's fine but pretty shaken up."

"Do you need me to come out there?"

"No. But I will need you to go to the gallery in the morning. We are getting a special delivery. The delivery service is scheduled to arrive at 8:00 A.M. James has special security in place, but I need someone on hand for the delivery. I would prefer that it be you."

"Okay. No problem." I glanced toward Mathias. He was probably awake. "Are you sure I can't do anything for Lisa?"

"Yes. I've finally got her down for some rest, but I just don't want to leave her alone. Shame is here and we're going to spend the rest of the night."

"Call me if anything happens." I closed my cell phone gently and put it on my nightstand and then turned to look at him. "Someone tried to break into Lisa Millhouse's place."

"Is she all right?"

"Yeah, just pissed. Have you met her?"

"Yeah. I oversaw the installation of her security system. They couldn't have gotten past the motion sensors on her property line." He sat up. "Maybe I need to go out there and check."

"Shame and Mercy are there. It's good that she called them; even a year ago, she wouldn't have called anyone but her security company. There was a part of me that figured her ex-husband had done such a number on her that she would never get back to the person she was before they married."

Mathias laid back on his pillow and nodded. "She was a passionate and engaging woman before she married. I didn't see her for several years, so when I came back to Boston and ran into her at Shame's . . . I was stunned by the difference in her. It was night and day."

"It's good to see her out and about. She's great with the kids at the academy."

"What did Mercy need from you?"

"I need to go to the gallery tomorrow to oversee the delivery of some pieces for a show." I laid back down in the bed and sighed. "She has motion sensors on her property line?"

"Yeah, and that's just the beginning." He laid back down beside me.

"Her ex-husband is a real asshole." I knew that was the heart of Lisa's security fears.

Her ex had done a number on her in several ways. Emotional and verbal abuse had often given into physical abuse. The woman I knew Lisa to be didn't jive with the image of a battered woman, yet she had been. After my first encounter with her, I'd thought she hated men. But now I know that more than anything she hated herself for staying with a man who hit her.

"He should be a dead asshole." Carefully, he pulled me into his arms and ran his hand down my back. "Get some sleep."

I chuckled softly. "Giving me orders?"

"Yep."

Since I'd never allowed myself to spend the night with a man before Mathias, I had no way to compare what I was feeling to past experience. Lying in his arms, his body pressed against mine, was a unique experience, and that was why it felt so amazing and perfect. It couldn't be anything else. I didn't have room for complicated crap like love or intimacy.

Yeah, I'm pretty good at lying to myself.

* * *

Two hours. I'd sat and watched the delivery man unload his truck for two hours. Once it'd been done and I'd signed all of the paperwork for delivery, I'd dashed back across town to my apartment and found it empty.

He hadn't mentioned leaving and there hadn't been a note. Disappointed and more hurt than I should've been, I put on some workout clothes and went down to the gym. Forty-five minutes on the treadmill had turned my disappointment into anger. I was totally furious with myself; it wasn't like he'd promised me anything more than he'd given. Except it wasn't Monday, damn it.

I took the stairs back up to my apartment, my leg muscles protesting every single step, but I figured the physical punishment would help. It didn't. It just gave me a damn cramp. I limped to my apartment door and stuck my key in the lock, frustrated at myself.

Mathias Montgomery was just a man. He certainly didn't meet my qualifications for a husband. He thought art was pointless and that was irritating, especially for the brother of one of the most influential sculptors in the United States.

I stopped in the entrance of my living room and stared at Mathias. Fury and happiness warred inside me for a few bare seconds while I considered what to say to him. "How'd you get in?"

"I took the spare key when I left." He stood from the couch and glanced over me. "That wasn't what you were wearing when you left for the gallery."

"I went to the gym when I got back." I frowned at him briefly before I walked toward my bedroom. "I need a shower."

Jerking my clothes off didn't cut the edge off my anger. I was so pissed that I cared that he'd come back. I wasn't supposed to care, damn it. Under the pounding water, I tried to separate out all of my feelings. It was difficult, as I'd never ever allowed myself to be put in a situation like the one I was currently in.

I barely glanced his way when he entered the shower stall and pulled the door shut. I was so damn mad at myself that I almost could have cried. Modern, smart, and collected Jane didn't get attached to men. But suddenly I was none of those things. He pulled me close and kissed my neck.

"I figured I would be back before you."

"Okay."

"Jane." He turned me gently to face him. "What's wrong?"

"Nothing. What could be wrong?"

Everything was fucking wrong. I'd gone and gotten myself attached to a man I barely knew. Hell, I wasn't even all that sure I wanted to get to know him. But here I was, my heart stuck in my throat like a teenage girl staring at her first crush.

Mathias sighed and rubbed his thumb over my lips. "I should've called you."

"What makes you think I care that you left?" I tried to pull free of him, but he gripped my forearms and held me still.

"It's written all over your face. I didn't mean to upset you." He released me carefully. "I went over to Shame's to talk to him about Lisa. Then he left to go back out there and pick up Mercy, so I came back over here."

"Did you tell him where you were going?"

"No." He pulled me closer and kissed my mouth in that soft way that made my knees weak. "Jane, what's happened between us isn't meaningless for me. I meant for it to be. I meant to be done with you on Monday, but I honestly don't think it's going to work out that way."

I'd meant to be done with him by Monday too. "Fuck."

I turned away from him and reached for my shampoo. He took the bottle from my hand silently and poured the liquid into one hand. I closed my eyes as he rubbed the shampoo through what little hair I allowed myself to have and resisted the urge to lean back against him. I was not going to let this man turn my life upside down. Even if he was the fuck of the century. No. It wasn't going to happen. Who was I kidding? It had already happened.

"You thought I wasn't going to come back."

"It doesn't matter."

"Of course it does." He maneuvered me under the spray of the showerhead and covered my mouth with his.

I moaned against the invasion of his tongue and wrapped my arms around his neck. Raising up on my toes, I pressed my breasts against his chest and then jerked when my leg cramp returned. "Damn."

"What?"

I leaned my head against his chest and moaned. "I got a damn cramp in my leg."

"Oh." He knelt down on one knee and grasped the leg that I had lifted off the tile instinctually. His fingers were firm as they kneaded the muscle, and it began to relax almost immediately.

"Thanks."

"Is it better?"

"Yeah." I sucked in a breath when his hands drifted up to my thigh and then to my waist.

He pressed me against the wall and lifted the leg that had cramped onto his shoulder. I closed my eyes as he slipped his tongue between the lips of my pussy. Every time his tongue drifted over my clit, I jerked against his hold. I ran my hands over his head and held my breath briefly. I'd never had a lover so interested in my pleasure.

Mathias pressed two fingers into my pussy and curled them against my G-spot as he lifted his mouth from my clit and met my gaze. "I love how you taste."

I pulled my leg from his shoulder and he stood. He pulled

his fingers away, slid his hands behind me to cup my ass, and lifted me off the floor. Clutching at his shoulders, I hooked my legs around his waist as he pushed into me. The hot, near pain of his invading cock took my breath.

He rested his forehead against mine. "I'll never get enough of you."

I wrapped my arms around his neck and nodded. "Take all you want."

"Can I have everything?" Mathias kissed my lips gently. "Will you give me all of you?"

"Yes." I arched against the tile as he started to thrust into me. "Yes. Everything."

Everything. I had no time to absorb the fact that I meant it. I would give him everything.

He turned, pushed open the stall door, and tightened his grip on me as we left the shower. Seconds later I was flat on my back; the cool tile beneath me was startling. I let my legs drop away from his waist and pressed my feet against the floor as he pumped into me. Each thrust was harder and more demanding than the last, and I took it all and demanded more.

The pressure of his body against mine, the glide of his cock into my body, was suddenly more than I could take. I came in a rush of wetness and arched hard off the floor. He slowed his pace and tucked his face against the side of my neck as climax rocked his body.

We lay there spent and breathless for at least a minute before he raised his head and met my gaze. "We didn't use a condom."

Second time that hadn't crossed my mind. "Do I need to worry about that?"

"Not on my end."

"Then we're good." I ran my fingers along his jaw and shook my head. "But this floor is cold and hard."

He lifted off me with a laugh and then picked me up. "Sorry."

"No problem."

Mathias tossed me on the bed and then crawled up to lay beside me. "I really didn't mean to upset you by leaving."

"It's okay." I turned my face away from him and sighed. "I shouldn't have gotten bent about it. It isn't like we've made any grand promises to each other."

"No promises." He sighed and rubbed his face. "No complications."

"You think I'd be a complication?"

He laughed. "Certainly. In fact, you could be the single biggest complication I've ever encountered. I don't know what I'm going to do on Monday."

"We'll get up and go to work."

"That simple?"

"It can be." I turned and looked at him then. "Nothing about this has to be difficult."

"Okay." He rolled to his side. "And if I still want you like crazy on Monday?"

"You'll have to smile and pretend that this never happened." I pursed my lips briefly. "And so will I. I've already done a really stupid thing recently. I don't have any room for maneuvering when it comes to James Brooks. Mercy might overlook it, but he wouldn't. Business is business."

"Yet Mercy Rothell had a flaming affair with my brother and he never blinked an eye."

"Yeah." I laughed softly. "She still is."

"They are good for each other." He reached out and pulled me into his arms. "So, why can't we?"

"Because I don't have an Ivy League college education to flounce about."

"You think James Brooks gives a rat's ass where you were educated?"

"Boston is about appearances, and I've had to work hard to project the right one. I don't have connections from college or old family friends to get me where I want to be. I've had to work damn hard to get here, and I'm not going to fuck up now."

"So this master plan of yours doesn't have a slot for a relationship?"

It did. At least, it had a slot for the right relationship. "Is that what you want with me?"

"Hell, I don't know. I just don't like the idea of being dismissed."

"This was all your idea." I poked him in the chest and pulled away from him. "I was going to suffer this attraction in silence. But you had to come over here and get me all worked up."

"I got you worked up?"

"Yeah!" I left the bed and went to the dresser for a T-shirt. I pulled it on and crossed my arms over my breasts. "Are we about to argue?"

"Probably." He left the bed and pulled on a pair of jeans.

"Mathias, you and I both knew what this could and could not be." I turned and rummaged through my panties. If I was going to argue with a man, I needed my drawers on. I pulled on a pair quickly and walked past him to leave the bedroom. "I don't have time for anything else."

"What about the mama's boy?"

"What about him?" I frowned. The last thing I wanted to talk about was Charlie. "That is none of your business."

"No, he's just another poor bastard in your life that gets half of you."

I glared at him, fury rushing all over me. "You're barely in my life. I didn't even know you two days ago. I fucked you, Mathias." I waved my hand around the living room and then sat down in my favorite chair. "It's what you said you wanted. Yet now you're treating me like I left you at the altar or something. What the hell is wrong with just having this?"

"Nothing." He rubbed his face. "At least, I thought so on Friday."

"And now?"

"Jane, I think I want more."

"I don't have it to give." I sucked in a breath. "And even if I did, I barely know you."

"Yeah, you've just spent the last twenty-four hours fucking me."

"And you barely know me." I glared at him when he started to respond. "How can I possibly take your interest seriously when all you do know about me is that I like to fuck?"

"That's bullshit."

"It's the truth."

"I know a lot more about you than you think," he murmured carefully. "I know you have nightmares about the shooting, that you believed yourself in love with your partner when he was killed, and that the last thing you ever want to do is be a disappointment to anyone."

I crossed my arms over my breasts and took a deep breath. "You don't know what you're talking about."

"The thing is, Jane, you couldn't disappoint a single person that ever spent more than five minutes with you. I've never known a woman like you, and it makes me furious that you hide so much of yourself away."

"I make my own decisions."

"Yes, you've made that clear. The sad thing is that you don't even bother to consider what you need in the process."

He turned on his heel and left the living room. I didn't follow, because I figured if I watched him gather his stuff I would start crying. It's terribly uncool to cry over a man. It's also fucked up to argue with someone and not get make-up sex afterward.

I sighed when he appeared with his bag. "You don't have to go."

"I do."

"Why?"

"Because, Ms. Tilwell, I'm finished fucking you." He tossed a small key ring, with my door key on it, on the table in front of me and left.

I sat where I was even after I heard the door shut. That arrogant bastard had actually said he was *finished* fucking me.

5

Monday sucks. There probably hasn't been a Monday in the existence of recorded history that didn't suck for at least one person. I'd endured good-natured teasing from the morning shift guards as I'd entered the gallery, but after that I'd managed to scoot into my office. Once there I glared at anyone who came near or stood in my doorway. So far, it had worked.

My assistant, Casey Andrews, was at her desk. I figured she was bursting with curiosity and found her restraint a relief. There wasn't a single cell in my body that was up to talking about a single part of this weekend, and that included Friday night. Since she was tied up in several large projects, she'd probably leave me in peace for most of the day.

I had over a hundred e-mails unanswered, a stack of phone messages, and little to no urge to address any of it. In truth, I was waiting for him to show up. I knew that he would be touring the gallery today. One security consultant had already come and gone. From my fishbowl of an office, it had been easy to keep track of my boss, Mercy, and the contractor as Mercy had outlined the gallery's needs.

Why the hell was I waiting for him to show up? He was *finished* fucking me. I've never had a man leave me like that in my life. I decide when I'm done with a man, and his deviation from his role in our empty physical relationship had me all twisted and, okay, pissed. I never should've gotten sexual with him in the first place. Mathias Montgomery may be the sexiest man I've ever known in my life, but going to bed with him had been a huge mistake.

I sat back in my chair and swung it around so I could look out the window. If he won the contract for the security upgrade, Mathias would be spending a lot of time in my workplace. I had to formulate a battle plan or there would be no telling what would happen. For all I knew, I could fall at his feet at the sight of him and beg for more. Not gonna happen. There was no way I was that far gone. Several things crossed my mind, but the last thing I was, was a black hole of need with no dignity.

"Hey."

I turned in my chair and smiled at Mercy. "Good morning."

She came in and closed the door. "I think that's the first time that you've ever done that."

"Done what?" I asked softly, worried that she could read me like an open book. All I could do was hope that I was doing a good job of keeping my anger and hurt in a deep place.

"You just fake smiled at me." She sat down in a chair in front of me and crossed her arms over her breasts. "What's up?"

"Nothing."

"I'm not buying it."

"That's good because I'm not selling it." I reached out and fiddled with my computer mouse and then sighed. "I'm not a morning person, you know."

"You also don't fake smile at people either." She glared at me pointedly. "Not even when that troll Milton Storey was here. So something is wrong."

"Everyone fake smiles at people. I do it every morning when I'm leaving my apartment and the twit across the hall from me comes out in his bathrobe to greet me. Ratty, green bathrobe and fake smile actually go hand in hand."

"You shouldn't encourage him."

"I breathe. That's all the encouragement he needs."

It was true enough. Though living beside a weird, nosy little man was actually sort of comforting. He always knew when there was a stranger in the building, and he would sign for my packages. Though I was pretty sure he kept the last thing I ordered from Victoria's Secret.

"You're upset about something." She was staring at me, that hard stare she gave people when she figured they were lying to her. I'd never been the recipient of that stare, and frankly it made me very uncomfortable.

"Yeah." I nodded. "The price of gasoline, global warming, rabid Republicans in charge of our country, and the fact that the networks have scheduled two of my favorite shows in the same time slot on Sunday nights. I'm gonna have to get one of those digital recorder things."

"Not funny." She tried to glare, but a little smile hovered on her lips.

"I know for a fact I'm funny and entertaining."

God, I wished she'd drop it. I couldn't, wouldn't discuss what had happened with her. Certainly not right now, and maybe not ever. But lying to her had me shaking on the inside.

"You got laid."

"Pardon me?" I sat up straight in my chair and swallowed hard. One statement and she'd reduced me to an outraged modern version of Scarlett O'Hara.

"Don't even bother lying. Your accent sneaks into your voice when you try to lie. It's like a built-in lie detector or something." She stood. "Fine. Keep your little secret. I'll find out eventually."

That was exactly what I was afraid of. "You know I'm not seeing anyone."

"Except that stuck-up lawyer." She wrinkled her nose. "But I thought you'd started pushing him off in a new direction. I mean, you haven't brought him up in weeks."

"Charlie is not stuck up and he's better than those nerds you used to date. We can all thank God Shamus Montgomery came into your life when he did. There is no telling what kind of man you'd have ended up with. Maybe a dentist." All I could do was hope she'd take the change of subject and move on. I was pretty damn close to losing it right then and there.

She laughed and shrugged. "I'm a very lucky woman."

"Get out of my office." I pointed toward the door. "I don't have to sit here and bask in your domestic bliss."

"That really doesn't fit." Mercy walked to the door and then pulled it open. "The last thing Shame is, is domesticated."

Okay, so fine. Now I'm going to think about my boss's future husband doing wild, freaky things to her. Considering they are both beautiful people, it wasn't an entirely unpleasant mental picture.

I shook it off and looked out into the bull pen just as Mathias walked past my office. He didn't even glance my way. It shouldn't have mattered, yet as I watched him walk away from me, it mattered a whole lot.

I wanted him to be as keen to see me as I had been him. Obviously, he had a lot more willpower, or our weekend together had meant absolutely nothing to him. Though he'd given me no indication that he was the kind of man who got past things that didn't work out his way. In fact, I figured he was furious. Furious with me and probably with himself for letting things get out of hand the way they had. He'd said at the very beginning that he wanted to get me out of his system, and I felt pretty comfortable in the knowledge that he had *not* accomplished that.

I sat back in my chair and plucked my PDA from its station.

Fiddling with it wasn't a big enough distraction, so the soft swoosh of my office door opening garnered my immediate attention. I swallowed hard and tried to smile pleasantly as Mercy and Mathias entered.

"Hey, can you give Mathias the tour? I have a conference call in ten minutes." She checked her watch and cut her eyes at me as if I might tell her no. I figured she suspected that he might be the cause of my sour mood.

Standing, I put my handheld down on the desk carefully and nodded. "Of course."

She smiled and with a little wave left me alone with him. I knew she was matchmaking, but I figured letting her win on this front might help me avoid another conversation with her about my sex life.

Mathias closed the door gently and sighed. He looked contrite, but I honestly wasn't sure if it was an act. "I owe you an apology."

I swallowed and tugged at my waist-length jacket. "Actually, I'd rather not talk about past events. If you'll follow me we can get this out of the way."

"Past events?" His tone had a soft but lethal quality that I found insanely attractive.

"Yes, that's what I said." I stopped just short of being within his reach, and when he started to move, I shook my head abruptly. "Don't."

"Don't what?" he demanded through clenched teeth.

"Touch me." I took a slight step away from him and met his gaze. "This is where I work, and everyone on the other side of that stupid glass wall can see us. I won't give them anything to talk about. There isn't a member of our staff who isn't fully aware that I earned my degrees in night school while they were getting too drunk to remember their own name in pricey Ivy League schools." I glanced out into the bull pen and then focused on him. "Please."

"Are they insulted that you're their boss?" He shoved his hands into the pockets of his dark blue slacks and for all the world looked casual and at ease. I could tell he was neither.

"Probably, but that doesn't bother me. I don't live to make them happy. That doesn't mean, however, I'm going to give them ammunition to use against me." I bit down on my lip briefly.

It occurred to me that I had never once voiced those concerns, not even to Mercy. Of course, I knew Mercy would've torn me a new one for it, but she came from a different world than me. She could afford to not care where my education came from.

"Fine. I believe you have a tour to give me." He opened the door and motioned me out ahead of him.

I inhaled deeply as I passed him. Aftershave, soap, and something I couldn't identify teased at my nose and reminded me of things I needed no reminders of. "We can start with the third floor. It's currently the home of several large exhibits, including your brother's collection. Lisa Millhouse's show came a few weeks after his. All of the pieces have been sold, and as you can imagine Mr. Brooks is very interested in protecting the pieces."

"Yes, that concern did come up several times during our conversation."

"Your demonstration was unnerving and would've been more so if I hadn't been here." I glanced back at him as I walked toward a narrow hallway that connected the administrative area to the third-floor viewing areas. "The current contents of the gallery have a collection worth $500 million."

"Because of the Impressionist exhibit on loan from New York?"

"Yes. If it became widely known that Holman can't provide adequate security we'd lose a great many relationships with artists and museums." I winced when the door to the admin area closed and we were alone. "This is the staff entrance to the third-floor show area. All patrons of the gallery must use the front elevator or the main staircase."

"This area isn't under surveillance." He glanced around the narrow hall. "What are these rooms for?"

I paused and glanced around the narrow hallway. "No surveillance, and two of the rooms are storage and the third is an empty office."

"There should be cameras in here. How deep are the background checks on the staff?"

"Criminal and financial background checks are done on all employees every six months. We have a firm that performs those reviews for the gallery. Random drug tests are conducted yearly, and if we find a user on staff, they are required to undergo a treatment program. If they refuse treatment or they've tested positive in the past they are immediately released."

"Fired?"

"Yes." I nodded and wished silently that I'd taken him through the public area instead of the private one. The last thing I needed to be was alone with him.

"Their key cards are immediately nullified in the system?"

"Of course. Only senior members of staff and security have key cards. They are updated weekly." I stopped at the door that would lead us to the show floor. "How did you get in?"

"I downloaded the program that handles the key card system for the building and then implanted a manual code to let me in."

"That easy?" My stomach tightened with nerves. That kind of vulnerability in our security was sickening.

"Possible, but it takes some work. The average B & E guy isn't going to make that kind of effort."

"Okay, but the average criminal isn't going to break into a gallery like this. We don't keep cash on hand, and fencing artwork isn't something a street thug will likely know how to do." It was comfortable talking about work things, but I knew he was only biding his time.

"Right." He nodded as he walked toward me.

I resisted the urge to back away or run. I'd done more than enough of that already. "But breaking into a place like this and vandalizing it would be a tempting target for gang initiation."

"So, we're looking at a variety of criminals that might find the gallery attractive for one purpose or another." He sighed. "I was frustrated with you on Saturday."

"I know." I crossed my arms over my breasts and looked down at the floor between us. "Frankly, I'm a little frustrated with you right now."

"Why is that?"

"You made a deal with me, Mathias, and then you changed the rules. It wasn't fair."

"That's childish."

"Fine. Then I'm childish and you're an insensitive jackass." I snapped and then grimaced at the emotion I heard running through my words. My eyes dampened, and I closed them briefly. "I'm not prepared for this."

"I know."

"Then you should have the decency to back off." I met his gaze as I said it and saw nothing that made me think he agreed with me. "You think that I don't know what I want? Why do men always assume they know what's best? I've been making my own decisions for at least 15 years, and I've managed to make them quite nicely without you."

He moved so fast that by the time he'd gathered me up and covered my mouth with his, all I had time to do was respond to the kiss. I moaned against his invading tongue and wrapped my arms around his neck. It had been easy to think that I wouldn't care if he never touched me again. Wrong but easy.

I let my head drop back as his lips left mine to travel across my jaw to my neck. "This is the wrong place for this."

"I know." His hands curled into fists against my back and then loosened his hold on me. "You wore *the* suit."

Swallowing hard I pulled my hands from his shoulders and shook my head as he released me. "Not on purpose."

"I don't believe you."

Hell, I didn't believe me either. It had crossed my mind as I'd dressed that he'd mentioned liking it. "It's my favorite." I crossed my arms over my breasts as he backed away from me. My nipples were hard and aching, and it took very little effort to remember the feeling of his very talented mouth on them. "We agreed that we wouldn't be personally involved after the weekend."

"It was probably the stupidest thing I've ever suggested in my life."

"But you suggested it. You did this, Mathias. I could have been fine without all of this emotional crap. This can't happen again. You and I both know the chances of you not winning this contract bid are slim. You impressed the hell out of James Brooks already, and that's hard to do. My work is important to me, and I worked too damn long and hard to have it endangered by a sexual liaison that shouldn't have happened and won't happen again." And I couldn't even look at him while I said it. I met his gaze but couldn't repeat it.

"Why?" he asked softly, his voice bearing none of the frustration that showed clearly on his face.

"I don't have room for complications." I pressed my lips together firmly to avoid saying anything else.

"What would you call your friend Charlie? He isn't a complication?"

Boring. I shook my head. It was obvious that I couldn't defend the nonrelationship I had with Charlie. "My relationships are none of your business."

"I've been in this game long enough to know when I find something special. You can't make me believe that what you have with him can even compare to what moves between us."

My attraction to him was so deep and elemental that I could

barely comprehend it entirely. Closing my eyes, it was easy to remember his body moving on mine, within me.

"He isn't part of this conversation."

"No, why would he be? He's just the man you allow to stay in your life even though you couldn't care one way or the other if you ever laid eyes on him again. Is that why it's so easy to say that you aren't involved with someone?"

"He's a distraction." I admitted, and then shrugged at the shocked look on his face.

"Christ, that's cold."

"I never claimed to be more than I am." Resisting the urge to rub my face in frustration, I took a deep breath and demanded, "Can we just get this over with?"

"By all means." He pushed the door shut as I tried to pull it open and pressed against me. For a few seconds we stood there, his cock pressed against my ass showing me exactly how much he wanted me. "We aren't done."

"You said you were finished fucking me." My hand tightened on the door knob.

"I lied." He slid one hand down my side and around to my stomach to press me back against his erection. "You think about how this feels . . . because before the day is out I'm going to be in you again. Hard and fast or gentle and slow—any way you want it—but it's going to happen."

"No" was my first reaction, and I regretted it immediately. Denying the attraction I had for him was stupid and juvenile, but it was too late to take it back.

"Yes, and you know it."

He released me then and opened the door. I slid past him and took a deep breath as I entered the show floor.

Suddenly, he was way too much for me to handle.

"How did the tour go?"

I glanced up and focused on Mercy. "Matchmaking?"

She shrugged and pulled the door shut behind her. "He's pretty, you're pretty . . . seems like it could be fun."

Yeah, it was fun. But it had to be over. I didn't have room for a man like Mathias. Demanding, aggressive, and complicated. "I'm not ready for anything serious, and when I am it won't be a problem for me to locate a man." She sat down in front of my desk and crossed her legs. I watched her bounce her foot for a few seconds before I met her gaze. "No more matchmaking."

"Can't make that promise. Being in love has made me into some creature that has to plot the romantic lives of others."

I laughed and shook my head as she smiled. "Well, be prepared for me to ignore you."

"Granted."

"You chose an interesting way to get James's attention."

"The security is bad. I've been saying it since I got here, and after I became director I realized that I needed to take drastic measures." She shrugged. "The point was made, and it also served to highlight the risks to the staff in the building after hours."

"I feel bad enough as it is."

"I'm not trying to lecture you. If it hadn't been you, it might have been someone else. I do hope that if the situation were to happen in the future, you would use better judgment."

"I sure would." I'd pick up a weapon on my way to the disturbance. A big, heavy blunt object. I tapped my fingers on the desk and thought about those first few moments with Mathias when I'd thought he was a criminal. His body pressed against mine, and the heat he'd teased in me before I'd even seen his face. "How many more contractors do we have to see today?"

"James called four firms including Mathias's. Their bids are due before end of business today."

"No pressure."

"I got my point across. He's hired ten off-duty cops to be in the building after hours until we have a new trained guard service and the new security system." Mercy stood and looked around my office. "You know, I kind of miss this fishbowl."

"Speaking of, the vertical blinds have arrived and will be installed by the end of the week." I looked toward the glass wall and the bull pen area that was almost empty. "How are things going with the lawsuit against Storey?"

Mercy sighed and slouched in the chair a little. "James is a little frosty with me on that subject, though he was just as aware of Storey's behavior as I was."

"It was his problem and he ignored it." I shrugged. "There were complaints against Milton Storey in the past, long before you arrived, and the board should have dealt with his sexist and abusive behavior long before now; perhaps being sued was exactly the kind of wake-up call that James Brooks needed."

"Ladies."

I sat up a little in my chair and offered James Brooks a smile. "I meant that in the best way possible."

He laughed softly and shook his head. Even white teeth gleamed against his neatly trimmed black beard. The man was quite fine, but I'd never thought of him sexually, which was weird for me, as I can imagine almost any attractive man in a freaky sexual position of my choosing. It's a talent I've always sort of reveled in.

"You couldn't have said it better. My willingness to put up with that man to avoid paying him a severance package is going to cost me big." He came in and sat down in a chair next to Mercy. "I've decided to settle with the woman."

"Oh really?" I raised an eyebrow in shock.

"Yes, the board isn't all that happy with it, but I'd rather settle now than deal with a public relations nightmare a year from now." He checked his watch and then glanced between the two of us. "She took far less than I thought I'd have to pay. I guess she's really planning to stick it to Storey pretty hard."

"Well, he did use his position in the gallery to lure her into a sexual relationship where she was promised advancements." Mercy sighed. "Her judgment was poor, and she never realized that he was using her to get back at me until the very end."

"You almost sound like you feel sorry for her." I frowned at her. "She wasn't a victim in that relationship. She traded sexual favors for professional advancement and then sued when she didn't get what she wanted."

"I feel like I failed her," Mercy admitted softly. "I should've intervened sooner or maybe fired her when I realized the situation was going on. Instead, I let her stay in the hopes that she would be enough of a distraction that Milton wouldn't be too difficult to deal with until we could oust him."

"You weren't alone in that decision, Mercy." James sighed. "Let's just chalk this up as a lesson learned."

"And the moral of the story?" I asked softly.

James chuckled. "Let's just all take our own lessons from it. I have a feeling you wouldn't appreciate my point of view on the subject." He cleared his throat. "Okay, tell me about the security firms that came through."

Mercy cleared her throat. "Well, I briefed all but Mr. Montgomery. All of them asked good questions about the history of the gallery."

James focused on me, and I frowned. It was uncomfortable reporting on Mathias, and after a few seconds, I nodded. "I would say the same of Mr. Montgomery. Though he does consider art somewhat silly, he understands the value that we place on it. He asked questions about the current system and mentioned several improvements during the tour."

"Are you still angry with him?"

"For what?"

"For the break-in," James answered patiently.

"Oh." Shrugging, I thought about how I felt about his behavior that night. "No. My pride has recovered."

He nodded and rubbed his beard in thought. "The bids are due this afternoon."

"Why so soon?"

"The bid process itself can take a long time. To avoid it and to test them, I set a one-day deadline. I want to know what they are made of."

"What he is made of," I correctly softly.

James laughed. "Well, yes. If he's as good as his reputation, then this little challenge will be nothing for him. His firm in New York does very well. Boston can be fortunate that his brother lives here."

Mathias had come to Boston to be closer to his family, and I'd moved here to avoid mine. Staying in Savannah, seeing the pity and the concern in their eyes every damn day, had seemed impossible. Unwilling to indulge in those feelings, I stood from my chair. "Well, I believe I'll do a walk-through of the sales floor and then take a break."

"Ms. Rothell, we're being dismissed." James stood, an amused smile lighting his nearly perfect face. I'd always wondered how he broke his nose, but I would never ask. Knowing would ruin the mystery of it, and we all need a little suspense in our life.

"She's been putting on airs since she moved into this office." Mercy pushed her red hair over her shoulder as she stood.

I laughed as James offered her his arm and they headed toward the door. "The two of you define 'putting on airs'."

People spend entirely too much time shopping. I'd watched the women browse through the gallery sales floor like vultures. Vultures with expensive and very specific taste. They'd spent half a million dollars in thirty minutes without blinking an eye. The sales staff were jumping to their every demand, just like they'd been trained to do.

When I'd come to Boston, I took jobs as sales clerks in several galleries around the city. I paid for college and lived a cushy life on commissions. The galleries, including Holman's, had been thrilled to have a sales clerk with a law enforcement background on the sales floor, even if I was female. My former career had paved the way for the new one.

I walked outside and took in a deep breath. Winter had been slow coming, but the wind had started to bite a little. As I came from the south, my first year in Boston had been a mixture of wonder and misery. Too cold at times but beautiful in a brisk, different way from home. I'd fallen in love with that difference and had learned quickly to deal with it.

A block down from the gallery, I walked into a deli and grabbed my usual. An espresso with a double shot of caffeine and a coffee-flavored brownie. Caffeine and chocolate weren't the ideal lunch but they satisfied a craving. The walk back to the gallery helped me settle a little; the last thing I needed was to be all jittery in front of James and Mercy.

I'd worked long and hard to earn a place in Holman's and I wasn't going to let anything stand in my way. No man was worth the expense of my dreams.

Any way you want it. I wanted it a couple hundred different ways, and I figured that Mathias would be game for most if not all of it. I was sitting behind the wheel of my car and had been for about twenty minutes. I'd spent the afternoon avoiding practically everyone and trying to forget Mathias. That had been painfully unsuccessful.

There were a few options. I could go home and wait for him to show up, find a place for dinner and let him wonder where I was . . . or I could go to him. Maybe it was time I turned the tables on him.

I pulled out my handheld and found the e-mail he'd sent to the gallery with his bid. I'd received copies of all of the bids. He hadn't cut corners on his despite the fact that he knew James Brooks liked to torture Abe Lincoln on an hourly basis. I'd expected to be impressed and hadn't been disappointed. Mathias was thorough, professionally and intimately.

He was staying in a swanky hotel downtown. The knowledge was both disconcerting and comforting. I knew where he was . . . but a hotel room didn't spell anything permanent. He'd come to Boston to start a business but would he move on if he found a better opportunity elsewhere? Did I even want him to stay in Boston? He represented a huge and practically insurmountable complication.

So I argued with myself all the way over to the hotel, through valet parking, and on the swift elevator ride up to his floor. I let the doors to the elevator slide shut without leaving. It wasn't nerves that made me hesitate . . . but the pure lack of them. I rested against the wall and closed my eyes briefly. I pulled my skirt up my thighs, hooked my fingers into the sides of my panties, and slid them off.

After shoving them into my purse, I pushed the button to open the door and left the elevator. The hall was wide and empty. The walk to his room gave me plenty of time to consider what to say when he opened the door. I stopped in front of his door and stared at the number for a few seconds. The gold swirly numbers embedded in the door below a peephole reminded me yet again of the fluid condition of his lifestyle.

I knocked briskly and heard activity on the opposite side of the door briefly before it swung open. My gaze drifted over his bare chest and muscled stomach to the worn jeans that clung to his slim hips. "Nice."

Nice barely described an inch of the man much less the whole package. He did it for me three ways from Sunday, and I figured that was the reason coming to his hotel room had been such an easy decision.

"This is a surprise." He leaned against the door a little and looked me over. "I called your apartment but there was no answer. I figured you were going to hide from me."

"That wouldn't be my style." At least it wasn't the style I'd worked very hard to perfect. He might rock my world sexually, but I was in charge, damn it.

"I see." There was a cool tone to his voice as if he, like me, was calculating risk and reward while we talked.

He backed up and motioned me inside. I dropped my purse on a small table near the door and watched him flip the lock on the door. A suite. Somehow I figured he wouldn't be the type to suffer with just a simple room. I turned and watched him as he walked toward me.

Oversized furniture dominated the impersonal sitting area. A television sat dormant in one corner. The walls were a rich burgundy to match the pillows tossed artfully around the couch and chairs. It probably should have felt inviting. But no matter its trappings, it was a hotel room.

"Is this you making a move on me?" he asked softly.

"Maybe I don't like waiting around for people to act." I glanced him over as I spoke.

"I didn't expect you to show up here," he admitted, and shoved his hands into his jeans. "I figured we were about to enter that stage of things where you played hard to get."

I unbuttoned my jacket and started to shrug it off.

"No." He came to me and took my hands. "Not yet."

Flushing a little, I frowned. "I wasn't about to take off all my clothes and beg for sex."

"You aren't the type of woman to beg for anything." He brushed his fingers along my jaw. "Just looking at you makes me a little stupid."

He knew exactly what to say. I leaned into him as he pulled me closer and wondered why that didn't bother me. In the past men as smooth as Mathias would have had me on edge immediately. Of course, the difference was that I believed him. "I came over here because I wanted to be in charge of this situation."

"And are you?"

"I don't know." I gasped a little as he slid his hands around my waist and under my jacket. "I don't think I want to be."

Mathias moved his hands down to my ass. "You have a decision to make."

"Really?" I curled one hand into the front of his jeans. "I think I've already made enough decisions tonight."

"Are you sure?" he asked softly as he maneuvered me gently.

I gasped when my back met with the solid surface of the wall. "I wouldn't be here if I wasn't."

"You make me want some pretty primitive things." He ran his finger along my jawline and then leaned in to kiss me. "I had plans for this suit of yours."

"I remember."

"But, really, I just want to get you naked, lay you out on my bed, and take you over."

He pushed my jacket over my shoulders, and I let it fall to the floor. The fine linen whispered against my legs as it settled near my feet.

"Tell me I can have you, Jane."

I sighed against his kiss and wrapped my arms around his neck. "Yes, you can have me."

He kissed me hard and then took a step back from me. I watched him, caught up in his eyes and the way he looked at me.

There had never been a man like him for me. Why was it so easy to give over to his control? I pushed off my shoes and followed along gamely when he took my hand and started toward what had to be the bedroom.

We stopped at the foot of the bed and I watched silently as

he gently unbuttoned my blouse. He tugged it from my skirt, and I shrugged it off. Pulling me close, he unzipped my skirt. His fingers brushed against the sensitive skin of my back with every movement he made. I wondered what he'd think of my missing panties.

I rested my hands on his arms, so relieved to be close to him again. The smoothness of his skin, the heat of his body, and the heady smell of soap and him had all of my senses on overload.

He stepped back as he released my skirt and it fell to the floor. I stood still in front of him clad only in a bra and a pair of thigh highs. The hose felt naughty, even risqué. It was almost worse than being naked.

"Very nice," he murmured as he ran his fingertip across the top of one breast. "Please tell me you were wearing panties earlier today."

I laughed at his tone, surprised at the near desperation I heard there. "I took them off in the elevator."

Mathias moved closer and covered my mouth with his. The sweep of his tongue against my lips made me gasp, and I opened to his sweet invasion. His hands moved down my back to cup my ass. I wrapped my arms around his neck as he lifted me. Being in his arms was amazing, and it was easy to forget everything that had already happened between us.

I released him as he laid me out on the mattress and hovered over me. He kissed my lips softly once more and then moved downward. Mathias placed soft kisses down between my breasts, his lips skirting the edge of my bra, down my stomach until he came to my pussy. I spread my legs and stiffened while I waited.

Carefully he tugged the thigh highs to my knees and then pulled them away. I unclasped the front closure of my bra, pulled it away, and tossed it in the direction he'd fired my hosiery.

He placed a soft kiss on the lips of my sex before he slipped his tongue inside to find my clit. A broken sound burst from my mouth as he pressed my legs apart with firm hands. I jerked against the delicious action of his mouth until he pushed his tongue into me and I shattered under the pressure of orgasm.

Rocking back and forth against his mouth, I let myself drown in pleasure for a few long minutes. The sweet sensation curled into my body and left me wanting more.

"More." I clutched at his head. "You have to fuck me."

He lifted off me and unbuttoned his jeans with shaking hands. "I love how you taste. I could eat you for hours."

I pressed my feet up against the bed as he stood up and took off his jeans. "Now."

"Let me get a condom."

I sat up and reached for him. "I need you inside me, Mathias. Just you."

"Jane." His tone was one of question.

"I have birth control covered." I stroked the side of his face and swallowed hard. "I just need you to be as naked as I am."

"Anything you want." His lips brushed over mine gently.

He came down with me willingly, the head of his cock pushing almost immediately against my entrance. I spread my legs wider as he thrust into me with ease. The hot, stinging pleasure of taking him stole my breath. I lay beneath him, impaled and loving every second of it.

"Yes. Yes." I dug my hands into his back. "Fuck me."

He thrust upward into me, stretching my insides and rubbing against my G-spot in the most amazing way I'd ever known. I was so wet, so hot for it that every thrust of his cock into my cunt sent heavy arcs of pleasure through me.

"I need more."

He pressed into me hard and stopped. "I'll give you everything you need."

I tightened my fingers into his as he took my hands and arched against my body. The feeling of being pressed between him and the bed swept over me, and I wrapped my legs around his waist in an effort to hold him closer. "Harder."

"Yes." He pushed his arms under me and started to slam into me.

Every pounding thrust of his cock into me was a tiny bit of satisfaction that layered and layered until another orgasm burst over me. My vision darkened, and I groaned with the pleasure of it. He rocked into me as my body rushed wet with the pleasure he'd given me.

Mathias stiffened against me as he came and buried his face in the side of my neck. "Perfect."

We held each other, rocking gently against each other as the hot feeling of orgasm drifted away. When I could, I slowly released my legs from his hips and sighed when he pulled his still-hard cock from my body. He rolled onto his back beside me, my hand still caught in his.

I turned into him and rested my cheek on his chest. He brought my hand up to his mouth and kissed my palm. It was the kind of intimate and personal thing that should've had me running for the door. "We do have some very amazing sex."

"Yeah." He chuckled softly. "We sure do. In fact, you could be the best time I've ever had."

Had there been many women? I could assume so; surely I'd had my share of men. "You're certainly the most interesting man I've known."

"That's not surprising."

I turned and looked at him and frowned. "What's that supposed to mean?"

"You date lawyers and probably investment bankers. It isn't like you to go out of your way to involve yourself with people who will actually challenge and excite you."

"Are you being insulting on purpose?" I demanded, wondering why he would ruin what had turned out to be a very pleasant encounter with another argument.

"I'm being honest."

"I'm perfectly fine with not hearing the so-called truth from people who barely know me." I started to leave the bed but he snagged my arm and pulled me close to him. I relaxed against the heat of him and closed my eyes. "So, if you know so much . . . why am I here?"

"Because it hasn't occurred to you that this thing between us isn't going to go away."

"How can you be sure?" I curled my fingers into his when he picked up my hand.

"Don't you feel it?" He maneuvered me onto my back and covered me with his body.

I moved under him and moaned softly when he pushed his cock up against the entrance of my pussy. Although swollen and overpleasured already, I couldn't help but spread my legs for him and accept, with a needy sound, the thrust of his body into mine. "Yes."

"Has it ever been so good before?" he asked softly against my lips.

"No." I shook my head abruptly and tightened my fingers against his. "Never."

He kept his gaze on mine as we moved together, the delicious friction of his skin on mine pushing a low sound from my mouth.

"I feel like you were made for me," he whispered.

I closed my eyes and pulled him down close. There was a part of me that agreed. No man had ever felt so perfect or so right. All of it was beginning to scare the hell out of me. I had plenty of things going on in my life. The last thing I needed was a complicated sexual relationship that kept me off balance and out of control.

6

Pleasure is hard to walk away from. Even when that physical feeling is surrounded by insecurity and guilt. I buttoned the shirt I'd pulled from the narrow closet across from the bed and walked out into the small living room of the suite. He was on the couch, remote in hand, staring intently at the television.

"Anything interesting?"

He tossed the remote aside and held out his hand. "No."

I slid into his lap with more ease than I liked and settled astride his thighs. Being comfortable with him would lead to things that I was just not ready for. "Tell me where you think this will go with us, Mathias."

He glanced over my face and plucked gently at the hem of the shirt where it rested on my thigh. "I don't know. I think it would be a mistake not to explore it."

"Don't you think that this kind of play could be bad for us professionally?" It was starting to sound like a very weak argument, but it was what I had.

"I'm an adult, Jane. I can keep my personal life out of my professional one, and I believe that you can too."

"And if you take over the security contract for the gallery?"

"I'll be there a few months solid getting things in place and working with the security personnel that I bring in, but Holman's isn't going to be my only project in Boston."

"It's not?"

"Of course not." He laughed softly and ran his finger along my jaw. "I came to Boston to be closer to my brother; this is no whim. I've been planning the move for nearly a year. My offices will be ready for occupation by the end of the week, and my team will move in."

"Where are they now?"

"They are all staying in the hotel, but we are using a conference room here for our office space at the moment." He rubbed my thighs gently, his fingers encouraging my muscles to relax. "You're getting tense on me."

"I don't know why." I did know why. The thought of him staying in Boston was a source of both relief and immense dread. He was the kind of man that I could spend my life drowning in, and I had plans that didn't jive with that.

"I do." He laughed softly. "You thought that there was a chance I'd leave if I didn't win the Holman contract."

I had. "You have family in New York as well."

"Yes, but Shamus is here and this is where he will remain. Once I realized that, I made the choice to come here. Our parents are getting older, and now that they are both retired, they are starting to travel more and more. Kane, our younger brother, will be graduating and coming to college in Boston in the next two years. There isn't much left in New York to hold me in the long term. I'll visit, of course, but Boston will be home. It's a good city for a man to have a family in."

"A family."

"Yeah. A snotty, expensive dog; sexy, amazing woman, and maybe a couple of monsters that we produce . . . a family."

"Monsters?"

"I was a horrible kid. I'm sure God will pay me back by giving me some of my own."

The thought of some other woman having Mathias's babies made me furious. But children certainly weren't in my future. I didn't have room for a family. "I see."

"You have that look on your face."

"What look is that?" I demanded.

"That look that a career woman gets when a man tells her he wants children."

I pressed my lips together and tried to think of what to say about that. It was true; I knew a lot of women who broke out into hives when they thought about having children. Pressing one hand against my flat stomach, I considered my future.

There was another part of me that feared that I would end up like my mother. Tied down to a man and children, and absolutely miserable. So miserable that I'd be forced to abandon them all.

I didn't make it a habit to talk about my mother, and I wasn't going to start now. Yet there was the thought that I might have the potential to be just like her. "But we aren't talking about that kind of future, are we?"

"Not yet."

Not yet. Christ, the man was shifty. "So, what are we talking about?"

"You, me, really good sex, dinners, movies, and no 2 A.M. friend."

He wanted me to stop seeing Charlie. I frowned and slid off his lap to move down to the other end of the couch. The man was making demands, and I didn't like it at all. I couldn't very well rearrange my life to suit a man I'd known only a few days. "You want an exclusive arrangement."

"Yes."

"No." I shook my head. Getting roped into an exclusive relationship is the beginning of a dead-end road. "I told you from the very beginning that I'm not in the market for something serious."

"It's what I need."

"But not what I want. You just can't decide for the both of us where this is going to go." I crossed my arms over my breasts and braced myself. We'd traveled this path once already. Mathias wasn't a man used to being told no.

"I need it, and if it's beyond you . . ." He sighed and stood. "I'm not going to share, Jane. If I'm not enough for you, then you can leave."

"Not enough?" I frowned at him. "The fact is that you are more than I can handle. I'm just not ready for this kind of thing." I waved my hand around. "I need space."

"Fine." He turned away from me and headed toward the small kitchen. "If you change your mind, you know where I am."

Dismissed. The smug bastard had dismissed me, again. Insulted and hurt, I stood from the couch and started to gather up my discarded clothes. "It doesn't have to be this way."

"I'm not going to share you, physically or emotionally, with another man. You've made your choice clear." He snapped, his voice hard and unrelenting.

"We barely know each other. You have no business making demands on me like this. You aren't the only person in this situation who has feelings, you know." I hugged my clothes to my chest and left the living area for the bedroom to locate the rest.

I gasped a little when he grabbed and whirled me around to face him. "Is that how it feels when I'm in you? Do you feel like I'm a stranger?"

My clothes fell to the floor between us as I grasped his shoulders. "No."

We came down on the bed in a swift, breathless movement, his thigh pressing between mine in a demand that felt so natural that I complied immediately. The flannel material of the pajama bottoms he wore rubbed against my bare thighs as he put his hands on either side of my head.

I could barely stand to meet his gaze, but I wasn't going to be weak; neither one of us deserved that. He looked angry and, yes, hurt. I felt like the worst person to ever live on earth. Here was a man who wanted me for who I was and had really asked for so little, yet I couldn't make myself give in to what he needed.

"Do you have this kind of connection with him?" he demanded.

I shook my head. How I felt with Mathias was unique—so unique that I couldn't remember ever feeling that way about anyone in my life. "No, of course not."

"Then why?"

"I don't have to explain myself to you."

He slid one hand under my head, fisted it in my hair, and covered my mouth with his. I sank into the hard, possessive kiss with all the neediness of a woman who had no control of herself. I wrapped myself around him and rocked against the erection he pressed against me.

Mathias lifted his head and shook it. "I want more than your body."

"It's all I have to offer."

He released my hair and shook his head. "You do yourself a disservice."

I closed my eyes when he lifted away, and I let my legs drop to the bed beneath me. This wasn't the way I wanted things to be between us, but I couldn't, wouldn't give in to his demand.

Mercy was sitting across from me in our favorite café, trying to be patient with me. I figured I had another minute or two of silence before I'd be forced to start talking. I'd called her as I'd sat in my car outside of his hotel.

"So, tell me."

I stared into my coffee and shrugged. "Nothing to tell."

Mercy laughed softly. "Come on, Jane. You're miserable."

"I'm fine." Fine as a woman could be considering she'd made a mess of the most intense and frankly wonderful relationship she'd ever had with a man.

"You and Mathias hooked up." She broke open her muffin and offered me half. "Don't deny it. It was written all over both of you yesterday. The man has a serious thing for you."

"I don't get physically or emotionally involved with strangers." I frowned at her for good measure. But I knew already that it was a lost cause.

"Oh yeah?" She snorted. "What's Charlie's favorite color? What did he want to be when he was six years old? His favorite subject in school?"

I couldn't have even guessed the answers to those questions. "That doesn't mean anything."

"Sure it does. You've been seeing him *casually* for nearly a year and you've never even spent the night with him. I know for a fact he's only been in your apartment like six times total, and he's barely gotten past the living room."

Okay, so what did that mean? I liked things to be neat, and spending the night with a man made things messy. Look what a mess I'd made with Mathias. "There is nothing wrong with that."

"No. Of course not. A woman can choose exactly how involved she wants to be with a man, and no one has the right to decide if it's right or wrong." Mercy sat back in the booth we were sharing and glanced around the cafe. "Yet if we put all that aside I can count on one hand the number of times that you've called me at 9 P.M. on a work night for something. You sounded like a nervous wreck on the phone. Otherwise I can assure you I'd be wrapped up in my man right now."

"Is it weird?"

"What?"

"Having a man in your life like Shamus. Don't you miss the freedom?"

"I'm not the man's slave." Mercy snorted. "We have a relationship, Jane, and it's not one sided. We both sacrifice things to be together, and at the end of the day knowing that I can go to him and not have to worry about anything else is priceless to me. I don't know what I feared about falling in love. If I'd known it would make me feel so complete I wouldn't have backed away from Shame once."

"And marriage?"

"Marriage." Mercy sighed. "It's a social obligation of a sort, isn't it? People expect it, sometimes even demand it if you want to be respected."

"Children?"

She paused and cleared her throat. "Lord, this man's got you thinking too much."

"I'm being real."

"Okay." She cleared her throat and nodded. "I think about children lately, in a way that I never did before. A baby is the ultimate commitment, ya know? Of course I've thought about having Shame's baby, and when I do, it won't scare me. I know he'll be there. I know he'll love our baby without reservation or stipulation . . . just the way he does me."

"No stipulations?" I shook my head. "Your relationship is full of stipulations."

"Name one."

"It isn't like you can still date."

"Well, that's hardly a sacrifice. I haven't looked at another man like that since I met Shame." She shrugged.

"Not once?"

"No, and worrying about the grass on the other side of the fence is a waste of time."

"I'm just not ready for anything serious."

"And you think Mathias is the kind of man who'd want it?" Mercy asked softly.

"I never said I was involved with him." Damn it.

"Come on. I'm your friend, right?" Mercy tilted her head and raised an eyebrow.

"You're also my boss." I sat back in the booth and crossed my arms over my breasts. "How would you feel if you discovered I was fucking a man who could potentially be in charge of protecting Holman's multimillion-dollar collection?"

She pursed her lips. "Your private life has nothing to do with the gallery."

"That's crap and you know it."

"Look, Jane, hiding behind your job is a fool's choice. Life is about chance, and if you never take any—well, then you're wasting your life." She slid from the booth, her hands shaking as she gathered her purse and coat.

"Mercy, I'm not criticizing you for getting involved with Shamus. This is about me." I swallowed hard and slid across the booth to stand.

"I involved myself intimately with a contracted artist. Shame's contract is worth twenty million dollars, Jane. Don't think I didn't think about what would happen to me if things hadn't gone well with Shame and he'd pulled his work from the gallery." She pulled her jacket on and met my gaze. "But I couldn't let that stand in the way, and I hope that you don't either. There are some risks worth taking."

I shoved my hands into the pockets of my jeans as she hugged me and hurried from the cafe. Fuck and double fuck. I slid back into the booth and buried my face in my hands. I just plain sucked in the personal relationship department.

"Would you like something else?"

I jerked and then glanced up at the waitress. "No, just the check please."

"Of course."

* * *

I pulled a towel free of the free-standing weight station and rubbed my face with it. Forty-five minutes of weight training and thirty on a treadmill hadn't come close to taking the edge off. Messing up with a man was one thing, but fucking up my friendship with Mercy because of my own hang-ups had me feeling like absolute shit.

Truth be known, I was of the opinion that a man can be replaced but finding a real friend who'll stand by you is priceless. The thought that I might have hurt her feelings had me feeling about two feet tall.

Disgruntled, I grabbed my keys and went back up to my apartment. My empty apartment. Its empty status had always been something of a relief, but not now. I blamed Mathias. He made me think about things that I'd never thought before.

The light was on when I entered the foyer. For a few seconds my heart jumped a little, and then I remembered that Mathias hadn't kept the key he'd used over the weekend. Frowning, I tossed my keys on the table and walked into the living room. Mercy was curled up on one end of my couch with her handheld.

"Hey."

"Hey." She poked at her screen for a few seconds and then put away the stylus. "I decided that we weren't finished talking."

I laughed a little and plopped down in a chair. "I gave you a key to my apartment?"

"Yeah. Did you forget?"

"Apparently." I pulled my legs up into the chair and jerked off my shoes. "Okay, so what's left to talk about?"

"I got all tangled up in my own situation and lost sight of yours." She dropped her handheld into her purse and focused on me. "That wasn't fair of me."

"I really wasn't talking about you and Shamus." I bit down

on my lip and considered what to say next. "In fact, I think your relationship with him is probably the best thing that's ever happened to you. I've never seen you happier."

"I know, and I was silly for being so sensitive about it." She looked me over as if she'd just realized what I was wearing. "You've been working out?"

I laughed at her wrinkled nose. "Yeah, we aren't all blessed with a curvy figure like yours. And bony with sagging skin isn't sexy. I'd give up multiple orgasms for big, natural tits."

"Are you smoking crack?" She laughed. "Big, natural tits cause back problems and grooves in my shoulders, and men rarely look me in the eye when they talk."

"At least they aren't staring at your chest trying to figure out where your tits are." I sighed. "Man, it would be nice."

"Besides, don't go giving up the best thing God gave us. Multiple orgasms are probably the most important thing we have."

"Yeah."

"And you can buy breasts," she pointed out sagely, "that won't sag like natural ones. And I know you are purposely try-ing to avoid talking about what is bugging you."

"No, I'm not. Small tits bother me a lot." I sighed and laughed when she frowned at me. "What's it mean when a man tells you that he doesn't want to share?"

"No real man wants to share his woman."

"Who said I wanted to be some man's woman?" Though it didn't sound so bad the way she said it. "Why can't all men just be simple and easy to deal with? There are plenty of men who would be content to fuck me whenever I want and leave me alone the rest of the time."

"Would you want to share him?"

The thought of him fucking another woman made me want to go get my gun. "I'm not the one making demands."

"There are plenty of women who would love to find a man

who turns them on and wants to see only them. How often do you even run across a man that actually makes your panties wet?"

It'd been awhile. At least until Mathias had tossed me on the floor and climbed on top of me. I'd wanted him in those first few seconds, and that hadn't changed at all.

"He's beautiful." I finally said, my voice breaking a little. I winced at that but looked toward her with dry eyes.

Mercy chuckled. "Yes."

"And a sex god."

"What a bonus! Don't you hate getting a pretty man who can't fuck?" She grinned when I laughed. "I'm for real."

Nodding, I stood from my chair. "Want a beer?"

"Yeah, Shame drove me over. He'll come get me when I'm ready to come home." Mercy followed me into the kitchen for the beer.

"Remember that guy Nigel that I dated?"

"Yeah, pretty face, great English accent . . ." She sighed and waved her hand.

"And he couldn't fuck his way out of a wet paper sack," I finished as I went to find a bottle opener. I popped her cap and passed her the beer. "Well, hell, since denying it has done me no good—I'll just fess up." I sat down at the kitchen table. "Mathias spent the weekend here."

"Oh." She sat down across from me. "Well, that's not what I expected to hear."

"What did you expect?"

"That you had sex with him and sent him packing."

"He spent the weekend in my bed doing things to me that I've only read in erotic romance novels. I don't have a single patch of skin on my body that hasn't been fully explored by the man."

"And?"

And it had been the most amazing sexual experience of my

life. It was the kind of sex I could imagine having for the next thirty or forty years, and thinking like that had me wishing I had a therapist to moan and groan to. I sighed. "And when I told him that sex was the only thing on my agenda—he got mad and left."

"And today?"

"And today I was trying to ignore it all happened, and he made it difficult. So difficult that when I left work I went over to his hotel room; we had some really hot, amazing sex; and then we argued again. Then I called you to whine, came home, worked out, and now it's 1:00 A.M. and we have to be at work in six hours." I took a deep swallow of beer. "The man has me at my wit's end."

"He wants to see you exclusively."

"Yeah, while we explore this thing between us." I motioned my hand around. "It's all about that risk stuff you were mentioning earlier."

"But you don't want that?" she asked softly.

I could see the confusion in her eyes. More women than I could count would give up their best Prada handbag for a man to be interested in them the way Mathias was interested in me. "Is that slutty?"

"No. It's certainly par for your course, but I wouldn't say slutty." She fiddled with her beer bottle and met my gaze.

"Par for my course?"

"Remember how I used to always date nerds?"

"Yeah."

"I dated them because I wasn't attracted to them. I didn't want to deal with sex so I avoided it."

"Okay." I nodded, suddenly a little more empty. Mercy had survived so much and learned to love again. It seemed possible that I could too, but why was I so afraid of it?

"The way I see it, you keep a man waiting in the wings so you don't have to deal with taking someone seriously. If you didn't have Charlie, there would be someone else there and he would be just as boring. Attractive, good in bed, but not someone you have to talk to every day." She took a deep breath and then a drink from her beer. "It's your pattern."

Since it *was* my pattern, I couldn't very well be very angry with her. Instead, I just sat there and considered what to say. "So I use men like Charlie to keep myself safe from what?"

"Love. You and I both know that you are in no danger of falling in love with Charlie or any man like him."

"Love hurts."

"Yeah, but it's also pretty damn cool."

"Love ends with commitment or heartache."

"Yeah, but life would be boring as hell without it." She laughed. "Don't look at me that way, I mean it."

I dropped my gaze to the table between us, because I figured I wasn't capable of not glaring at her. "I don't have room for a man who is serious."

"Okay, then tell him and he'll move on."

He'll move on. "Even thinking about him moving on makes me want to crawl into my bed for a few years and moan."

"Wow."

"Yeah." I nodded. "This shouldn't be so damned complicated. I like the man. I enjoy being intimate with him. He's fun to hang out with."

"Then telling Charlie to hit the road should be a walk in the park."

"It isn't about Charlie."

"Then what is it?"

"It's about me. I promised myself a very long time ago that I would never let a man maneuver me into making decisions that I don't want to make. That's how my mother ended up trapped in a marriage she didn't want with three kids. She destroyed our family because she didn't have enough strength to acknowledge even to herself that she never wanted a family to begin with. My father ate his own fucking gun because she broke his heart."

Mercy cleared her throat. "And you don't want to be your mother."

"No. Not in a million years." I bit down on my lip. I couldn't remember ever discussing my mother with Mercy. "I see her twice a year, you know. And never once in all the times that we've met up for a weekend together or whatever have I ever asked her why she left."

"Are you afraid of the answer?"

"Yeah, I guess so." I pursed my lips together. "She came to the hospital once after the shooting. I know she meant well, but after about an hour of her hovering, I exploded. She hadn't bothered to be there for me before and it was infuriating that she wanted to be there then. I didn't try to contact her for a year after that."

"Was it difficult?"

"Stella is pretty damn good at playing the victim. I felt guilty for a long time about how I treated her, but it only served to remind me of my own anger and hurt. I also realized that I blamed her for my father's suicide. She might as well have put that gun to his head herself." I cleared my throat. "My older brother, Stan, refused to let her attend his funeral. I guess I'm not the only one who blamed her."

"Jane, you don't honestly think you are anything like that selfish woman, do you?"

I met her gaze and shrugged. "I could be."

"You are anything but selfish, and I've never known you to break a single promise."

"I try to be as honest as I can be." I took a deep drag of my beer and shrugged. "But I've never been faced with the kind of choices that my mother had to make."

"Do you think about having children?"

Wow. I sighed and then finally nodded. "Yeah, I mean, I'm in my thirties so my clock is thumping along just the way it's supposed to. I have the urges, and I think I'd probably be a pretty good mom."

"And?"

"And, maybe sometime in the future I could see myself having a family. I'm just not sure at this point, and now there is this man in my life expecting me to make choices and changes based on what he wants. Well, I'm way past living to please a man." I put the beer bottle down on the table with a thud and nodded to myself since she was staring at the table between us.

"Love is about changing and growing with another person."

"Well, I don't see him offering to make any grand changes to his life."

She laughed softly. "Have you even asked?"

I paused and then frowned at her. "That's just it. I'm not even prepared to start demanding things from him, and it's really unfair that he's that far ahead in this whole situation. What makes him know what he wants? How can he even be sure I'm worth his time?"

"He'd be an idiot not to know that. You are a smart, intelligent, successful woman, with a great sense of style and excellent choices in friends."

I flushed a little. "I'd still like some big tits."

"Maybe you can get some next year with your bonus."

"I would have already if the whole process didn't make me want to run for my life. They honestly should refrain from showing those kinds of surgeries on cable. It costs them a lot of money."

"Yeah. I've seen a few of those. It's pretty damn horrific. The childbirth one is practically medieval. I don't know how they get away with treating women that way." She shuddered. "Just don't ever make the mistake of watching one of those things on a big-screen TV. You'll be ruined for life."

I laughed at her expression. "I'll make a note of that." I went to the refrigerator and got another beer. "Want another one?"

"No, I'm still nursing this one."

"So, what should I do?"

"Well, you aren't going to like this."

"Just tell me what you think." I tossed the cap of my beer into the trash and leaned against the counter.

"Mathias strikes me as a man who is ready to find a partner and settle down. If you can't ever imagine yourself being that woman, you would be doing him a favor to avoid further interaction with him on a personal level."

"Did I tell you that he was a sex god?"

"Yeah, you mentioned it."

She was right, and the knowledge of it hurt more than I anticipated. "I never asked for this."

"Life has a way of kicking you in the teeth."

"He's a grown man, and I've been real with him about how I feel and what I've got to offer."

"Then he can come to you if he wants to play with fire."

He seemed the type that wouldn't deny himself. Wouldn't it be best if I turned him away? Since there was little chance of that happening, I sighed. "And if he wins the bid for the gallery?"

"James notified Mathias a couple of hours ago that his company won the two-year contract for security. He'll begin work immediately."

I rolled over on my back and stared at the clock on my nightstand. It was barely 7:00 A.M. Since I should already have been at work I managed to get the sleep out of my voice before I picked up my ringing cell phone.

"Jane Tilwell."

"I'm at the deli down the street from the gallery getting coffee. Will you join me for breakfast?"

I loved the sound of his voice. "Mathias."

"Just say yes."

"Yes." I sat up and rubbed my head. "I'll be there in thirty minutes."

I closed my phone and tossed it on the bed. It was a stupid thing to do and it didn't jive with the plan I'd made after Mercy had left. Of course, since he was going to be in the gallery long term, none of my plans had really been viable. Ignoring him was simply out. Forgetting what had happened between us would be damned impossible.

I was most sincerely screwed.

7

He stood up as I approached the table and reached out to help me with my coat. "Thanks for coming."

I smiled and slid into the booth. "I shouldn't have."

"It's good to break your own rules every once in a while."

The man looked and smelled amazing. I stared at him for a few seconds, as if I hadn't seen him in weeks, and then plucked up the menu on the table in front of me. "I should be at work."

"Late night?"

I frowned. "Pardon me?"

"I was at Shame's when Mercy called to be picked up." He sat back in the booth. "He told me that the two of you were together."

"We had a bit of a girl party."

"Yes, that's what she called it. She knows, right?"

"She already suspected." I smiled for the waitress and ordered quickly. All I really wanted was coffee, but I figured that I needed to get some real food down. "We're good friends. Mercy is probably the closest friend I have in Boston."

"Is it going to make things difficult at work?"

"No, but she might look at you funny. I told her all about the sex and everything. So if she looks at your crotch a couple of times while she talks to you, she's just getting used to knowing things about you that she shouldn't."

"Christ, women suck." He sat back in the booth and glared at me. "If we talk about a woman like that, you act like we betrayed your entire gender."

"It's a horrible double standard." The waitress came back with coffee, and I snagged a flavored creamer as she left. "But to be real, no—there shouldn't be any problems. Mercy is a very discreet person, and she understands already that I'm uncomfortable with the whole thing."

"I won't give anyone in that gallery something they can use against you, Jane. No matter who they may be."

"Mercy wouldn't."

"This isn't about you and her, this is about us." He reached out and took one of my hands. I loved the strong, calloused feel of his fingers. "You're important to me. Important enough that I'm going to back off and leave you alone like you want."

It wasn't what I wanted, but on the other side of it, I couldn't give what he wanted. "Leave me alone?"

"I've pushed and pressured you since we met because my attraction to you knocked me off center." He sighed and released my hand as our food arrived.

"Okay."

"I'm telling you this because I want you to be comfortable with me."

The man was trying to manage me. I unrolled my silverware as I considered what I wanted to say. "I won't do anything to interfere with your contract at Holman, Mathias. I didn't help you get it, and I won't stand in the way of it."

"I didn't think that you would."

"Then why are you so interested in making me comfortable?" I inclined my head. "Wouldn't I be easier to manage if I was off balance and worried about what your next move will be?"

He laughed softly. "Perhaps, but I enjoy a challenge. I'll play fair with you, Jane. It's the only way I want you in my life."

"Even if I'm not willing to play by your rules?"

"We'll take it one step at a time. You were right about one thing; I had no business making demands on you. It's too soon, and I'll make every effort to keep my arrogance in check. So, I'm going to try things your way."

Somewhere between coffee and his promising to try things my way, battle lines had been drawn. He was saying all the right things. Being reasonable and charming and sexy came easily to him. The man was *so* up to something.

I watched Mercy walk across the bull pen toward my office, several folders clutched to her chest. She looked excited—as excited as she'd let anyone see. I envied her reserve and her ability to hide what she was thinking. My heart and temper are displayed all over my face, despite years of work to change.

"You look like you just won a million dollars."

She closed my office door and leaned on it. "Samuel Castlemen is coming to do a site visit. He's agreed to bring six pieces for display in the special focus gallery on the first floor, provided that he likes the setup."

Samuel Castlemen, genius of canvas and world-renowned womanizer, was coming to Boston. "That's awesome."

Mercy came to my desk and offered me a folder. "I want you to handle it."

"Me?" My stomach dropped to my feet as I accepted the folder. "I've never done a show, Mercy."

"This is a special focus show. It will be invitation only on the opening night, and Castlemen doesn't want anything grand.

Something simple and classy to showcase the six paintings he is bringing."

I opened up the folder and swallowed hard. "Oh." He was bringing *Phases of a Woman*. It was one of the most sought-after collections in the country and the only work he'd ever produced that he refused to sell. It was, in fact, one of the few modern collections that could be called priceless. "Did he insist on the charity deal?"

"Yes, and I agreed to give fifty percent of the ticket price for the special focus display to the breast cancer foundation in his mother's name. That wasn't hard to agree to. I donate to them myself on a yearly basis. I'd like you to compile a list of the most influential and powerful women in Boston. They go on the list first."

"Total head count?"

"One hundred invitations—so two hundred."

Two hundred people. I cleared my throat. "Are you sure you want me to choose?"

"Yes." Mercy stood and smiled. "Just remember to include our big buyers. While they are here for Castlemen's show, we can provide private tours of the rest of the gallery. You'll need to spend some time with the sales staff and the rest of the support staff regarding the tours."

I watched her for a few seconds and pressed my lips together. When I was fairly sure that I wasn't going to beg her to take the show back, I cleared my throat. "This is huge, Mercy."

"Yes."

"Why are you giving it to me?"

She sat down again and glanced briefly toward the bull pen. "Castlemen will be in here in two weeks and he would agree to no other time."

I hadn't even looked at the date. Two weeks wasn't even reasonable, but that wasn't why she'd passed it off to me. Mercy would be in New York in two weeks, testifying in the trial of the man who raped her. "How is that coming?"

"The DA thinks I'll spend two or three days on the witness stand, mostly under cross-examination. His assistant sent me a list of questions that the defense might ask—some of them are just so horrible that they make my heart hurt. I don't know how I'm going to get through this." She'd kept her gaze on the floor in front of her until she'd finished speaking, and then she looked up at me. "But knowing that you are here handling the show and the gallery is one less stress for me."

"You know I can still call my brothers and have them go to New York and kick his ass."

"I have enough trouble keeping Shame from killing Jeff; I don't want to add your relatives to the mix."

I laughed softly at her frustrated tone. "Must be horrible to be loved like that."

"Yeah, sometimes it is." She sat forward a little, her gaze focused on mine. "The other night you compared being in love with a lack of freedom. I've been thinking about it, and in some ways you are right. There are times when I would like nothing more than to hide in my apartment until the trial is over. Then I remember how strong Shame has been for me. How he's put aside his own anger to comfort me time and time again, and I know that I can't hide from my past."

"So love forces you to do things that you wouldn't normally do."

"Yes."

"Have you ever been *naked* with Shame?"

Mercy stared at me for a few seconds, frowning. "Jane, you've seen the sculpture of me at Shame's . . . of course I've been naked with him."

"Not that kind of naked." I waved my hand dismissively and then used it to rub at my mouth. She was my friend—I should just be able to ask the question outright, but I found I couldn't. "You know when I was in school, we received yearly lectures about safe sex and AIDS prevention. I watch the news now, about how people are trying to prevent schools from teaching sexual education and instead are trying to promote abstinence, and I wonder how those people could be so stupid."

"OH." She was silent for a moment, then her lips curved into a little smile as if she was remembering something particularly hot and amazing. "Yes. Though it wasn't something we planned. Shame is very careful about birth control. We've talked about alternate methods, but he insists that he wants to take care of it. Pills and shots have side effects."

"Yes, but condoms aren't 100% effective."

"True." She nodded in agreement. "But on the other hand, neither of us would be unhappy if I got pregnant. It might move our plans up a little . . . but the prospect isn't a scary one."

Pregnancy wasn't a concern for me, and it wasn't about disease. It was about a level of intimacy and trust I'd given Mathias.

"You forgot a condom with Mathias."

Forgot twice, requested he not use one a third time. Even now, I didn't regret it. I was just left wondering why it had been so important to me last night. "Actually, I asked him not to use one."

"Oh."

I looked up at her and sighed at the shock on her face. "Primitive, huh?"

"Is that what it was about?"

"I don't know. I just needed him to be as vulnerable as I was. *Naked.*"

She nodded her head in silence and bounced her foot a little as she digested my words.

I sat there tense while she thought, wondering why I'd told

her and why her opinion on the matter had me all twisted up. Her perspective had always been important to me, and maybe I wanted her to tell me that what I was feeling was natural.

"That kind of intimacy can be overwhelming. I mean, it's one thing to have sex with a man . . . it's another to open yourself up to him completely."

Had I done that? I started to shake my head, but she laughed.

"No, really, Jane. Getting *barenaked* with a man like that is intimate. It's a base and entirely primal reaction to sexual attraction."

I crossed my arms over my breasts and sighed. "You spend too much time with your therapist."

She stood with a grin. "My therapist would tell you that deep down you are starving for an emotional connection and you are using sex to fill that need."

"I don't buy psychobabble."

"Fine." Mercy stopped at the corner of my desk and met my gaze. "Just be careful."

"I am."

"I don't mean birth control, Jane. I mean with your heart. I've never known you to be so intimately involved with a man. You've already told me how you feel about serious relationships."

Insulted, I sat up straight in my chair. "I've had relationships."

"Yes, but this is no ordinary relationship for you. You let him spend the night in your bed." She tapped the desk with one fingernail. "Just be careful."

Just be careful. I watched her leave and let my gaze drop to the desk in front of me. How can I be careful with my heart when my body is set on doing whatever it wants? Not that my body was totally to blame; Mathias was just as stimulating intellectually as he was sexually. That was part of the problem I suppose—I couldn't forget about him when I left the bed.

I spread the contents of the folder out and stared at the picture of Samuel Castlemen from his press kit. He looked like exactly what he was . . . a big mountain-man artist from Alaska. Black hair fell on his shoulders, he wore a neatly trimmed beard, and sharp green eyes looked right at the camera. The photographer who had done his head shots for his press kit knew exactly what made Sam so attractive, both as an artist and as a man.

And he was all mine. All one hundred eighty pounds of him. What the hell was I gonna do with him? A special focus show usually took months of planning . . . it wasn't like a large coming-out party for an artist. It was intensely personal, and it wasn't about buying. The small shows had been Mercy Rothell's first contribution to the gallery, and the people in Boston had taken to them like a moth to a flame.

Being invited became a bragging point, and a special focus show featuring Samuel Castlemen would be a coveted event. The first thing I had to do, of course, was to contact the breast cancer foundation. Well, it wasn't the first thing I had to do.

I stood up and closed the folder. There was a slight buzz of activity in the bull pen as I left my office and hurried to the service hall that led to the show floor. It was the only truly private place except for the bathroom, and I couldn't do what I needed to do in there.

Closing the door to the hall, I took a deep breath, walked sedately to the small unused office in the middle of the hallway, scooted in, and had myself one fine ass-shaking victory dance. I heard a chuckle just as I'd gotten to the Rocky Balboa arms-in-the-air part.

I jerked around and found Mathias sitting at a table in the office that apparently was no longer unused. "Oh."

"Christ, if I give you a hundred bucks would you do that again?" He leaned back in the chair he was in and grinned at me.

I flushed and shut the office door. "What are you doing in here?"

"Mercy gave me permission to use this as the command center for the security team. Currently I'm using it to study the building plans."

I glanced briefly at the blueprints on the desk and then met his gaze. "I see." Slowly, I relaxed and walked toward the table. "I just had the best thing happen."

"Yeah, the Rocky part sort of sealed that up for me." He stood and walked around the table. "That was adorable, by the way."

"Grown women don't appreciate being called adorable." I took a step back from him when he got too close. "We're at work."

"Yeah, and then you came into my office and shook your sexy little ass."

"I didn't know it was your office."

"So tell me your good news." He touched my jaw with his fingertips, and I had to take another step back to keep from jumping on him.

"Mercy is giving me my first show. It's a special focus show, so it's not like a big pay event."

"Special focus?"

"Yeah. Samuel Castlemen is bringing a special collection that is not for sale to display here. We'll have a limited ticket-only viewing after the opening of the show."

Mathias sighed. "Not the *Phases of Woman* collection."

He actually looked like he was begging me. "Of course it is."

"Fuck." He turned his back on me and walked back to his table. "Where in the building?"

I walked to the plans. "First floor." He flipped through the pages and presented the first floor. I put my finger on the special focus gallery. "Here. We've used this room with the veranda for these events since we started doing them."

He sat down. "When?"

"Two weeks." I frowned. "This is good for the gallery."

"Yeah, perhaps, but that is a high-profile project, Jane. Two attempts were made to take it from the last gallery it was in. That's one of the reasons he hasn't allowed it to travel from his own gallery in Anchorage in nearly two years."

"How do you know so much about this artist and his scribbles?" He'd already made his position on how much he valued art very clear, so his knowledge of Sam was a bit of a surprise.

"Sam is a good friend of my brother's. I designed the security system in his gallery in Alaska."

"So you've seen the collection?"

"Yes, and even met the woman who inspired it. Alicia Castlemen was a truly beautiful and amazing woman, and her son barely did her justice in those paintings. I can understand why he won't part with them." Mathias rubbed his face as he stared at the plans. "Is there anything in this room right now?"

"No. We'd planned to use the space next week for a special showing for the local high school students I work with. They have a regular show space, but we were going to do a special focus event for them as a reward for all of their hard work."

"These events are big?"

"It's invitation only. Over the summer there was a couple who actually included the invitation in their divorce proceedings."

"Who won the invitation?"

"Since it was issued to the wife, the gallery withdrew the invitation and reissued it to her in her maiden name. Her husband wasn't a patron of the gallery, and when we heard that he intended to auction it off . . . well, that was intolerable."

"So all guests will be required to sign in, show ID, and have the original invitation?"

"Yes."

"Who prints the invitations?"

"A company downtown. The invitation will have a distinct

watermark, but we've had someone duplicate it at least once in the past six months."

"How did you know?"

"We keep the number down to make the event feel more important and special to those who make it through the door. When the guard told me that we'd processed one hundred ten invitations, I knew that there were at least ten fakes in the mix. After that we started putting the invited guest's name on the invitation instead of just on the envelope."

"When will you have the invitation list?"

"Within the next four days. There are several names that are automatic, including the board of the Holman Foundation. They receive formal invitations while staff does not."

"All members of staff will be required at the event?"

"Yes, the event will have food but we never allow the catering staff to stay. Our sales team will handle the food. At a designated time, the front doors will be closed and locked."

"Then your guests will have access to the entire gallery."

"Yes. Though most will prefer a guided tour." I glanced up from the plans and looked over his face. He looked fierce and determined, as if I'd just given him an impossible mission. "What are you thinking?"

"I'm thinking that I've got a lot to do in a very short time." He reached out, grabbed me, and pulled me into his lap before I could realize his plan.

I gasped a little when he brought me close to his chest. "Mathias."

"Shhh." He kissed my mouth softly. "Congratulations, Jane."

"Thanks."

"I'll make sure my end of things is perfect."

He kissed me again, and I opened my mouth against the gentle invasion of his tongue. I curled my hands into his shoulders and moaned softly when he released me. "What? I wasn't done being kissed."

Mathias laughed softly and brushed his lips against my forehead. "Do you really want to come out of this office looking like you've been kissed thoroughly?" He let me go with exaggerated slowness. "I promised I wouldn't do anything in this gallery that could be used against you, Jane. That includes creating situations where people have something to speculate about."

"Okay." Good thing one of us was sane. I slid from his lap. "Thanks."

"Save your thanks for later."

"Oh yeah?" I laughed softly and walked toward the door. "When?"

"I'll let you know."

It was almost one o'clock when Charlie showed up. He'd never once, in all the time that I'd known him, showed up without an invitation. I watched him cross the bull pen and tried not to frown when he came into my office and shut the door.

"Hey."

"Hey, I was hoping I could take you to lunch." He leaned on the doorknob as he spoke.

Charlie Wallace was everything I thought I needed, yet as I looked at him, I found nothing about him attractive. Mathias had ruined me, and that was irritating. "Sure, sounds good."

It was also probably a good idea to get Charlie out of the gallery before he and Mathias crossed paths. Promises aside, I doubted seriously that Mathias would take meeting my 2 A.M. friend with any kind of grace. I stood up and went for my coat.

Charlie met me at the coat stand and helped me with gentle hands. "We should see more of each other; I've missed you."

I frowned as I buttoned my coat. That did not sound good. He'd never even come close to saying something like that to me in the past. "What's going on?"

"We're going to lunch."

He said it in that patient tone that I'd seen him use on people he thought were stupid. I went back to my desk and grabbed my purse and my PDA. "Do you have reservations?"

"Of course—you know I hate to wait."

I turned to watch him run his fingers through his blond hair and thought he probably practiced that a lot. Not only had Mathias ruined me, he'd made me cynical of men. I wondered what Charlie's moves were and if I'd fallen for any of them.

We made it all the way to dessert before I found out why he'd come to see me out of the blue.

"My mother is canceling lunch."

God loves me. I tried to frown. "Oh, well, that's okay. You didn't actually take me out to lunch to 'break it to me' did you?" I laughed softly.

"The thing is, Jane, she's had you investigated."

Investigated. Did average people really do that?

"I see." I put down my fork and picked up my napkin. "And?"

"She finds your past distasteful."

"I find her investigation of me presumptuous and distasteful." I folded the napkin and put it beside my plate with exaggerated care.

"Presumptuous?"

"Yeah. It obviously wasn't clear to her that I was just fucking you." I was angry. Angry that Katherine Wallace had investigated me and found out things that were none of her business.

"We're more than that."

"No. We weren't."

"Jane."

"Look, Charlie, you're a decent guy and I enjoyed seeing you, but it is obvious that your mother has plans for you that don't include a woman of my background."

"I don't care about any of that." He reached across the table and covered my hand with his. "I defended you, Jane. You're an amazing and thoughtful woman, and I'm honored to know you. Once my mother gets to know you . . . things will be different."

"Gets to know me?" I asked with a sigh.

"Jane, we're good together. I can see us together long term."

Now, that thought made me want to run away. Fast. "Charlie, I'm not interested in anything serious, and if I were I certainly couldn't be serious about a man whose mother is such a—a . . . nosy, interfering witch. She thinks I'm not good enough for you, and I'm not all that interested in changing her mind."

"You aren't being fair to her."

I pulled my hand free from his. "You be sure to let her know that I have no intention of sullying her precious family tree with my questionable background."

"Jane." He stood when I did and reached out for me.

"Don't touch me." I jerked on my coat with shaking hands. I was so angry that I could barely think, and this asshole thought it was no big deal. "I'm sure you'll have no problem replacing me for your event on Friday."

"Janie."

"Ask your mommy, Charlie. I'm sure she has a list of acceptable women for you."

"She finds my past distasteful."

"You take that witch off the gallery mailing list." Mercy propped her bare feet up on the corner of her desk and glared at me. "I want the whole family off the list."

I laughed. "She's stupid with her money; it would be a mistake to exclude her. It isn't personal for me."

"The woman had you investigated and found you unacceptable for her son." Mercy opened a desk drawer and pulled out a hair clip. "I hate people like that."

"The truth is that I'm sort of relieved."

"You wanted a reason, outside of Mathias, to get rid of Charlie."

I laughed softly and shrugged. "I can't have the man thinking that I'm giving in to his demands. Though I have to tell you, I was finished with Charlie the morning I opened my apartment door and found Mathias standing there. Today when I was at lunch with him, I couldn't even imagine getting naked with him."

"I see."

"Mathias isn't a man you can just put out of your head when it's convenient. He's penetrating."

Mercy laughed outright. "Yeah. I imagine he is."

"Dirty mind." I smiled against my will and then laughed softly. "I'd hate to meet their daddy; he must be one fine, amazing man."

"Will Montgomery is certainly a stunning man and not just for his face. I find him to be entertaining and thoughtful. He made every effort to put me at ease in his home when I went to visit."

It was weird how she talked about meeting Shame's parents. Like it was no big deal. But then maybe for her it wouldn't be. Mercy Rothell came from old New York money and could trace her family back to Jamestown. It wasn't fair to think about her like that, and I was almost immediately ashamed of myself.

I cleared my throat. "Katherine Wallace will talk. It won't take long for her entire social set to know where I come from and what happened to me. My past is probably more violent than most of those people can deal with."

"And?"

"Are you sure you want me to handle the Castlemen show?"

"Yes." She frowned at me. "Don't make me mad."

Laughing, I stood and shoved my hands into the pockets of my slacks. "I just don't want the gallery to suffer."

"Katherine Wallace may be a big deal in her little world, but she's nothing in the scheme of things. James Brooks could buy and sell that woman and her entire family ten times over and still have enough money to roll around in naked every Friday night."

The image of the very manly and sexy James Brooks rolling around naked in money was actually rather interesting. I considered it for a few seconds. "You know who he reminds me of?"

"Pierce Brosnan."

"Yeah." I glanced at her. "Like in that movie with Rene Russo." Okay, I had to get that image out of my mind or I'd never be able to look at James again. "We went too far."

"Agreed."

"I'm going to go out and see Lisa. Want to come?" I looked toward her.

"I have plans or I would. Tell her I'll be out later in the week."

"Sure."

8

─────────────

As naked men went, the one in front of me was a stellar example of the male of our species. Every bit of him was cut and defined. His cock, semi-erect, lay against his thigh, and he had one arm thrown up above his head. Dark red hair was spread out on the pillow he had his head on, and I thought for sure that I'd seen him before.

"I can never get a pretty man to lay around my apartment like that."

Lisa Millhouse glanced over her shoulder at me and grinned. "Jane."

I walked into the barn and closed the door. "I should've called."

"No, we're running long. You've actually saved Marshall from another hour of torture." She picked up a towel and rubbed at her clay-covered hands. "Darlin', you can dress and go. I'll need you again tomorrow."

Marshall stood from the platform he was on and offered me a grin as he stood. "Ms. Tilwell."

My mouth dropped open as I made the connection as to

where I'd seen him before. It took me a few seconds to find his full name. "Marshall Banks, go put on some clothes." I turned my glare on Lisa as he walked off toward a stall to dress. "Lisa!"

"What?" She laughed and walked toward a sink in the back of the barn.

"He's a child."

"I'm nineteen, ma'am." Marshall yelled from the stall. "And my dad said it was okay."

"Shut up and go home, Marshall." I followed Lisa to the sink. "Is this a conflict of interest?"

"Look, Jane, he's of age."

"What would James Brooks think if he knew you were trolling the Holman Arts Academy for models?"

"My involvement in the academy is minimal, and besides, James knows." She glanced up from washing her hands. "I had him help the kid with the contract. Don't be such a prude."

"I'm not a prude." I crossed my arms over my breasts and glanced back at Marshall, who was wearing a pair of jeans and a T-shirt. "Go home."

He laughed softly. "You sure are cute, Ms. Tilwell. I'll be at the gallery on Monday as planned. I have permission to work with your high school project through the end of the semester for credit."

"Fine." I was silent as he left the barn and then turned to look at Lisa. "How am I supposed to look at him now?"

"With more appreciation. That young man is stunning. I can't believe you've never noticed how yummy he is." Lisa yanked off the flannel shirt she was wearing, tossed it on a beat-up desk next to the sink, and stared at me. "What's up with you?"

"What do you mean?"

"You're wound up like a little kid's toy top. Something happen at work?"

"I've had a difficult couple of days."

"Yeah." She snickered and walked away. "For real, I've heard all about the incident with Mathias. So, did he really pin you down on the floor and hold you there?"

"For a few minutes." I followed her out of the barn and toward the house. "Did Mercy tell you?"

"Actually, no, Shamus told me. Apparently his brother is quite taken with you."

"I haven't done anything to him."

"Yeah, sure." She smirked.

"You suck." I shrugged off my jacket and tossed it across the back of a kitchen chair. "I'm not really here to talk about Mathias."

"Okay." She went to the coffeepot and set a pot on to brew. "So, what are you here to talk about?"

"Charlie's mother had me investigated."

Lisa paused as she digested that information and then went to the cabinet to get cups. "Okay, and he dumped you."

"Well we weren't in a relationship, and hell no he didn't dump me. Men don't dump me." I glared at her as I sat down at the table. "I'm a freaking amazing woman . . . he would've been an idiot to do that."

"Then what?"

"She finds my past distasteful. I'm sure she'll tell everyone she knows how she feels about me too." I dropped my head onto the table. "Mercy doesn't think it matters."

"No, but Mercy, as wonderful as she is, grew up in a very different world from you and me." Lisa took the cups to the counter and leaned there for a minute in silence. "When I was eight we lived in a trailer in a little city outside of Knoxville, Tennessee. Sometimes it was so cold that I'd be afraid to get out of the bed to go to the bathroom. . . . I knew the moment my feet hit the floor I'd pee my pants."

"I spent most of my childhood huddled in my bed trying to figure out what I'd do when my daddy got shot. My mother bailed, and I figured that God just didn't love me enough to keep my daddy safe." I focused on the coffee as it dripped into the pot. "Cops don't make good money, but we got by okay. I never had to worry about food or getting kicked out of our house."

"Do you think that how you grew up makes you less than anyone else?"

"No." I shook my head. "I'm stronger for my past, and anyone who can't deal with where I come from or what happened to me can just fuck off."

"Yet you are worried that Katherine Wallace is going to run her mouth about you."

"Yeah."

"She's not stupid, Jane. There are very few people in Boston who'd cross James Brooks, and everyone knows that he values you and your place at Holman Gallery." She tapped her fingers on the counter. "I've read about the shooting, of course, but I've never asked because I didn't want to cause you pain."

"I don't remember all of it. I remember the road being hot underneath me . . . so hot that I had burns on my back. My left leg was numb by the time I went down, and all I could think was that I couldn't drop my gun."

"And you didn't."

"Not until it was empty."

She poured the coffee silently and then brought it over to the table. "Cream?"

"What flavors?"

Lisa laughed softly. "Maybe vanilla."

"Sure."

"You were in love with your partner, the one who died."

"We had a great relationship that could've extended beyond the job, but it never had the time to get that far. When we were first partnered up he was married, and I don't mess with married men." I doctored the coffee with the creamer she'd set in front of me and plucked a plastic spoon from the collection in a glass in the middle of the table. "His divorce had been final about five months when he was shot and killed. His ex-wife blamed me for both."

"The divorce and the shooting."

"Yeah."

"Did he leave his wife for you?"

"I never asked." I looked up and met her gaze with a shrug. "I guess I didn't want to know; maybe if I'd known it would've made wanting him wrong."

"If it wasn't wrong . . . why didn't you hook up with him the moment you could?"

Excellent question. One that I'd asked myself plenty of times, and the only answer was so horrible that for a few seconds I considered not answering the question. "Because the moment he became available . . . the attraction withered on my end. I still had feelings for him, but it wasn't the same."

"Well, it's easy to love someone you don't have to worry about committing to. Once he was available, having feelings for him became risky."

"Yeah." I held my cup in both hands and took a sip of the coffee. "So, about that kid."

Lisa burst out laughing. "It's perfectly legal, Brooks finds me amusing, and the kid's father volunteered to model too."

"Good lord." I paused. "How does his daddy look?"

"Like his son . . . only better and more yummy. I had to tell him no."

"Why?"

"Because if I had him out here naked for any length of time I'd be fucking him . . . and that would be a conflict of interest considering how much money he puts into the Holman Foundation on a regular basis. I want to pursue my craft, but I'm not going to do it at the expense of the Holman Foundation. They've done too much for me."

"You were a student at the academy."

"Yes, until I made the mistake of getting married. Volunteering there was the only thing I had during my marriage that made me happy."

"And you didn't meet James until you signed a contract with the gallery?"

"I'd seen him a few times at the academy, but at the time he was far more involved in his father's law firm." She sat back in her chair. "Look, I've been very polite to the man."

"Yes. You've done very well."

"Well, the man did cut me a check for five million dollars." Lisa chuckled. "And carried me over to the bank to make me get a savings account."

"Well, you needed one. How'd things go with that investment broker we set you up with?"

"I had to spend a few weeks breaking him, but we're getting along okay. The biggest trick was making him speak English to me on a consistent basis." She got up from the table and poured herself more coffee. "Still, Brooks and I are getting along as fine as anyone can expect."

"I'm sure he expects more."

Lisa chuckled. "Yeah, he does. Actually, I'm beginning to enjoy the whole thing. It's been a long time since a man has actually put any effort into pursuing me."

"And are you going to let him catch you?"

"Haven't decided." She flushed a little. "I'm not sure what I'd do with him if I did. He isn't the average man."

"Not by anyone's standards." I laughed and then dropped my gaze to my nearly empty coffee cup. "The thing is this . . . men suck."

"They sure do."

"But there is just so much time I can spend with my vibrator, ya know?" I jumped a little when a high-pitched shriek burst through the house. "What the hell is that?"

"It's my alarm. I flipped it on as we came inside." She stood and went to a control panel. "The county will send out a patrol car unless I cancel it. I need to go check the cameras. Would you check the front door?"

"Sure." Frowning, I hopped up and walked out into the living room. "Who could it be?"

"No clue. You are the only scheduled visitor, and the delivery service knows better than to come out without calling."

I watched her go down the hall and went to the front door. There was a man on her front porch. For a moment, I stood where I was, frowning at him, and then I reached out to push the door shut. He beat me to it, pushing it open and coming in like he owned the place.

"Where the hell is Lisa?"

"The real question, asshole, is who the hell are you?"

"He's my ex-husband."

I turned and looked at Lisa, who was on the stairs, her face pale with fear I'd never thought her capable of. "Go get your gun."

Lisa jerked her head in a nod and hurried back up the stairs.

I watched Greg Carlson start toward the stairs and I moved in front of him. "No."

"Get out of my way, bitch."

Men should know better than to call a woman they've never met a bitch. I mean, for all he knew, I could've been a psycho killer and being called a bitch was my "on switch." Didn't he watch movies? "Back off and get out of here."

"Get out of my way or I'll make you regret it."

"Get away from him, Jane." Lisa hurried down the stairs with a rifle in hand. "Greg, get out of here. You aren't even supposed to be on my land."

"We need to talk." He pointed a finger at her, and Lisa actually jerked.

"Dude, don't make her nervous; she's got a fucking gun

pointed at you." I pulled at Lisa's arm and pushed her toward the kitchen. "The cops are on their way."

"I cut the phone line before I tripped the alarm. The system had no way to call the police."

"You know that was actually pretty smart, except for one thing. Her security company would've been notified the moment her line went dead. They'll send cops." I took the gun from Lisa's shaking hands and leveled it at him. I'd never seen her like that and it worried me. "Here's the difference between me and your ex-wife, Greg—I never once had an inkling of feeling for you. I could blow your head off without blinking an eye."

"You'd kill me?" He laughed and took a step toward me.

"You wouldn't be the first man I put in the ground." I primed the rifle and his eyes widened. "Get out of here."

"Lisa."

"Don't talk to her." I pushed Lisa back farther into the kitchen with one hand while keeping an eye on him. "She's not interested in anything you have to say."

"Jane, be careful," Lisa whispered.

Then it occurred to me. It was her paintball gun. The only thing between us and her abusive ex-husband was a couple ounces of paint. The moment he realized that, our situation was going to change drastically.

He came at us. Since the damn gun in my hand wasn't going to be much of a weapon from a traditional perspective, I shoved it into his gut and then used the butt of the weapon to hit him in the back of the head.

"Holy shit." Lisa swallowed hard, her gaze glued to the sprawled form of her ex-husband. "Jane, you're freaking awesome."

I laughed softly. "Get some rope or something before he wakes up."

She nodded and went to a drawer by the sink. "You'd better not tell anyone what a pansy I turned out to be."

I kicked Greg in the head when he started to move and then straddled his back. "The only pansy in the room is this guy. Christ, Lisa, he must outweigh you by a hundred and fifty pounds."

"Yeah." She came back with a roll of duct tape. "This is all I got."

"That works." I jerked his arms behind him and pressed his wrists together. "Tape them."

"So, Mr. Carlson entered through the front door."

"Yes, it wasn't locked." I glanced over at Lisa, who was also getting questioned. "I told her to go get her gun, but I guess she was so freaked out she grabbed the paintball gun instead."

"Okay."

"So we told him to leave and he wouldn't. Then he tried to come at me."

"And you used the paintball gun to subdue him."

"Yes."

"Did you threaten to kill him?"

"Is that what he said?" I asked softly. I was trying hard not to be amused. "He's going to whine the whole way to booking, you know that."

"Yes, I do know that." The deputy cleared his throat. "He said that you told him that he wouldn't be the first man you'd killed."

"Oh." I straightened in my chair. "Okay, when you run my name you'll see that I was on the job in Savannah, Georgia. I was involved in a shooting that lead to the death of a man. He killed my partner and put holes in me."

"I see." He stood. "I think we're done here. The security company is already out here repairing the damage done to her system."

"Thanks."

I laid back in the recliner and closed my eyes. I still wish I could have put a few holes in Greg Carlson. The son of a bitch was huge. I don't know how Lisa survived her marriage, and I doubted I'd ever be able to ask her. Even now, I could see her face—pale and almost lifeless—when she'd realized who was in her house.

"Jane?"

I jerked up in the chair at the sound of Mathias's voice and relaxed in relief at the sight of him. He pulled me up from the recliner as soon as he reached me. His fingers were gentle but firm on my arm as he pulled me as close as he could without wrapping his arms around me.

"Are you okay?"

"Yeah." I glanced toward Lisa. "He didn't touch us."

"Good." He touched my cheek with gentle fingertips and nodded. "I saw Carlson out in one of the squad cars."

"Yeah, we kicked his ass and hog-tied him with duct tape until the cops showed up." My hands tightened against his fingers as he took up one of my hands. "We need to fix her security system, Mathias. If I hadn't been here . . ." I shook my head. "You need to build her a safe room."

Mathias looked toward Lisa and nodded. "I'll discuss it with her as soon as the cops leave."

"Lisa? Jane?" Mercy came through the door, and Mathias released me immediately.

I frowned briefly at him and then turned to Mercy. "Hey. How'd you get here?"

"We were in a meeting when the security company called me and told me Lisa's system had been tampered with. I just beat them here." He rubbed his head in frustration. "After the other night, I contacted her monitoring firm to let them know I was back in town. I'm on her list of contacts."

Mercy glanced between us and cleared his throat. "James is outside talking with the sheriff. He'll be in soon."

I took a step back from Mathias and looked around. "Maybe

I should make coffee." I looked pointedly at Mercy as I turned toward the kitchen and was relieved when she followed.

"How is she?"

"Shaken." I went to the counter and poured the coffee out to make a fresh pot. "She fell apart the moment she set eyes on him. Did you get a look at him?"

"Yeah." Mercy nodded and went to the cabinet with the cups. "I wonder what he wanted."

"He wasn't too chatty after he woke up." I pursed my lips. "I should've used more duct tape; he didn't howl nearly enough to suit me when the deputy started removing it."

"So you really are GI Jane."

I laughed and shook my head. "It was a strange situation, especially when I realized that she'd brought the paint gun."

"I was in a hurry."

We both turned to look at her as she came into the kitchen. She let Mathias put her in a chair at the table and then he sat down across from her.

"Next time I'll be more specific."

Lisa laughed sadly and folded her hands in front of her. "Let's just hope there isn't a second time." She focused on Mathias. "A safe room? Like the one in the Jodie Foster movie?"

"Yeah, we can build it on the ground floor or in the basement."

I watched Mathias dealing with Lisa, drawing on a scrap piece of paper what he could do to make her feel more safe, and I realized that just his arrival had made me feel more safe.

"You've had one hell of a day."

"Yeah." I nodded as I tossed my keys on the foyer table and pulled off my coat. "I'm gonna get a beer. Want one?"

"Please."

I pulled two from my fridge and then walked into the living

room. Mathias had slipped off his shoes and was staring at the blank screen of my television.

"I can turn it on."

"Nah, come here." He took his beer and tugged on my hand.

I slipped into his lap with a sigh. "There is no shortage of excitement in my life lately."

"Yeah, you seem to make a habit of running into arrogant, overbearing men."

"Don't compare yourself to that asshole." I ran my hand over the top of his head and down his neck. "I don't want to talk about him."

"Okay, one thing."

"Okay."

"*If* you ever get the opportunity to kick him in the face again, you are to do it at least five or six times for me." He ran his hand down my back and sighed. "When Mercy told me you were out there I got a little bent. I might have cursed out half of Boston leaving town to get out there."

"I'm sorry you were worried." I drank deeply from my beer.

"Worried, angry . . ." He pressed a soft kiss on my neck and then leaned back against the couch. "You've got me all twisted, Jane. It's not fair."

"Not fair?" I put down my beer and concentrated on his face. "You think you don't have me in the same condition?"

"I do?"

"You do." I touched his lips with my fingertips and sighed when he caught one finger with his lips. "I wasn't going to tell you . . . but I guess I should."

"Tell me what?"

"I broke off things with Charlie. I won't be going out with him on Friday or ever again."

"So why weren't you going to tell me?"

"Because, frankly, I didn't want you thinking that I'd given in to you."

He was still for a few seconds and then he started to laugh.

"What?" I frowned at him.

"I doubt seriously I'd ever make the mistake of thinking that you gave in to me on anything."

"Okay, fine. It also doesn't mean that I'm ready to start talking about exclusive arrangements or anything."

"I get it." He stood from the couch, holding me tight against his chest. "But I have a plan."

"Oh yeah?"

"I figure if I fuck you stupid every chance I get, you won't have much time for anything else."

I swung my feet a little as we entered the bedroom. "I'm digging that first part, but I can guarantee that I'm not that easy to manipulate and I've got lots and lots of stamina."

"We'll see." He dropped me on the bed. "Want to take a shower?"

I stared at him pointedly and scooted to the edge of the bed. "Are you doing one of your 'moves' on me?"

"No." Mathias laughed and pulled off his shirt as he walked toward the bathroom. "I worked all day. I need the shower."

"I'll be in there in a few minutes." I watched him for a few seconds and then laid back on the bed.

There was a sick feeling in the pit of my stomach. It'd been there since I'd realized that I was face to face with Lisa's ex-husband. I rolled over on my side and took a deep shuddering breath. She was so small and fragile compared to the man. I was angry for what she must have suffered at his hands, but more-over I was overwhelmed by my own potential for violence.

I could have killed him. I knew it, and I think in that last second he'd known it too. I looked toward the nightstand where I kept my gun and swallowed hard. There wasn't any part of me that could even pretend to find death foreign. I'd crossed that line long ago. Some cops are lucky enough to never have to draw their gun in the line of duty. It's rare, of course, but it happens. I could only wish I'd been that fortunate.

The rush of running water reached my ears and I rolled into a sitting position. Wallowing in self-pity was a poor choice.

9

I braced myself against the shower wall with both hands and stiffened my legs as Mathias gripped my hips. His cock pushed between my legs, thick and hard, and I shuddered at the contact. Hands left my hips, moved up my rib cage and upward to cup both breasts. Talented, gentle fingers plucked at my nipples until they were so hard I could barely feel them.

"Stop teasing me." I rested my forehead against the tile and tilted my ass up in brazen demand. "Put your cock in me."

He pushed my legs farther apart with his thigh and pressed one hand against the small of my back as he brushed the head of his cock against my dripping entrance. A soft sob broke free from my lips, and I thrust back against him in a desperate attempt to get him inside me.

"Mathias, please."

He drove into me with one heavy movement and wrapped one arm around me to keep me still. His cock pressed up against the upper wall of my pussy as he carefully began to move. A shudder ran down the length of my back as he deepened his thrust. His balls slapped against my labia each time he slammed home.

"Fuck me." I clutched at the wall, the heady pleasure of our merging bodies washing over me again and again. "Fuck me."

He pulled from me abruptly and turned me around. "You make me crazy."

I laughed softly as he lifted me and pressed me against the wall. "I won't tell anyone."

Mathias clenched his teeth as he pushed back into me. "Your pussy feels amazing."

I tightened my legs around his waist and clutched at his shoulders as he began to move in a steady but gentle thrust. My nipples rubbed against his chest with every move, and every single sensation was delicious.

"Yes. Yes."

He pushed open the shower stall door abruptly. "Turn off the water."

I struggled with the faucet briefly before getting it turned off. "You look like a man with a plan."

Laughing softly, he stepped out of the shower and gently placed me on the bathroom counter. I gasped a little when he pulled his cock free from my body. My womb clenched around the sudden emptiness.

"I do have a plan."

"Is this part of that 'fuck me stupid' thing?"

"Oh yeah."

"Okay, good." I smiled and leaned back on my hands. "What should I do?"

"Go lay down on the bed."

I scooted down off the counter and went out into the bedroom. By the time I'd crawled up into the middle of the bed he was standing at the foot, watching me. His cock, still erect, thrust out from his body.

"Spread your legs for me."

Following his instructions, I planted my feet flat on the bed and gasped a little at the cool air that brushed over the heated flesh of my pussy as my legs fell open almost of their own accord.

"Grab the bars of the headboard and don't let go until I say."

Raising one eyebrow, I lifted my hands above my head and wrapped both hands around the bars there. At least he wasn't thinking to tie me up. "What are you going to do?"

"Anything you'll let me."

Christ, that certainly didn't narrow the list. I gasped a little when he lowered his head and nuzzled my labia with his mouth. I loved having his talented mouth on me. I rocked against him until his hands clamped down on my hips.

His tongue slid between my parted labia and thrust without pause into my pussy. I moaned against the invasion, and my hands tightened on the headboard until the square cut of the bars hurt my palms.

He licked upward and sucked my clit into his mouth. I bucked against his hands and mouth until I came in one excited burst of energy and emotion. The orgasm rolled over me in one wave after another, and all I could do was lay there and shudder. After a few intense seconds, I tried to pull free from his mouth.

Mathias released my clit and then went back to lick the throbbing nub just once before he crawled fully on top of me and pushed his cock into my clenching pussy. My body yielded to his invasion, and I stiffened underneath him as I came again.

Every move he made sent shudders of pleasure through my swollen and constricting pussy until I could do nothing but hold onto the headboard, as he demanded. I was slack beneath him, taking the pounding of his body in and on mine like it was my due and loving every single second of it.

He arched against me as he came, his orgasm making him

groan, and then collapsed against me. I welcomed the weight of his body and turned my head to kiss his cheek.

"You could be the best sex on the planet." He lifted his head.

"Could be?" I asked softly, amused.

"Yeah, I figure it's one of us."

I rolled onto my back and watched silently as Mathias dressed. When he'd left the bed, I'd immediately wanted to ask him to stay. Yet I couldn't. My stubbornness would mean that I would spend the rest of the night alone, but I couldn't bring myself to ask.

He came back to the bed and sat down on the edge while he put on his shoes. "I'm bringing some contractors into the gallery early in the morning before operating hours. I'd like to seal that special focus gallery off so my men can work on a few things today."

"Okay."

"When did you need the space back for the kids?"

"Thursday to set up."

"Invitations went out some time ago, right?"

"Yeah."

He sighed. "I'll get them to work fast, but I won't be able to release the space again until I'm sure it's safe for the Castlemen collection."

"This has got you a little nervous."

"A little."

"Why?"

"Well, beyond the fact that I don't want to be the man to lose even a single piece of that collection . . . it would ruin me professionally if I couldn't even be counted on to protect six paintings."

"I have total faith in you." I sat up, letting the sheet I'd covered up in fall to my lap. "And if we have to move the kids' show somewhere else we'll make do."

"They'll be disappointed."

"I'll tell them why if it comes to it. They're all artists, and trust me, they understand the value of someone else's work." I touched his face, pleased that he cared about the things that were important to me. "I'll see you in the morning."

"I'll need to see you around ten unless you are booked up for the morning."

"About what?"

"About the security personnel I'm hiring to replace the current team."

"You'll be replacing all of them?" I asked softly, concerned about some of the men that had been there for years.

"No, not all. I've started working with your current head of security and he's agreed to move to my contract. Between the two of us, we've weeded out those that I'm uncomfortable with. He was surprised by the level of surveillance I did on the gallery, but I find him honest about his position and what he's willing to do to protect Holman. I trust him."

"Okay."

"Carl Wilkes has been grossly understaffed for years, and the security company he answered to ignored all of his suggestions and concerns."

"They ignored Mercy too." I raised an eyebrow. "Hence, you."

He laughed. "Well, I don't ever make the mistake of ignoring women. You creatures can be vicious."

I sighed when he leaned in and kissed me. "I'll bring in some food; we can brunch while we meet."

"Yeah, sounds good." He stood from the bed and started to walk away.

I snagged his hand. "Hey."

"Yeah?" He turned my hand over and ran his fingers across my palm.

"Take my spare key. It's where you found it the first time."

Mathias paused as if he was waiting for me to say something else and then nodded. "Okay."

I dropped back on the bed when I heard the front door to my apartment close and the locks click into place. For a few minutes, I laid there wondering when I'd gotten so reckless. I'd just given a man I'd known only a few days a key to my apartment.

Giving a man the key to my apartment was huge, especially since I'd never even let one spend the night until Mathias. Yet this huge thing didn't feel overwhelming at all. It felt awesome and relieving.

The morning passed in something of a blur. The administrative staff was in a tizzy, helping me compile a list of people to invite to the Castlemen show and alternately being grilled like spies by Mathias and his crew.

His crew consisted of six silent, serious men who walked around the gallery like a little army. They were dressed well, but they also looked like they could take over a small country. Something would have to be done, and I honestly didn't know what.

My assistant, Casey, was out at her desk looking pointedly at me. I motioned her inside. I felt a little guilty; I'd had very little time for her since she was promoted and in a lot of ways had dropped her into a strange pond with little or no training. She'd landed on her feet and performed well, but it still hadn't been very fair of me.

She shut the door and walked to the chair in front of the desk she favored and took a seat. For a few seconds, she sat there and then sighed. "The guys with the guns are freaking out the sales staff, the whole building is bursting with rumors about the new security firm, and there is this absurd story going around about how you foiled a robbery over the weekend."

For a few seconds I just stared at her, and then I started to laugh. "Okay, one thing at a time. I'm going to talk to Mr. Montgomery about the guys with the weapons. They don't freak me out, but I can see how they might be a less than wonderful addition to our work environment."

"Why new security?"

"Because our collection is growing in expensive ways and something has to be done to protect it and make our artists more comfortable."

"So there was a robbery?" Casey's eyes got wide and she leaned forward. "You stopped a burglar?"

"*Stopped* is a strong word, and it was a staged break-in to demonstrate to Mr. Brooks how vulnerable his collection was." I looked out toward the bull pen and then looked back toward her. "How are things going?"

She pursed her lips and then crossed her legs at the knee. "Well, there are a few people who resent me, especially since I came up from the sales floor and into such a high position."

"And?"

"I'm dealing with it. I knew it would happen. They'll either get over it or not. I worked hard on the sales floor. I haven't been the head of sales for a year without learning how this gallery works. I've earned the position of senior buyer, and everyone will just have to deal with it too."

"Good." I looked over at my calendar and then sighed. "I have to meet with Mr. Montgomery in Conference Room 2 in about twenty minutes. I want you to sit in and then I'll want you to go over to the academy and pick up the two students who'll be starting their internships today. Make sure to keep track of your gas and mileage so that you can be reimbursed."

"No problem." She stood and straightened her short jacket. "Anything else?"

"Make sure the coffee is fresh in the conference room; since I'm going to be arguing with the man I'd like to at least offer him coffee."

"Sure thing. I'll get out some bagels as well. Men always argue less when they have something to eat."

I doubted that would be true of Mathias, but I figured it couldn't hurt.

Mathias was already in the conference room when we entered. I sat down across from him and glanced briefly as she went to the refreshment table to get us both coffee.

"Coffee?"

He nodded, barely glancing up from the laptop he had in front of him. "Thanks."

I arranged my folders in front of me, placed my handheld on my left, and then waited for Casey to bring the coffee.

Closing his laptop, he gave me his attention as Casey set a cup down just to the right of him.

"Ms. Tilwell." He looked briefly at Casey. "Ms. Andrews, it's a pleasure to see you again."

Casey blushed and fiddled with the folders in front of her. "Thank you."

Great, if he was going to turn all of the female employees into little wet spots I couldn't see how things were ever going to get done.

"I have a few things." Starting with the problems seemed to be the easiest course.

He met my gaze and grinned. "Yes, I imagine that you do."

"First, the guys with the guns are freaking everyone out and they can't be great for our clientele's morale either." I folded my hands on the folder in front of me and took a deep breath. "Now, I realize that you have a job to do around here, and while I don't want to interfere with that I can't have a small army marching around the gallery scaring the crap out of everyone. It's not good for our image."

He nodded and then to my amazement laughed softly. "Seth and his team are only here for the day. After that you won't see them again until they provide me with an in-depth report on the staff currently employed here."

"All of our employees are thoroughly investigated before being hired." I picked up my coffee. "You have those reports."

"Seth does things a little differently, and one weakness in your staff could be a vulnerable spot in my security system. I have to be sure." He tore the bagel that Casey had slipped his way in half and shrugged. "I realize that the interviews are making the sales and administrative staff nervous, but if they have nothing to hide then there is nothing to worry about. You might as well know I've scheduled a drug test tomorrow."

"What percentage?"

"Nothing random about it. I'm testing everyone."

My mouth dropped open briefly and I glanced toward Casey, whose gaze had dropped to the table. "Everyone?"

"Everyone. It's in the employment agreement that they signed. I'm bringing in a lab first thing in the morning to take blood and hair samples from every staff member."

"Okay." I glanced down at the list I'd made and pursed my lips. There were a few questions about the drug testing running around in my head, but I wanted to ask them in private. "The staff interviews are a part of that process as well, I can assume?"

"Yes, I have to be sure of everyone in the building."

"The special focus gallery?"

"Isn't going to be ready for your high school students' show. I'm sorry, but I'm going to have to rewire the entire room and the veranda."

That sucked. I looked at Casey. "Any ideas?"

Casey raised an eyebrow and cleared her throat. "Well, I know we're saving the central space for the Abigail Grayson show. Since the high school show will be only two days, we can set it up and still have three days to clean up and prepare for the Grayson show."

"It would be tight but workable." I nodded. "Why don't you get started on that?"

She bounced up with a smile. "Sure thing."

Mathias said nothing until she left. "You just made that kid's week."

"She's hardly a child. She graduated the top of her class at Berkeley."

"Last year?"

"Four years actually; she just looks very young." I laughed softly. "Now, about the drug testing?"

"We've found trace evidence of marijuana and cocaine use in three different employee bathrooms. Seth wants to bring in a drug dog, but I thought that would be excessive."

"Pot and cocaine." I rubbed my mouth in disgust. "I guess our antidrug program is not as effective as we could hope."

"Male and female bathrooms."

"Could it be the cleaning crew?"

"If the staff tests clean, we'll approach the cleaning company with our concerns and get those people tested. But I'm fairly sure of who it is."

"Based on?"

"I watch these people a lot," he reminded carefully. "I've been watching them for nearly two weeks. If you spent a week or so observing them, you'd know too."

"Am I going to be disappointed?" I asked softly, thinking of Casey. I didn't know her as well as I should, but she'd never given me any cause to think she had a problem like that.

"You and Mercy both have a few perceived favorites, and from what I can tell they are all clean, including Casey. But to prevent any rancor, all staff will be tested."

"Sales?"

"The male is in sales and the female is in administration."

"Great. Any other stellar news to share?" I asked, dejected but relieved.

"I handled your employee background check personally." He pulled a folder out of the briefcase that sat in a chair next to him and pushed it across the table at me. "No surprises for you, I'm sure."

I opened it up and stared at the picture of me, and then skimmed through the report. "I can assume that Mr. Brooks will get this."

"Yes, and Mercy."

They both knew I'd been a cop in my past, but I doubted either of them had dug this deep. The previous security firm had only ever provided a yes or no on the people we submitted to them for review. When asked, they would provide a summary on those who failed to meet their standards, but we rarely requested that.

"That's fine."

"It's not. But there isn't much of a choice." He sat back in his chair and picked up his coffee. "I realize that Seth and his men are making people uncomfortable around here."

"I guess that's their purpose."

"In a way."

"Your regular staff won't look like them?"

"There will be armed men in the building at all times, but those on the sales floor will not be armed in an obvious way. It'll be your job to train them to meet your needs. They'll already have met mine by the time they walk into the building."

"Okay."

"I promise, no blunt objects. I save those kinds of guys for more varied assignments and bodyguard situations."

"What about the earpieces?"

"Those will stay, but the regular staff will have a more sophisticated and less visible system. You'll be able to contact any member of security throughout the building without alerting the patrons."

"Good."

"Relax, Jane, by the time I'm done this gallery will be the safest place in Boston and people won't even know why. They'll come in here and think for all the world that they are not being watched and scrutinized."

"Yet they will be?"

"Yes. I have a man coming in from Vegas to help with the security cameras and the face-recognition software. He's designed some of the most sophisticated systems in the world."

"Facial recognition?"

"Yeah, they use it in Vegas to watch for known cheaters and to do background checks on their guests without alerting the guests to the scrutiny."

"And we need that?"

"I've been in the gallery ten times in the last two weeks and there isn't a member of your security staff who has ever remembered seeing me."

"Oh."

"Carl is vastly understaffed, as I've already told you; his system is outdated—it was outdated ten days after it was installed. If the man didn't have an overdeveloped sense of personal honor and deep appreciation for art he would have changed jobs by now. The stress and frustration level is so high in that man I'm surprised he hasn't given James Brooks an earful every chance he's gotten in the last five years."

"Milton Storey rarely ever let complaints get out of the building. He liked to show a profit and as a result never fully informed Brooks of the gallery's security issues. Honestly, it wasn't much of an issue in the past.

"The Holman Gallery is an institution in Boston—popular and moderately successful in the past because it is run to support a charity organization that the blue bloods love to contribute to. All of that has begun to change; with new artists in our collection and a series of vibrant shows, we are growing popular in a way we never have before."

"Every penny the gallery makes goes back into the Holman Foundation?"

"Yes. After salaries, bills, and the like are taken care of. The gallery was opened to fund the foundation and its various community activities." I stood up and went to the coffeepot. "Would you like some more?"

"Please."

I went back to the table with the pot and topped off his cup. "Are you comfortable with Mr. Wilkes remaining here?"

"If I wasn't, he would be on my list of removals."

I put the pot back, went back around to my chair, and sat down. "How many?"

"You have fifteen security officers. Only three are on my list to stay."

"Including Mr. Wilkes?"

"Yes."

"Can we afford to do such a mass replacement so close to the Castlemen show?"

"We can't afford not to."

"Okay." I nodded. "Have you told Mr. Brooks?"

"Yes. He told me that you could handle the details and that we should go to Mercy with any concerns." He opened his laptop. "You were CC'd on that e-mail."

"I haven't checked my e-mail this morning." I was avoiding it. The last time I'd opened it two hundred messages had downloaded.

He closed the laptop again and focused on me. "Okay, now enough business."

I laughed softly. "It's supposed to be all business when we're here, Mathias."

"I know. I just have a question."

"One question?"

"Yeah, one question."

"What is it?"

"Will you have dinner with me tonight?"

I jerked a little and blushed at his amused smile. The man sure knew how to throw a woman off. A real date? We'd really skipped over that part.

"Aren't we passed dating?"

"No, and we'd be cheating ourselves not to indulge in that little ritual." He chuckled when I frowned at him. "I can make moves on you, you can make moves on me, and we can pretend that we don't know how the night will end."

"A little dating game?"

"Yeah, of sorts."

It sounded fun and dangerous. That much time together would lead to real conversations and getting to know each other.

"Okay, a date. I pick the place and you take me dancing."

"Deal."

I'd made a deal with a devil and he was standing there in my doorway looking like sin on a stick. The suit was dark blue, was tailored, and looked perfect on him. I wanted to invite him inside and get him out of it.

"I hope you have a jacket to put over that or you're going to freeze to death."

I laughed and glanced down at the barely there black dress I'd chosen from my closet. The skirt was swingy; it was cut too low in the front and so low in the back that it probably wasn't legal in some states. No butt crack, though; I have rules about showing my private parts to strangers.

"I have a cape in the closet." I walked to it and opened the door. "Did you have problems getting the reservations?"

"No; it pays to have a famous brother."

I laughed. "You know, I've had him book a few places for me as well. He's a good sport about it, and people do tend to fall over themselves to make him happy around here."

"They don't want him to leave Boston. Having an internationally famous artist in the city is good for tourism."

"Perhaps."

"Let's go before your dress does me in."

Great food, a little too much wine, and an hour of dancing later I could hardly remember why I ever thought that there wasn't a place in my life for Mathias Montgomery. Perhaps it was foolish to think of him as a fixture in my life, but I'd already passed some crazy line in my mind. I could barely imagine life without him in it. It was insane to be so wrapped up in a man I barely knew, but there it was, and I couldn't very well ignore it.

He pulled me closer and ran his hand downward to rest on the small of my back. "We should probably leave soon."

"Yeah." I glanced up at him and sighed. "I need to be at work early in the morning."

"Then we definitely need to go, otherwise I won't have time to do all the perfectly filthy things I've been thinking about doing since I picked you up."

"Sounds like a plan."

I curled my fingers against his as he led me off the dance floor and toward the front door. The jazz club wasn't very crowded, but it was busy enough that it took us about a minute to get to the door. He retrieved our coats and we slipped out. Preoccupied with my own dirty thoughts, I barely took note of getting in the car or anything else until he parked in front of a building that did not look like mine.

I frowned at the window and turned to him. "Where are we?"

"I thought I'd show you my place."

"Oh." His place. Not a hotel room, but a place. "Renting?"

"No. I purchased the building." He left the car.

I watched him walk around the car and open the door for me. "The whole building?"

"Yeah, it has two apartments."

"One on each floor?"

"Side by side, but neither of them was big enough on their own so I had the building gutted and renovated. The floors and walls are in. The majority of the furniture will arrive in about a week."

I followed him up the stairs and waited patiently while he unlocked the door. The first floor was wide and open with a set of stairs against one wall. A large flat-panel television was on one wall in front of a leather couch, and a pool table was to the left of the front door. He flipped on the lights.

"So, a TV, a couch, and a pool table." I looked at him and laughed. "Basic necessities?"

"And a bed."

A bed. I pursed my lips as I pulled my cloak off and walked toward the couch. Past the couch and TV I saw that the back part of the building had been turned into a kitchen with bar and table seating. I couldn't even begin to speculate how much money he'd spent renovating the place.

I dropped my purse and cloak on the couch and turned to look at him. "It's beautiful."

"Thanks." He shoved his hands into his pockets and glanced around. "It's starting to feel like home."

I walked back to him and stopped just short of touching him. "Wanna show me upstairs?"

"Yeah."

Mathias touched my jaw with the tips of his fingers and then pulled me close. His mouth covered mine, and I wrapped my arms around his neck without another thought. I nodded and moaned a little when he picked me up. I'd never really enjoyed being carted around until him. I figured I'd let him carry me wherever he wanted.

The upstairs appeared to be divided into several rooms, but only one really mattered to me. Once we were in his bedroom, he put me down on the bed and knelt at my feet. "What are you doing?"

He chuckled as he picked up one foot and pulled my shoe off. "I figured I would take off all of your clothes and then spend at least the next hour exploring those filthy plans of mine."

"Oh yeah." I winced briefly as he tossed my shoe aside. "You'll scuff them."

"Don't tell me you're one of those women with a shoe fetish." He plucked off the other shoe and put it down gently.

"Yes, I am." And I wasn't remotely ashamed of it either.

My breath caught in my chest as his hands slid up one leg to the edge of my stockings. Seconds later, his fingers caught the strap of my garter belt.

He paused and sucked in a deep breath. "Are you trying to make me stupid?"

"Of course not." I laughed softly when he stood and pulled me from the bed. "Most men would appreciate lingerie." I slid the straps of my dress down my arms and dropped the dress.

"Well." His gaze dropped to my breasts and then slowly downward. "I'm not complaining."

I slipped back on the bed and watched him undress through half-closed eyes. Spreading my legs, I laid back on the bed when he joined me. I lifted my hips when his fingers grasped both the garter belt and my panties. He pulled them carefully away and tossed the tangled mixture of hose and silk aside.

He sat back on his heels and spread my legs wider with firm hands. My fingers twisted into fists against the blanket beneath us, and my body tensed with both arousal and anticipation. It didn't matter what he had planned for me, I knew I would enjoy it.

"You're already wet for me."

"Always."

Mathias released one knee and pressed his thumb against my

clit. The pressure felt amazing, and immediately I rocked against his hand, trying to add friction to the mix. He lifted his hand from my body, and I groaned in frustration.

"Bastard."

He laughed softly and moved over me until we were eye to eye. I moved against the weight of him, pleased by the heat and feel of his body against mine. It felt amazing and perfect.

"You make me want things I've never even thought about before."

His lips brushed against mine briefly before he drifted downward and latched onto one rigid nipple. I arched my back, and a shiver ran down the length of my body. Teeth grazed and lips pulled at my nipple until I was twisting and shaking beneath him.

When I thought I could take no more of the gentle war he was waging against me, he lifted his head and sought out my other breast. My hands, still fisted in the blanket, clenched further, and I shuddered against the heady and vivid pleasure of his mouth.

Mathias released my nipple and raised his head to meet my gaze. "Tell me what you want."

"You know."

"Yes, but I want to hear it." He shifted and pushed the head of his cock against my clit.

Gasping, I stilled and waited for him to move again. "Do that again."

"Is this all you want?"

"No."

"Then tell me."

I cried out when he moved again, the large head of his cock rubbing my clit in just the right way. "Put your cock in me."

"More. Don't hold back on me, Jane."

"Fuck me, please."

I arched against his body as he lifted and without pause

thrust his cock into me. Wrapping my legs around his waist, I pulled him tight to me and rocked against his invasion.

"Relax, baby."

I laughed softly at his whispered demand and lifted my hands from the bed to stroke his back. "I need it hard."

"I know." He kissed me, and then slid one arm underneath us to support me. "You know I'll give you everything you need."

I did know and it wasn't scaring the hell out of me. He pushed deep into my body and withdrew so fast that I gasped, and then he sank in hard. I arched against the heavy thrust of his body and clung to him as our pace became frenzied.

He pulled free of my body abruptly, and for a few seconds I clung to him. "Please."

"Relax." Mathias kissed me briefly and then slid downward and pushed his tongue into me.

"Oh my God."

I spread my legs for him and rocked against the invasion of his tongue until he moved upward and claimed my throbbing clit. Lifting my hips, I silently begged for his attention, and each swipe of his tongue sent me a little further away from reality. Finally, when I thought I might burst from my skin, I came in a rush of physical and emotional pleasure.

Hot, unbearable seconds passed as he lifted away from me, grasped my hips, and pushed his cock back into my pussy. My inner muscles clenched and clung to him as he started to rotate his hips. I hooked my legs around his body and lifted to meet the demanding pace he'd set.

He pulled me up off the bed and guided my arms around his neck as his hands cupped my ass firmly. I wanted to make him come, needed to. I followed the pace his hands demanded, sliding up and down on his cock until he shook against me and clutched at me with shaking hands.

"Come for me," I whispered against his mouth.

"I'm close." He groaned against my lips and held me still suddenly. "Yes."

Carefully, he lowered us both to the bed and rested his weight on me for a few seconds before he pulled free and rolled onto his back.

I hated leaving him, but I found I couldn't stay. I sat down on the edge of the bed and slid my shoes on. Just as I was about to stand, he reached out and took my hand. "Hey."

"Sorry, I didn't mean to wake you."

"You aren't all that good at sneaking around." He sat up and ran his hand down my back. "You weren't going to try to catch a cab, were you?"

"Yeah."

Mathias sighed, and I bit down on my lip. "I'll take you home."

"I'm an adult, you know."

"That's beside the point." He left the bed and walked into the master bathroom. "I don't put women in cabs."

I stood up and hurried downstairs, wishing that I'd managed to make my escape without waking him.

10

I leaned against the door and listened for the steps as he walked away. Relaxing a little, I turned and flipped the rest of the locks. There was no rhyme or reason to my need to sleep in my own bed.

I pulled off my cloak and dropped my purse on the table close to the door. The answering machine was there . . . blinking madly as if I'd been gone for days rather than hours. I pushed the button and stilled as the first message began.

"Hey, it's me, Charlie. I think we need to talk. I totally understand your anger and frustration concerning my mother. She had no business invading your personal life, and I've made it clear to her that she's not to tell a single person what she found out." He sighed. "Jane, we have a good thing together, and it would be a shame to let it all go because of one mistake on my mother's part."

I hit the delete button and glared at the machine as another message started.

"Look, it isn't like you to ignore me so I'm not sure what's going on."

His tone was tense and almost angry. I'd never known Charlie to be either. Disgruntled, I shoved off my shoes and sat down on the bench that was beside the small table.

"I'm not going to be dismissed like this. I've invested entirely too much time in you to be pushed aside like I don't matter." The call ended abruptly as if he'd slapped his cell phone shut in a tiff.

He invested time in me? Another message began, and it was him again. Frowning and a little unnerved, I turned to stare at the machine.

"You're out with someone. I never should have agreed to that nonexclusive bullshit of yours. I didn't spend the last year taking you to the best restaurants in town and showing you the proper way to be for nothing."

Showing me? Maybe he was drunk.

"Where the fuck are you?"

I jerked and stood up abruptly. After stopping the answering machine, I went in search of my phone. I found it on the couch. It was nearly two o'clock in the morning, but if he was going to call and berate my answering machine, I didn't feel guilty about calling so late.

"It's about damn time you got home," he snapped the moment he answered the phone.

"What's wrong with you?" I demanded, furious at his messages and, moreover, his tone.

"I've been calling you all night."

"No, you've been calling and leaving stupid messages on the machine all night." I sat down on the couch. "I dumped you, Charlie. I'm not sure what deluded world you live in, Charlie, but in Jane-land that means that whatever relationship we had is over."

"That's not how I see it," he ground out. "I'm not going to be dismissed like this."

"It's the only way it's going to be. I don't care how you see it." My fingers tightened on the phone as I listened to his breathing.

"Look, I've spent the last year grooming you into a woman I could take into my social set."

"Grooming me?" I demanded. "I'm not a horse!"

"Do you know how long I had to search for a woman I could fuck regularly that would be presentable to the people I work with?"

Stunned, I sat there in silence. It was a difficult moment for me because there was a part of me that had been searching for the same thing. It made me sick, emotionally and physically. Stomach churning, I walked into the kitchen and pulled out a glass.

"I'm finished with you, Charlie. Don't call here ever again."

"You wait a damn minute—"

"No." I ended the call and tossed my phone on the counter.

Grooming me? The son of a bitch. I filled the glass with some water and downed it in one gulp. Had he really been trying to sculpt me into a society wife? I probably had the right look and the right job, but the background issue must've been something of a stumbling block for him. Suddenly all of his good-natured teasing over my using the wrong utensil at dinner no longer seemed like teasing.

I was an idiot, twice an idiot in fact. Once for thinking that a man like Charlie Wallace was worth my time and twice for thinking that I wanted a man like him. I put the glass away and went to my bedroom. Finding the list was easy; it had been in my bedside table for as long as I could remember. Perhaps since my first night in the apartment.

Jane's Perfect Man
. . . is educated and cultured
. . . is ambitious about his career
. . . understands that my career is important

. . . loves art
. . . is even tempered and thoughtful
. . . is NOT interested in marriage
. . . has no ex-wife
. . . has no children

Not one mention of love or even passion. Was this emotionless man really all that perfect? Disgusted, I wadded the paper up and tossed it back in the drawer. I was certainly no better than Charlie. I'd been dating him because of that stupid list. A list I'd made one lonely night years ago when being so far from home had been too much for me.

I stripped off my dress and panties and went into the bathroom for a shower. The middle of the night was not a good time to make life-altering decisions. I needed a clear head and some sleep. Both, I'm sure, were going to be in short supply by morning.

"So, I get home and the damn machine is overflowing with messages from Charlie." I glanced around the café and then looked toward her.

Mercy wrinkled her nose and swished a cinnamon stick in her coffee. "How many?"

"At least four, but I stopped listening to them when he started to talk crazy. My answering machine was full when I came home." Shrugging, I tore my muffin apart and reached for a little packet of butter from the basket between us. "I called him, and he informed me that he hadn't spent the last year training me to be a good, presentable society wife for nothing."

"Training you?" Mercy asked softly. "And he's still breathing?"

"Yeah, I'm trying to avoid racking up a body count this close to Christmas." I sat back in the booth and silently munched on the muffin.

"I hope you told him where to go and how to get there."

"I behaved in a civil manner."

"Bah, you're no fun. Obviously he didn't upset you enough to get your hackles up or you would have started to sound so country that he would've been glad to be free of you."

"Yeah, I thought about it."

"You broke off your relationship with him because of Mathias."

"No."

"Stop kidding yourself. You can say it was his mother or his sudden confession that he was grooming you for marriage all you want, but at least be honest with yourself."

Honest with myself. I haven't been honest with myself in years it seemed. "Okay, so maybe Charlie just wasn't all that attractive or entertaining compared to Mathias, but that doesn't mean it's got to be something serious."

"I've seen you go through men like shoes . . . at least four since I met you. Denis, the accountant, who met your every demand but was boring in bed. Jacob, the doctor, who certainly qualified—"

"He was impotent." I frowned at her. "You didn't honestly expect me to date a man who couldn't perform, did you?"

"What about that stockbroker guy?"

"He had a little dick." I frowned as I thought about it. "I've never been so disappointed in my whole damn life."

She raised an eyebrow. "Oh yeah? What about that jewelry designer guy?"

"Yeah. How can a man who spends that much time with diamonds be a total asshole?" I wasn't entirely sure that Simon was even human. Diamonds always put me in a superior mood, and as far as I know it worked that way for most normal people. "Anyways, Charlie met my criteria to a T. Except, of course, for his recent admission. If I'd thought for a second that he was planning to marry me I would have run so fast from his ass that I would have left a trail of flame behind me."

"Do you think he'll come around?"

"It would serve Charles Wallace III to keep his distance." I frowned as I said it. "I'd really like to punch him in the face."

Milton Storey's lawyers were the first meeting of the day. I'd put them off as long as possible, but they'd threatened to have me served if I didn't meet with them willingly. I'd spent nearly four years in the gallery under the semidirect supervision of Milton Storey and I had nothing good to say about him. I didn't imagine his lawyers were going to be too pleased with me.

There were two. The man, Oliver Keener, was small boned and delicate in a way that was not attractive at all. The woman, Mara James, was matronly and her hair was one or two shades from blue. Both were from a law firm that had more names on their sign than actual employees.

"Do you mind if we record this?"

"No."

I crossed my legs, sat back in the chair, and cupped my coffee with both hands. "I only have an hour, so if you can just get to the point that would be great."

"You worked for Mr. Storey for four years."

"Yes, one year as a sales clerk and then three as the senior buyer for the gallery."

"At any time during your employment did Mr. Storey express a sexual interest in you?"

"No."

"Did you feel that others were given opportunities within the gallery because of how attractive they are?"

"No, Mr. Storey rarely gave anyone a chance unless he wanted them to fail. He takes great joy in making others uncomfortable."

"That isn't what I asked," the woman snipped through clenched teeth.

"That's my answer and that will be my answer if I'm called upon to testify."

"Ms. Tilwell, you do realize that the gallery is at risk with this lawsuit."

"Actually, Mr. Brooks has settled the suit against the gallery. So as you can see we have nothing to gain or lose by what happens with the civil suit against Milton Storey."

"Brooks admitted fault?" Mr. Keener's face was flushed red with anger.

"I'm not privy to the terms of the settlement."

"This is a violation of the agreement that Brooks made with our client." She stood and snapped her fingers. Oliver leaped up, snagged his recorder, and grabbed his folders. "You'll be seeing us again, Ms. Tilwell."

"Tell that troll client of yours I say, 'hi'."

Now, if I could start every day like that it would make the world a better place. Getting someone else wound up like a two-dollar toy was enough to set anyone's world to rights.

"Don't you love making lawyers mad?"

I looked up and laughed. "Yes, I do."

Casey came all the way in and shut the door. "I've cleared your afternoon."

"Why?"

"The maintenance contractor will be putting up the blinds and I've been informed that drilling into all of this metal is going to be something of a nightmare. The rest of the staff will work in the large conference room, unless you'd prefer something different."

"How are we coming on the list?"

"We have a partial." She flipped through the folders in her hand and offered me one. "We'll have a better one once the computer guy comes to fix the network."

"It's down?"

"Not down, but we can't access the secured server where the client information is stored. Something funky involving 'shares' and some other such nonsense that made my eyes cross." She sat down in a chair in front of my desk and sighed. "Well, the walking mountains are gone, and in their place is the fine, unbelievable man with an accent. The sales staff has spent the morning falling all over themselves to make him feel at home. The women *and* the men."

"I see. Should I tell Mr. Montgomery he'll have to go?"

"Lord no, the whole staff would revolt. They'll calm down once they realize he's mine." She grinned and looked down at her folder to the Post-It note she had stuck there. "I've booked the hotel suite for Mr. Castlemen, and as far as I know everything is going well on his end. His publicist called three times this morning to confirm details. I get the feeling that he hasn't left Alaska in some time."

"I wonder why."

"It's strange, that's for sure. There are like ten men to every one woman in Alaska." She frowned and pursed her lips. "Do you think they'd let me pick out the ten I wanted?"

"Something tells me that you wouldn't be that lucky." I opened the folder containing the partial list and browsed the names. "Any calls yet?"

"Oh yeah. We have the answering service answering the phones right now. How do people find out these things?"

"I'm sure his publicist has already started the ball rolling, and you did book the suite in his name?"

"No. I booked it in the gallery's name. I figured he would demand privacy. A man can't live on a mountain in the middle of nowhere and actually crave a lot of human contact."

"Good thinking." I looked toward her, and she was frowning. "What?"

"There was a message on your voice mail this morning that was . . . unpleasant."

"From Charlie?"

"Yeah, he certainly wasn't acting his best. It's still there if you want to listen to it."

"Give me the highlights."

She cleared her throat. "I'd rather not. As I said it was unpleasant."

I took a deep drink of coffee and glanced toward my phone. "Delete it and inform security that he is no longer allowed in the office areas. If he causes a scene they are authorized to remove him by any means necessary."

Standing, I straightened my jacket and handed her the list. "I'm going to go check out the new guy and then I'll be ready to meet with Mercy."

"She's currently in a phone conference, but I've been given strict instructions to rescue her in ten minutes." She cleared her throat. "The people from the lab are set up in the small conference room on two. Each employee has an appointment time."

"Reactions?"

"A few here and there. Mostly they seem to be personally affronted by the whole process, but that's to be expected. No one has refused the testing."

Connor Grant stood about 6'5" and was a tight 195 lbs. Dark brown hair, blue eyes, and a wicked smile completed the picture. He had a voice like melting chocolate—soft, warm, and delicious. I wasn't remotely attracted to him, and I blamed Mathias.

"How long have you been in the U.S.?"

"I met up with Mathias a few years back when he was doing some wet work for Interpol." He glanced me over and smiled. "I think the hair suits you."

"You tell Shamus Montgomery that my hair is not too short."

"I sure will."

"Where is Mathias?"

"He's in the security office." He jerked his thumb behind him. "Last door on the left."

"Yes, thank you."

I walked down the hall toward the office quickly and found Mathias sitting alone at a bank of cameras. "Hey."

He turned and raised an eyebrow. "Get a good look at Connor?"

"Yeah." I shut the door and leaned on it. "We have this many cameras?"

"We do now. I had them installed last night."

"Cool."

"Am I going to have to fire him?" He motioned toward the camera that showed Connor at his station.

"Well, he does have the sales staff all wound up, but I have it on good authority that he'll be off limits soon enough."

"The guys tell him all the time that he's too pretty for security work."

"But a good choice for the gallery. I know plenty of bored housewives that would come down here if he were giving out tours of the place." I leaned against the edge of the table and looked over his face. "When I got home last night my answering machine was brimming with messages from Charlie."

"I see."

Sighing, I couldn't figure out why I was telling him this, but I felt like he should know. "I'm not filling you in on this because I want you to do something about it. It's just that I've asked Casey to pull him from the authorized list of visitors to the office level and I figured you would see it. I didn't want you to think I was keeping secrets from you or anything."

"Okay." He plucked up one of my hands and kissed my palm. "What did he say?"

"Basically that I wasn't allowed to call things off with him."

"And?"

"And that he'd spent the last year *training* me to be his wife."

"So I take it you plan on punching him square in his mouth the next time you see him."

"You bet your ass."

Mathias tugged gently, and I sighed as I went willingly into his lap.

"I can go find him and kick his ass. He'll never know what hit him."

"No. He's just not used to things not going his way. I'm sure he'll get over it and go on. I mean, he's hot tempered but I wouldn't call him stupid." I hoped. But then I'd also never believed him the kind of person to leave psycho-stalking messages on a woman's answering machine either.

"As long as he keeps his distance."

I was so wrong, and that irritated me. My knuckles whitened on the handle of my briefcase as I walked toward my car. Charlie was leaning against it and offered me an easy-going smile once he caught sight of me.

Glaring, I pushed the button on my remote that unlocked the doors and went directly to the driver's side door. "Obviously one of us needs to bone up on our conversation skills."

"I came on a little strong last night." He reached out to touch me, and I jerked back. "Hey, I'm not going to hurt you."

I tossed my briefcase into the passenger seat, gaze centered on him. "I won't make that same promise, Charles."

"Janie, I'm trying to be good about this, you know. I spent several hours convincing my mother to overlook your background and get to know you."

"My background is nothing to overlook." I slammed my car door shut and glanced around the empty parking lot. The last thing I wanted was a big scene anywhere near my job, and he knew it. "It isn't like I did drugs or spent time in jail. I put on a badge and served others. If that somehow makes me deficient in your mother's eyes, I feel sorry for her. Living with that kind of narrow thinking must make for a miserable life."

"My mother is not narrow minded. She gives to the under-privileged and volunteers annually for various children's charities."

I stared at him for a moment, and then frowned. "So?"

"What do you mean *so*? If she felt poor people were beneath her, she wouldn't work so hard to help them."

"For the love of God, Charlie, the woman had me investigated because she wanted to make sure I was good enough for her baby boy!"

"She was looking out for me."

"Sure she was." I jerked open my car door and looked at him. "It doesn't matter anyway. Hell, if she hadn't come over to your apartment uninvited she never would have met me at all."

"You really mean that. I was nothing more to you than an occasional fuck?" His face flushed red with anger. "I invested too much time and money into you. What am I going to tell my friends?"

"I don't care."

He grabbed my arm and jerked me toward him. "The people I work with expect to meet you on Friday night. I won't have you embarrassing me like this."

"You can let me go or you can explain to the people you work with how you got a black eye. It's really up to you." I glanced toward the gallery and sighed as Connor came through the front doors at a near run. "Let me go before the security guard gets here."

Charlie looked over his shoulder and released me quickly. "We aren't finished."

"Ms. Tilwell." Connor looked pointedly at Charlie until he backed up a few paces. "Mr. Montgomery wanted me to make sure you didn't need any assistance."

I looked between the two of them and then slid into my driver's seat. "No, but thank you, Connor."

Locking the door, I turned on my car and whipped out of the parking space without looking back at Charlie. In the rearview mirror, I watched him slink away toward his vehicle.

My cell phone started to ring before I was even a block away. I picked it up and sighed. "Thank you for not coming out."

"I told you that I wouldn't give anyone in the gallery reason to believe that we are more than coworkers." His tone was clipped, even, and very angry. "Just make sure that's the last time I have to watch him touch you."

"Okay." I pursed my lips wondering exactly how I was going to control them both.

Honestly, I had no chance in hell of ever controlling Mathias, and I was at a loss as to what to do with Charlie. He was hurt and angry, despite the fact that I'd always been very clear about how I saw our relationship. Obviously, he'd never really paid much attention to what I said or even wanted.

"I'll be at the gallery until late," Mathias said.

"Then I'll see you tomorrow?" Did that question sound needy coming out of my mouth or eager?

"Yeah, lunch?"

"Sounds good."

After our good-byes, I closed my cell phone and tossed it into the passenger seat. Relationships are too complicated, that's why they should be avoided at all cost. Did I even want a relationship with Mathias? Would I be able to live with myself if I turned him away without exploring it?

I parked my car in my slot, walked to the corner deli, and bought dinner. It was a crowded little place but had great food and I enjoyed the atmosphere. I also wasn't all that interested in going home to an empty apartment, which was disconcerting. My apartment had been my haven from the world for a long time and now it was just a bunch of empty rooms. That was Mathias's fault as well; before him, my life had seemed full and I'd been content.

My answering machine was full again when I got home. Frustrated, I unplugged the thing and tossed it in a closet. I wasn't about to let anyone use something that belonged to me to invade my space and insult me.

I woke up suddenly, reaching out and into the nightstand drawer. With the comforting presence of the 9mm in my hand, I reached out and flipped on the light. My gaze settled on Charlie, sitting in a chair on the opposite side of the room.

"What the fuck?"

He held up a key ring. "I took your keys a couple months back and made duplicates. I guess that's another reason you aren't a cop anymore. You aren't very observant."

"You're right." I shoved the covers back and leveled my gun at him. "I certainly never realized how freaking weird you are."

"I thought I'd come over here and find you with another man." He tossed the key ring on the carpet between us. "There is someone, right?"

"Yes, and you're fortunate that he's not here. He probably would've shot first." I stood from the bed and pulled my robe on. "You shouldn't have come here."

"I know." He picked up a glass I hadn't noticed before and drained the contents. "Good whiskey, by the way."

Glaring, I took a deep breath. "You come into my home un-invited and help yourself to my alcohol?"

"I've certainly had better judgment. I didn't realize how in-vested I was in you until you decided we were finished." He put the glass down and stood from the chair. "I have every right to be here."

"The hell you do," I ground out through clenched teeth, freaked out because I had no idea how long he'd been in my bedroom watching me sleep. "I decide who I see and don't see."

"This isn't done, Jane. I don't lose when it comes to anything." He picked up his coat and motioned toward the keys. "Those are the only ones I had made."

It hardly mattered. The first phone call I was going to make would be to a locksmith to have the locks on my door changed. "Don't come around anymore, Charlie."

"I don't plan to give up on you."

"Your plans don't matter." I followed him to the front door and watched patiently while he pulled on his jacket. The drama of the whole situation was beyond absurd. If it were happening to someone else, I might've laughed. Mama's boys do not make good stalkers.

He opened the door. "About my mother?"

"Yes?"

"I hope you won't remove her from the gallery's preferred guest list."

"She was on it before we met, and I don't let personal matters get in the way of business." I rested my gun against my leg; the cool metal actually felt reassuring.

Charlie paused and then gestured toward the phone. "I plugged the answering machine back in and deleted all of my calls. I'm sincerely sorry for that; it wasn't my intent to verbally abuse you. I was just angry."

"Okay." But deleting the evidence didn't make that behavior disappear. "What are you now?"

"Determined." He reached out to touch me but backed up when I jerked and lifted my gun. "You have two messages that aren't from me."

He pulled the door shut carefully, leaving me alone in my apartment.

I went to it, flipped the four bolts, and then put on the chain. Leaving the chain off on the off chance that Mathias might show up was foolish, and it was the only reason that Charlie had gained entry to my apartment without my hearing it.

I hit play on the answering machine and put my gun down on the table beside it.

"Hey, kiddo, you'd best call before one of us hops a plane to Boston. Some cop outside of Boston ran a check on you. Right now, Wes and I are drawing straws to see who gets to come up there and kick some ass. You'd better hope he wins. Call me!"

I laughed and shook my head. Stan was the oldest of my brothers and certainly the most protective. He'd been there, strong and determined, the day our father had told us quite simply that our mother had bailed. Bailed on her job, her children, and her husband.

Wes and I would've been at a loss without Stan to pick up the slack and keep our world spinning. I don't think any of us ever thanked him properly for that.

Stan had gotten us all fed and put to bed that night and every night after that until he'd moved out on his own. I glanced toward the clock; it was probably close to five in Savannah. Picking up the phone, I dialed his phone number and walked into the kitchen to rummage through my cabinet for breakfast.

He answered on the fourth ring. "Detective Tilwell."

"Good morning, detective."

"Jane, what the hell is going on? I got word that you were involved in a domestic dispute. If some guy you're dating messed with you . . . I swear to God—"

"No, no, it was nothing like that. I was at a friend's house and her ex-husband showed up." I poured myself a glass of milk and went looking for a snack. "I kicked his ass."

Stan laughed. "Well, okay, as long as you came out on top. What took you so long to call back?"

Frowning, I wondered how to address that question without revealing the fact that I'd been involved in something of a domestic issue myself. "I had a few problems with my answering machine. Why didn't you call my cell?"

"We all figured if it was really bad you'd have already called one or more of us."

"You were just looking for an excuse to come to Boston."

He laughed. "Maybe. I haven't seen you in a while. Will you be home for Christmas this year?"

I wrinkled my nose as I considered the last Christmas I'd spent at home. "That depends, is Mom bringing a date?"

"Gawd, I hope not. That was a disaster. I kept waiting for a brawl to break out." He sighed. "So, what's up?"

That's a loaded question. "I'm arranging my first show solo."

"That's good?"

"It's excellent." I grinned as I sat down at the table. "The promotion is working out great, and I've met someone."

"Wow." He was silent for a moment. "I don't think you've ever mentioned your love life to me, ever. I mean, there was that kid you dated in high school, but I can't really call that a love life since we had him scared half to death. He probably didn't even breathe hard on you."

"I always assumed so. Come to find out, he was just gay and didn't know it."

Stan chuckled. "Yes, I got an invitation to a housewarming a few months back."

"Did you go?"

"Yeah, even found a company to do his and his towels."

"How perfectly modern of you."

"I try." He paused. "So about this guy?"

"He's a security consultant. Army and FBI background."

"Nice. Name?"

"Are you going to run him?"

"Of course." Stan snorted. "Name?"

"Mathias Montgomery."

"Whoa. I know that guy."

"No way."

"Yes way."

"How?"

"He was here a couple of years back with an FBI task force. Did antiterrorism training for the whole department. Slick, professional, excellent aim."

Black. I kept waiting for it. I'd never known any of my brothers to speak or behave in a racist way, but I was worried nonetheless that they might be uncomfortable with it.

"Of course, he caught a lot of flack at first. But once people got to know him we mostly forgot he was a Yankee." Stan chuckled. "Tough bastard too. He went three rounds with Wes in the boxing ring down at the gym. Had Wes on his knees gasping for air."

Christ. My new boyfriend had bonded with my brothers before he ever met me. "You took him to your gym?"

"Yep."

I sighed and he laughed. "Great."

"He's a good guy, Jane. Excellent choice."

"We're nothing serious."

"Funny, I never took the man for an idiot and only an idiot wouldn't be serious about my baby sister."

After the phone call ended, I sat in my living room with my gun in my lap. The fact that Mathias had never once mentioned knowing my brothers had me thoroughly confused and, yes, of course, pissed off. It was a lie of a sort and I hate lies.

I dropped a bag of bagels on the table in front of me and looked right at Mathias. "Can I have a moment of your time?"

Mathias glanced around the table at his team and nodded.

"Give us ten, guys." Connor grabbed the bag of bagels and they all left without uttering a word. "What's up? You look serious."

"You know my brothers. You hung out with them in Savannah a few years back."

"Yes." He nodded.

"When were you going to tell me?" I demanded.

"I made the connection a few days after I got here. I'd done a superficial check on you, and Stan called wanting to know why I was investigating his baby sister."

"And you should've told me, first thing." I crossed my arms over my breasts and glared.

"Jane, I shared beer and a few rounds of boxing with those men several years ago." Mathias shrugged. "I've done that with a lot of people, on friendly and unfriendly terms. Your brothers are good guys."

"How often do you and Stan talk?"

"I hadn't spoken with him in over a year until he called me last week. He called me early last year about a case he was working. I did some research for him and forwarded the results." He stood and went to the coffeepot to refill his cup.

"They talked about me?"

"In general terms. They are proud of you and the success you have here. Both of them remember the day you were shot with some level of pain. They never talked about that day with me, or the weeks that followed. I only knew you'd been shot because your brother Stan has your badge on his mantel with a picture of you straight out of the academy in dress blues." He went back to his chair and sat down. "I should've told you, but frankly it just never came up."

"It should've come up," I snapped. It felt like a lie rather than an omission.

"Okay, so at what point? Oh hey, not only do I want to fuck

you but over the years I've trained literally hundreds of cops in antiterrorism and two happen to be your brothers."

"Trained, yeah, but you also socialized with them." I frowned at him. "This is serious."

"Jane, it wasn't something I kept from you on purpose. You were all prickly and standoffish from the very beginning. I honestly didn't think telling you I'd seen you dressed up like a duck when you were six would help my case."

"He still has that damn picture out?"

"Right beside your academy graduation photo." He covered his mouth as if to hide a grin and then cleared his throat. "Getting close to you is no walk in the park, lady."

"I know."

"So forgive me if I haven't made the best choices in all areas."

"You haven't talked to Stan or Wes about us?"

"No, of course not. I've spoken with my brother in general terms but nothing beyond that."

"Okay, well I need to think about that for a while." I sat down at the table with a sigh. "I woke up this morning and Charlie was sitting in a chair across from my bed."

"Excuse me?"

Glancing up, I found his expression a mixture of anger and irritation. It probably matched the one I'd had earlier in the morning as I'd stared at Charlie. "Yeah. He had a set of keys made. I don't remember the keys ever being gone."

"Have you called in a locksmith to change the locks?"

"Yes, of course." I pulled a silver key ring out of my jacket pocket and held it out. "Reason number two that I broke in on your meeting. I'll be busy the rest of the day, so I wanted to make sure you had the new key."

He took the key and then stood from his chair. "You need to file a restraining order against this guy."

"I don't believe he'll be around again."

"Jane." Mathias pulled me gently from the chair with a sigh. "The guy broke into your apartment. How long was he in there before you woke up?"

"I have no clue."

"Why didn't you have your chain in place?"

"I left it off in case you came over." I ran my fingers along his forearm and then met his gaze. "He won't be back."

"If you're sure."

"Fairly. He's a decent guy; he just got bent for a few days. We all have our moments."

"He has a history of this kind of crap."

"What?"

"His last girlfriend filed assault charges against him. They were eventually dismissed because she withdrew her complaint."

"You ran a background check on him?"

"Yes." He met my gaze without flinching and apparently wasn't remotely sorry that he did it.

"He hit her?"

"The details were sketchy. Just keep your guard up." He leaned in and kissed my lips softly. "Now, I'm going to go find the guys and wrangle a bagel free."

"Okay."

"Be careful."

"I will." I curled my fingers into his shirt briefly. "Don't keep secrets from me. I don't like it."

"Okay."

"Is there anything else I need to know?" I raised one eyebrow and looked over his face, carefully searching for a sign that he was hiding anything else.

"I was a sniper in the army."

"Okay." I swallowed hard.

"I worked antiterror in the FBI."

"Okay." Christ, was there anything horrible this man hadn't seen?

"And I stole a piece of candy when I was five."

I stared at him for a moment and started to laugh. "I knew it."

"Several pieces, but my mother made me take them back to the store."

"Good for her." I touched his face, suddenly so pleased with everything about him that I could barely stand it.

"And I expressed a box of pens to my old bank in New York anonymously yesterday because I'm pretty sure I stole at least fifty while I was their patron."

"That could be the single most charming thing I've ever heard." I pulled him down for a kiss and then sighed against his mouth. "I kept two bagels for you in my office. The food was just distraction for the guys."

"It worked." He brushed his lips over mine again, and I moved closer. "You make me want things I've never wanted before."

"I know." I linked my hands around his neck and sighed. "We're probably both in a bit of trouble on that front."

He released me with a sigh. "I need some space or I'm going to start taking off your clothes."

11

"Charlie has a history of violence with women."

Mercy lifted her gaze from the guest list she was reading and frowned. "Really?"

"There was an assault arrest, but the charges were eventually dropped. I can assume he bought her off." I pulled my bagel apart and sighed. "And this morning when I woke up he was sitting in that big blue chair we got at that estate auction last year."

"In your bedroom?"

"Yes."

"Well, that's creepy and stupid." She put the list down and glared at me. "You called the cops."

"No. I let my gun do the talking. I also had the locks replaced first thing this morning. You won't believe how much those jerks charged me for it." I stood. "Would you like some more coffee?"

"No." She shook her head and watched me with dark eyes as I went about refilling my cup. "I don't like this, Jane. Stalking behavior just turns into really horrible things."

"If he comes around again, I'll call the cops."

"And you think he won't?"

"Honestly, I just don't know if he has it in him to keep this game up for very long. If I come to think differently, I'll address it then." I put my cup down on the table. "Now, back to the list."

"If you're sure."

"I am."

I really wasn't all that sure. But I couldn't stand the look on her face. Mercy had survived a heinous act of violence with more grace and good will than I could've ever mustered, but I hated to bring up topics that reminded her of that past violence. The flashes of stark pain in her eyes made me want to go to New York and put a few holes in a man named Jeff King.

"This is good."

Glancing toward her, I found her concentrating on the list. "Casey and I started with a list of two hundred and pruned based on purchases made in the last five years and current net worth." I sat down. "I feel like I'm setting up a backroom poker game."

Mercy laughed. "Well, money does make the world go round."

"Yes." I flipped to the next page in my agenda. "Mathias has the special focus gallery closed for refitting. It won't be available for the high school show. However, Casey suggested we use the Grayson space. It'll give us three days to remove and prepare for her show."

"That works."

"And we are already fielding over two hundred calls a day about the Castlemen special focus show."

"Okay."

"So, I was thinking . . ."

"I love when you do that." She grinned and sat back in her chair to listen.

"I was thinking that we might hold a formal party on the

main gallery floor about a week after the special focus. A much larger invitation list, food to graze on, and private tours that would include the entire collection."

"Go on."

"Well, fifty percent of the money we bring in for the special focus is leaving the foundation for another charity. Holding a formal gala-type event with a much larger invitation list would allow us to market the collection and bring in money for the Holman Foundation that we won't have to share." I tapped my pen on the table. "We could make it an annual event; it'll be the start of the holiday party season anyway, and the only thing rich people like more than spending their money is putting on obscenely expensive clothes so they can attend parties for charity." I put the pen down and watched her as she considered my idea.

"It's good. Draft a proposal and we'll approach James in a few days. It's short notice, but everything apparently is recently. The gallery should already have a formal annual event anyway. As soon as Casey is finished with the special focus list, have her start working on an invitation list for the formal event."

"You know, meetings are more productive now that Milton isn't here to disagree with us."

Mercy laughed and nodded. "Yes, I noticed too." She stood and went to the coffeepot. "You know, a few months back when you told me that you'd been a cop I realized that I hadn't spent as much time on our friendship as I thought I had."

"I don't talk about it much."

She turned and looked at me. "I read the report Mathias submitted and I did some searching last night."

The Internet really sucks. I really didn't know what to say. "Okay."

Mercy walked back to the table and sat down. "You said you couldn't be a cop anymore."

"That's right."

"It wasn't just an emotional thing, was it?"

I picked up my coffee and took a drink before I spoke. "Getting shot was emotionally taxing."

"Jane. I know you. And the woman I know wouldn't let an emotional issue interfere with what she wanted. You're so much stronger than that."

"I have nerve and muscle damage in my right shoulder. It's gotten better over the years, but after the shooting the doctors made it pretty clear that I would never have the range of motion I had before the shooting. I couldn't see riding a desk. To me, the badge came with responsibilities that I could no longer be counted on to uphold. When I finally faced that, I resigned."

"I see." She nodded abruptly. "Did you know sometimes you limp when you're really tired?"

"Yeah, the bullet in my hip did some muscle damage as well. Physical therapy helped me get most of my motion back, but sometimes it's difficult to keep from limping."

"Do you hate that man for ending your career?"

"No." I shook my head. "I hate him for killing my partner and for making me kill in return. Until that day, I'd never even drawn my gun in a real-life situation."

"Talking about this makes you uncomfortable."

"Well, yeah." I looked over her face. "But we've had conversations that were difficult for you. It wasn't a good day for me, and there isn't a day that goes by that I don't think about it."

Assholes go to hell. I'm totally convinced of this fact and often tell people the danger they are putting themselves in just by being who they are. I'd been called to the sales floor exactly twice since I'd become assistant director, but I had a feeling this wasn't going to be just the average disgruntled patron. This person just looked like an asshole.

The woman, who had just recently stopped shouting at the

top of her lungs, was flanked by security guards, and half of the sales staff was huddled in the far corner of the gallery. The other half was lingering in the doorways of the other wings of the first floor, watching.

"Good afternoon."

"I demand to see the owner of this gallery."

"Mr. Brooks is not here. If you'd like I can put you in touch with his personal assistant so you can make an appointment." I paused, watching her face for signs of another outburst. "My name is Jane Tilwell, and I'm the assistant director of the gallery. Is there anything that I can do for you?"

"One of your little sales clerks refused to sell me an item."

"Yes, I was made aware of your demand. The sculpture in question has already been purchased and is on display by courtesy of the owner. As far as I know he is not interested in selling it at this time."

"If it's here, I should be able to buy it."

"I can do nothing about your assumptions." I checked my watch and then glanced around. "Your tirade has disrupted the sales floor long enough. You can leave on your own or I can have you escorted all the way to your car by security."

"Do you know who I am?"

"No, ma'am, I don't, and more importantly I don't care. If you cannot treat the employees of this gallery with the respect they are due, you are not invited to return, ever."

"I'll have you fired."

"You're welcome to try." I motioned toward the guards. "You have your choice, ma'am."

She turned on her heel and stalked out. I stood there for a few seconds and then looked at Connor. "Any idea who she was?"

"She took great pains to explain exactly who she was about a minute before you arrived," he muttered. "Julia Stansworth-Fitzgerald, wife of Derek Fitzgerald and granddaughter of Harvey Stansworth III."

Second tier in the social scheme of things. Lots of money, but it was mostly new. Her husband was a stockbroker and her grandfather an old industry baron who had the name, but the money was long gone. A new-age blend of prestige and wealth that equaled snotty society wife with poor taste and no class.

"Put her on the watch list and let Mr. Wilkes know that she caused a scene."

"Of course."

I watched him walk away and then glanced around the room. I'd yet to spot the new cameras. The placements had been clever, and I appreciated the thoughtfulness Mathias had put into the arrangement. Though, for real, I was pretty sure hiding them was part of some elaborate spy game he was playing with the rest of security team.

"One is on your immediate left above the unfortunate ficus tree, and there are four more near the entrance. In total, there are fifteen cameras in this room."

Turning, I met Mathias's gaze and raised an eyebrow. "Fifteen?"

"Yes."

"And what have you learned so far?"

"The sales staff does an excellent job of guiding those who will buy through the gallery. The browsers, and there are plenty, who come in for peace and quiet are left alone unless they seek out someone with a question."

"But?"

He laughed softly and shrugged. "They dismiss some people too easily. Maybe they know they aren't here to buy, but someone who was casing the place wouldn't be here to buy. Giving everyone equal attention in that respect, at least with a cursory stop, lets everyone who comes into the gallery know that they've been seen."

"How is the testing going?"

"We're almost done. I've asked for a full workup to avoid

mistakes with cold medicine, approved medications, and food. I'll have the results in about a week."

"I see." I glanced around the main floor and then focused on the ficus tree. "What's wrong with my tree?"

"A certain member of staff perpetrates acts of environmental terrorism against it daily. I can't even count on one hand how many cold coffees that tree has absorbed today."

"It's a perfectly lovely tree."

"Apparently she doesn't agree." He laughed softly and walked away.

Disgruntled, I went to the tree and peered down into the pot. It seemed that I was going to have a little investigation of my own. I glanced toward the receptionist desk, and the three women standing there immediately averted their gaze.

"Again."

Tempted to ball up my fist, I forced my body to relax and then swung my leg around and struck his padded arm with as much force as I could.

"Good. Good. Use that hostility." He moved around me and pushed at me with one of the pads. "Again."

"Did I thank you for working out with me?"

Ken Banks laughed softly. "Come on now, again."

I punched at his chest padding solidly and followed it up with a kick that sent him sprawling across the mat. "How was that?"

He sat up and coughed. "Excellent."

I watched him roll to his feet and shake his white blond hair back. He was one of the few men in the apartment building who I trusted enough to work out with. The others left me with the feeling that they would be rougher with me than necessary to prove a point.

"I saw that you have a new man."

"Oh yeah?" I jabbed and bounced on my feet as he took position.

"Yeah, looks like the likable sort. Much better than that stuck-up lawyer you used to hook up with." He motioned me forward. "Come on, you haven't even broken a sweat. You're turning into a real pansy, Janie-girl."

"You really don't have to carry me."

Ken laughed. "It's my fault you hurt yourself."

"I really didn't mean to kick you so hard."

"Well, if you broke your toe you have only yourself to blame."

I glanced down at my sneaker-clad foot and wrinkled my nose. I did not look forward to taking it off. "You shouldn't have called me Janie-girl. You know how I hate that."

"Yeah, but you get this really cute look on your face. It's really much too charming to pass up." He stopped in front of my apartment. I shoved the key into the lock and turned it.

"Do you have ice?"

"Probably."

He shoved open the door and carried me inside like I weighed about ten pounds. It was funny, but when he carried me around I sort of felt like a sack of potatoes. The difference was startling, and it made me realize that I was getting in way too deep with Mathias.

Ken carried me into the living room and came to a dead stop at the sight of Mathias on the couch with remote in hand. "Looks like you got company."

"Hey." I smiled and then frowned when he looked pointedly at Ken. "Mathias Montgomery, this is Ken Banks. Ken is my downstairs neighbor."

Ken set me down carefully on the couch and tucked his

hands behind his back. "She hurt her foot and probably needs some ice."

I glanced between the two of them. Men can be so unbelievably stupid.

"How did she hurt her foot?"

It was like I wasn't even sitting there.

Ken glanced at me and then laughed; I guess my expression said everything he needed to know. "She can explain. See ya later, Janie-girl."

He dodged the pillow I threw at him and left with a little wave. I swung my injured foot up onto my knee and pulled my shoe off gently. Easing off my sock took more willpower than courage, and when I was finished, I sighed with relief. With the pressure removed, the toe didn't hurt nearly as bad.

"Who is he?"

"I told you."

"Yes, Ken Banks."

I looked toward him and raised one eyebrow in question. "So, there, you know who he is."

"Jane."

"He's my neighbor and a kickboxing instructor professionally. I worked out with him in the gym and I kicked him too hard and hurt my foot." Exasperated, I stood from the couch. "Of all the things you could get bent out of shape about, this doesn't even rate in the top twenty."

"Why is that?"

"He's very married for one thing." I hobbled into the kitchen and slapped at his hands when he tried to help. "I don't need any help from you."

"But you let him carry you around like it was no big deal."

"It wasn't a big deal!" I pulled out a clean plastic bag and opened up the freezer for ice. "He's a friend. A married friend, and I shouldn't have to explain myself to you." I shoved ice into the bag and tried vainly to ignore him. "And to be frank, even if he was more than my friend you wouldn't have anything to say about it."

"You think so?"

"I fucking know so!" I jerked my bag up off the counter, slammed the freezer door, and tried to move around him. He cut me off and, despite my efforts to evade him, picked me up and carried me toward the couch. "Put me on the bed, jerk."

"You know something?"

"I happen to know plenty of somethings," I snapped in response.

He dropped me on the bed and then stepped back, mostly because I tried to hit him with the bag of ice. "Are you angry with me because I was jealous or because you like it?"

As if I liked a man being jealous over me! Okay, maybe a little. I put the ice on my foot and reached for the TV remote. "You officially suck."

"Do you need anything besides the ice?"

I turned to look at him. "Why?"

"Because I thought I'd go out and get us dinner."

"Who says I'm going to eat with you?"

He leaned down until we were eye level and spoke softly. "Jane, you are *officially* the biggest pain in the ass ever known to mortal man."

"Fuck you."

"Fuck you back." He kissed my mouth hard and stood. "I'll be back in a few minutes."

I watched him leave the bedroom and scooted down on my pillow. The jerk hadn't even asked me what I wanted to eat. My foot hurt, my lover was a jerk, and I wasn't even going to get the comfort food I wanted. Still, he was certainly a pretty jerk. Even mad he looked good enough to eat.

Jealousy is a petty emotion I'd promised myself a very long

time ago that I wouldn't indulge in. To be honest, there hadn't been a man in my life in recent memory in whom I had been so invested that I had reason to be jealous.

Would I be jealous if I saw Mathias with another woman? Okay, that was irritating to even think about. Yes, I would be jealous. Stark-raving-mad jealous.

Disgusted with myself, I flipped through the channels until I heard the door to my apartment being opened and closed. There was the clang of keys in the lock, and then he came into the bedroom empty handed.

Frowning, I put down the remote. "Food?"

Mathias laughed softly. "I came in here, Your Highness, to ask you if you wanted to eat in here or at the table."

"What did you get?"

"Pizza."

"In here." I crossed my arms over my breasts and glared at him as he pulled off his jacket and tossed it on my blue chair. "I have some bottled water in the frig."

He left the room with a nod and left me there. I wondered what he was thinking about and what I should do about my own feelings. It had been a long time since I'd been emotionally invested in a man. It also rankled a bit that I hadn't meant to get so invested in Mathias. Though I had doubts that I could've planned on meeting a man like him.

His re-entry jerked me free of those thoughts. I watched him arrange the tray and shove off his shoes so that he could join me on the bed.

"I'm sorry that I was irritated over your friend." He glared at me as he said it. "But it would help if your friends could be unattractive trolls."

"You think Ken is hot?" I asked, amused.

"Hell no." He opened up a bottle of water and handed it to me. "But I could understand how some women might find him appealing."

"Uh-huh." I took the bottle and laughed at the outraged expression on his face. "Okay, so maybe he does look like he stepped off the cover of a Viking romance novel. You should see his wife; she could be on the cover with him. All tits, ass, and big pouty lips."

"You think his wife is attractive?"

"Yep, I'd fuck her if I were a man." I snagged a piece of pizza.

He shook his head and laughed softly. "Christ, Jane, I wouldn't trade you for anything."

"That's because I'm awesome."

"Indeed." Mathias plucked his own plate from the tray and rested against the headboard of the bed. "How's your toe?"

"So cold that I don't think I would feel it if someone sawed it off right now." I took a healthy bite of pizza and looked at my foot. "In fact, my whole foot is sort of numb at this point."

"How did you hurt it?"

"The fucker called me Janie-girl. You know I hate that."

"And you overextended, missed the body shield, and actually connected with that big Viking's body."

"What's a body shield?"

"The piece of padding he should've been putting between you and whatever he might value."

"Then, yeah, that's what happened." I took another bite of pizza and chewed slowly.

"So, let's talk about Charles Wallace."

I shook my head and grabbed my water. Tipping it up, I drank deeply and considered how I was going to dissuade him from his current line of conversation. Seriously doubting that I would get far, I cleared my throat and put the bottle down.

"There is nothing to talk about."

"The man entered your home and spent God knows how long watching you sleep. That is seriously depraved behavior, and I don't care what excuse he offered." He grabbed my water bottle when I reached for it. "Jane. I'm serious."

"I honestly don't think he'll be around again."

"Yeah, you say that. What happens when you have to choose between killing him and letting him do what he wants with you? Do you honestly think you're up to pulling the trigger again?"

I closed my eyes and looked away from him. "I don't know."

"I know the damn thing isn't even loaded."

"You shouldn't have messed with it!" I picked the bag up off my foot and started to leave the bed. He grabbed my arm, and I stilled briefly. "Let me go, Mathias." A chill ran down my back as his fingers slid down my arm and away. "I don't even have bullets for it, to be honest."

"It was your off-duty weapon."

"Yes."

"So, it isn't the gun you used . . ." He took a deep breath and sighed. "Jane, baby, I'm only trying to look out for you."

"I'm a grown woman." I stood from the bed and walked to the bathroom despite the fact that the feeling returned to my toe the moment I put weight on it. The stinging pain wasn't nearly distracting enough. "I don't need anyone to look out for me."

"You've proved that."

"What the hell does that mean?" I tossed the bag of ice in the bathroom sink and turned to face him.

He stood from the bed and walked to me. "You moved here, to Boston, to prove to your brothers that you could live on your own. You didn't want them to think you were weak."

"I'm not weak."

"And they know it. They've known it since the day your parents brought you home." He touched my face and shook his head. "Stan called me this afternoon and told me that if I was fucking around with his baby sister he was going to kick my ass."

I laughed and shook my head. "What did you tell him?"

"I told him you were fucking around with me and that I was

in way over my head with you." He touched my face and rubbed his thumb across my lips. "The fact is, Jane, I'm not sure what I'm going to do about you."

"What do you want to do about me?"

"I don't even know." He moved closer and brushed his lips across mine in the softest of kisses and then sighed. "All I do know is that I want you. I want everything you have, and I can't even think about a day when I can't have you."

"Mathias."

"I know." He pulled me close and wrapped his arms around me.

It felt so right and perfect in his arms. The heat of him was soothing and exciting in the same instant. I'd never known the kind of intimacy I had with him, and it had nothing to do with sex.

I sat down on the edge of the bed and used my towel to rub briskly at my hair. Showering with Mathias wasn't exactly efficient, but it was fun. Out of the corner of my eye, I watched him leave the bathroom, a towel wrapped around his waist.

He gathered up the remnants of our dinner and took it into the kitchen. A part of me knew that whatever was happening between us, it was too fast. Suddenly he'd become the most important thing in my life, and I hated the way it made me feel. Desperate. Needy. Love had too many risks attached to it, and I couldn't afford to fall into that trap.

I dropped my towel and laid back on the bed in defeat. Was I falling in love with him? Mathias ran his hands up my legs as he crawled onto the bed and came down on top of me with a rush of heat and gentle hands. I moaned against his mouth and spread my legs wide for his body.

He settled between my legs briefly and then lifted away long enough to get rid of the towel. "Tell me what you want."

Pushing my feet flat against the bed, I thrust upward against him and sighed when he slid his cock against me in return. I rocked against him, my clit suddenly throbbing from the intense stimulation. "Mathias."

"Say it."

I lay beneath him shuddering at the intense pleasure of his body moving against mine. His mouth left mine and then moved downward until he could take one hard nipple into his mouth. I arched against him and clung with all of my strength.

He lifted away and pushed the head of his cock against the entrance of my pussy. I cried out at the contact and lifted my hips in an effort to take him in.

"Say it."

"Fuck." I curled my hands into the blanket beneath me and closed my eyes against the torment of physical and emotional sensations inside me. "Fuck me. Put your cock in me, now."

"Tell me how you want it."

"Deep." I moaned with relief when he slid into me. My body clenched and then gave way to his invasion. "Hard. I need it hard."

He withdrew almost completely and then slid into me hard, then rocked against me. Gasping, I let my legs drop to the bed and used my feet as leverage as he repeatedly withdrew and then hammered into me. It was perfect, he was perfect, and I was a goner.

Our bodies dampened with sweat, and I lost myself in the steady slap of his skin against mine until I came in a rush of emotion and physical relief. I collapsed against the bed and held him tight as he rocked against me and found his own release.

12

"So which one of those witches is poisoning my ficus?"

"The one that wore red today." Mathias ran his hand down my back gently and then back up again. "Cold-looking blond with the fake tits."

"They're fake?"

"Yeah." He laughed softly. "I can't believe you can't tell."

"Normally, I'm very good at judging plastic surgery or real."

"She's fake all over. I think her ass might be fake too."

"No way."

"'Check it out next time you see her."

I lifted my head and met his gaze. "Why are you looking at her ass?"

"Cause I'm a man and that's what we do." He touched my face with gentle fingers and sighed. "I know I'm pushing you, trying to take more than you want to give."

"No." I shook my head as his fingers drifted over my lips to shush me.

"Listen, please. I came into your life without even asking.

We made a deal, which I violated the first chance I got, and I've pushed you at every turn since then. I know I need to back off and give you room, but I'm afraid if I do I'll never get this back." He moved his hand to the back of my head and held me there for a few tense seconds. "On the other side of things, I'm worried that if I don't give you some space you're going to kick me out of your life for good."

I leaned in, kissed his lips, and then lifted my head. "You may be the pushiest man on earth. You're high handed and arrogant, and sometimes I get so frustrated with you that I could take a full-on swing at your head, but if I didn't want you here, you wouldn't be here. Yes, you have forced me to make choices and decisions that I should've made a long time ago. Yes, you've made me rethink the things that I want and the things that I need. But, in all honesty, Mathias, I really dig all those things about you."

"For real?"

"Yeah." I laughed softly, amused at his reaction and at myself for meaning it. "It actually really turns me on when you're arrogant, and having a man like you want me makes me feel like a million dollars."

"A man like me?"

"Strong, intelligent, powerful, and worldly. I've never known anyone like you, and while I thought for a few seconds there that once the novelty of that wore off, I wouldn't want anything more to do with you, I don't think that way anymore. I feel more with you than I have with anyone in a very long time."

"So you aren't going to kick me out of your life?"

"Not at the moment. It's true that I find you a tad overwhelming at times, but I don't think being overwhelmed a bit now and then is a bad thing."

"And the sex is mind blowing."

"Yeah." I nodded. "The sex is, indeed, mind blowing. I think we could medal in the Olympics if fucking were an event." He turned me over abruptly and held me to the bed. "What are you doing?"

"I figure if we're going to compete in a world-class event like the Olympics then we might want to practice. I'd prefer to win the gold."

I laughed as he covered my body with his and slid one thigh between my legs. Parting for him was like breathing. "Yeah, I agree. Gold is the only thing to bring home."

"I'd never live it down with the guys if I took home the bronze."

"I can't have anyone doubting my man." I pulled him down and sighed against his mouth. My man, indeed.

My man was an ass, and as soon as I found him, I was going to fill him in on that bit of news. I shoved open the door to the new security office where he spent most of his time and stared at the faces that turned to look at me. "Where is he?"

"Mr. Montgomery is not in the building, Ms. Tilwell." Connor stood. "Can I help in some way?"

"No, you wouldn't want to play stand-in on this conversation." I pulled the door shut with a satisfying smack and stalked back toward my office.

Casey hopped up from her desk and followed me in. "I'm sure he didn't realize what kind of problem it would cause."

"He's not here." I slouched down in my chair. "He closes off the largest exhibit in the gallery without notice and he knew damn well we were having that snotty ass women's league in here today. It's on the fucking calendar."

Casey pursed her lips and sighed. "Ma'am, your language has deteriorated to that point we discussed once."

"Oh yeah?" I glared at her.

"Yes, and you told me to remind you that a real lady doesn't use the word *fuck* like it's her only adjective."

So I had. Sighing, I glanced toward my computer screen and then back to her. "Okay, fine. So what are we going to do with those witches?"

"I have an idea."

"I'm all ears."

"I figure if we start them in the Montgomery exhibit, either they'll be blown away and not need to see more of the gallery *or* their sensibilities will be so offended they'll leave in a collective snit, never to darken our door again."

I laughed softly and sighed. "Unfortunately, James is very interested in their money for the Holman Foundation. The whole point of today was to pry them loose from their money."

"So how about the high school project?"

Straightening in my chair, I focused on her. "Go on."

"What better way to show them how their money will be spent? If they are true patrons of the cause that's all they'll need. Parting with their money once is okay, but getting them to part with it on an annual basis would be another."

Yes, it would.

"We could give them a tour here, invite them to the special focus event for the kids, and then take them over to the academy for an in-depth look at the creative process. Show them how their money can help the kids in high schools in the area get into the arts academy."

"You could be the smartest person in the building."

Casey laughed softly. "You'd have thought of it if you hadn't gotten your panties all in a twist."

Maybe.

"Go pitch it to Mercy, and if she agrees, get started on the arrangements. You've got about three hours to make it happen."

"Sure thing."

I watched her dart away and then focused once more on my decimated calendar. He'd ruined the planned events for the rest of the week with the closing of the Impressionist exhibit. I had four elementary school tours coming through the gallery on Friday, and now the biggest part of the second floor would be closed off.

Opening up the Holman Gallery for cultural lessons had been Mercy's idea, and the local schools had embraced it immediately. What the hell was I going to do with three hundred elementary school kids for an hour? The hour that had been slotted for a very guided and supervised tour through the Impressionist exhibit. It was the last part of the tour that I had arranged with the teachers over a month ago.

I lowered my head to my desk and tried to think. But, of course, all I really wanted to do was vent on the man responsible. He could have at least asked. The Holman Gallery was more than just a gallery, and since Mercy had become the director, we'd worked hard to make it more. It was a centerpiece for the city, an arts center of a sort, which offered museum-quality exhibits, hands-on exploration for young children, and a wide variety of adult art in the private galleries on the second and third levels.

"Connor told me that you were looking for me."

Lifting my head, I stared at Mathias as he shut the door. "Dude, you've fucked up my whole calendar."

"Yes, I know." He crossed to my desk and put a shopping bag down in front of me. "I figured I'd start with that."

I peeked into the bag and sighed. "You can end with this too." I pulled out the beautiful gold box and ran my fingers along the word *Godiva*. "You could've warned me last night."

"Then we might have argued, and I really prefer sex to arguments."

I opened the box, lifted the paper, and stared at the three rows of bliss in a box. "We could've argued and had angry sex." I glanced up at him briefly and noted the speculation on his face. "Angry sex can be really good."

"Yeah." He sighed as if he was thinking about it. "I bet it would've been awesome."

"You'll just have to find another way to make me mad."

"You aren't still mad?" he asked.

I laughed and shook my head. "No woman can stay mad while she's holding a pound of Godiva chocolate. It would be one of the signs of the apocalypse."

"I am sorry, but I honestly had no choice. The Impressionist exhibit is at risk. The wiring in that wing is a disaster, and half the pressure plates are malfunctioning with the new electronics we've installed. The risk is too great."

"I understand."

Mathias chuckled. "You're just mesmerized by chocolate."

I closed the box carefully and put it down on the desk. "I'd eat a piece but I have strict rules about having orgasms where I work."

"You'd actually have to eat several hundred pounds of chocolate to have an orgasm."

It was an entertaining prospect. I put the box in my briefcase and shut it. "You aren't to tell a single person about it."

"I wouldn't dream of it."

I wasn't sharing it. I probably wasn't even going to share it with him. I'm a total chocolate hog, and I'm not ashamed to admit it.

"I'll just have to think of something to do with all of those kids on Friday."

"Yes, I saw the tours were coming through."

I met his gaze and frowned. "I will not cancel on them. Those kids sent me little thank-you notes on construction paper for being invited."

"That kind of chaotic scene would give someone a lot of room to move around in the gallery."

"You'll just have to make sure that nothing goes wrong." I paused and watched him digest that. "Also, I'd like you to tell all the guards to watch all other visitors in the gallery on that day, especially if they interact with the visiting children. School trips like these attract undesirables."

"Like?"

"Pedophiles for one."

"Christ, that never even crossed my mind." He grimaced. "Yeah, I'll brief the team on it."

"It's a harsh world we live in, and bringing beauty into the lives of these children shouldn't be marred by something so horrible." I stood from my desk and walked to the window. "I'll think of something."

"I know you will."

"It would help if the Impressionist exhibit were ready to re-open by Friday morning."

"It might be, but I can't guarantee anything. It would be best to make plans for something else entirely."

"Okay, fine. You officially suck again."

He laughed. "I'll make it up to you."

"My goodwill isn't always up for sale, you know." I glanced pointedly at my briefcase. "Chocolate only goes so far."

"Sex?"

"Not likely." I glared at him and then sighed. "Get out of my office before I get mad at you again."

He left with a laugh. I sat in my chair, stewing over the fact that I'd stopped really being mad at him the moment I set eyes on him. It did not bode well for future encounters.

"So you didn't even yell at him for ruining your calendar."

I glanced up from my sandwich and sighed. "Mercy, the man is making me just plain stupid."

"I figured as much. Everyone knows better than to mess with your calendar. He decimated it in a matter of minutes, and I haven't even seen a whisper of a conniption come out of your office." She grinned and sat back a little.

"It would be difficult to argue with him considering the worth attached to the on-loan exhibit. Christ, if we even came close to losing a piece of that collection it would be disastrous for the entire foundation, much less the gallery."

"Frankly, as pleased as I am to have it here, I'm really looking forward to seeing it go back to New York." She glanced around her office and then shrugged. "It reminds me too much of . . . everything."

"That collection was an important part of your past, and it was just one of the things that Jeff King effectively took from you."

"Yes." She nodded and then shook her head as if to clear something bad from her thoughts. "After I was raped, I thought my world would end. Hell, I hoped my world would end."

"But it didn't."

"No, and eventually I picked up the pieces of my old life and built a new one here in Boston." She used her fork to stir around her salad and shrugged. "With the trial approaching and Shamus trying so hard to make everything feel normal, I'm left at odds with my feelings."

"How so?"

"Happy and sad in the same rich instant. I've never been in love before, and it's changed how I see the world and also what I want from it."

"Do you resent that?"

She shook her head and then shrugged. "Sharing your life with someone comes with a set of challenges that are hard to anticipate. We don't always agree with what we want in the future, but we do understand that we want that future to be together. And that's the important part."

"Is it?" I picked up my drink and sucked on the straw as I frowned. "I mean, really? You make that choice to be with someone and that's the big step . . . the rest of it can come as it will?"

"Something like that."

"Sounds practically religious." And that made me itch. I'd spent too much time as a child in church listening to the ambitious lead the blind. Maybe it was his job or my mother's departure from family life that turned my father toward religion.

"Something is bothering you."

"Tons of things are bothering me," I responded, and then shrugged. I wrapped up the remains of my lunch and tossed it in a nearby trash can. "How come I didn't know that Charlie was sort of psycho?"

Mercy stared at me for a moment and then kind of laughed. "We all kind of think we should be able to tell, right?"

"Yeah, I mean, he seemed normal enough." So had my father. I cringed at the thought of that day and stood from the table. "I'm going to take a walk."

"Sure. James will be here in about an hour. He wants to talk about the Castlemen show, and then Casey and I will be handling that women's club."

"Okay."

I went to my office and pulled on my jacket. At 32, I had lived enough to understand on a really finite level that life is anything but fair. My mother had bailed on our family when I was ten and our father had bailed four days before my seventeenth birthday. Even now, when I spoke to my mother I could barely stand to think about the time she'd spent in our home. She must've felt so trapped by marriage and children. So trapped and desperate that one night she'd packed her clothes and walked out on all of it.

I shoved my cell phone into my pocket and hurried out of the gallery. Why the hell was I thinking about this? It was a stupid question because the answer was obvious as hell. Mathias was making me want to think about the future.

In the small park across the street from the gallery, I sat down on a bench and pulled out my phone. My brother, Stan, picked up on the first ring.

"Do you remember the day Mom left?"

Stan sighed in my ear. "Yeah."

"Am I like her?" My fingers tightened on the phone as I waited for my brother's response.

"No. You couldn't be less like her. Ever since you were a baby you took life and everything in it so seriously," Stan murmured. "When you were five years old you promised me that you would never lie to me."

"I remember." I smiled and then laughed.

"And as far as I know, you never have. That's the kind of person you are, Jane. You honor your commitments. Keeping your promises and holding true to the things you say are part of you."

"So you think she abandoned us."

"Stella wasn't meant for marriage or children. You and I both know that about her. Wes tries to make excuses for her, but he wasn't there the night she packed up her shit and left."

No. Wes, the second oldest of us, had been away at a friend's house. I could remember how cold it was sitting out on the front porch steps with Stan waiting for him to come home so we could tell him what had happened. We knew that Wes had to know what had happened before he came into the house, because our father was barely hanging on.

He'd yelled and screamed at her the entire time she'd packed. Stella hadn't said a word. She continued to pack and pack until she had every sock, every shirt accounted for. Then, despite his attempts to prevent it, she'd taken her things out to the car and left.

"I kept wondering why she wasn't packing my stuff."

"I know." Stan groaned a little. I knew this was the last conversation that he wanted to be having with me. "Why are you thinking about this stuff?"

"Did Dad kill himself because she left?"

"Jane, rehashing all of this stuff isn't going to change anything."

"Stan."

"Dad killed himself because he hated his life and wanted it to end. Was it because Mom left? God knows. I mean, she'd been gone for years at that point. I know they still saw each other, kept in touch. In some ways it was like their marriage hadn't really ended."

"The day I was shot . . . when I was laying on the road waiting for help to come, I kept telling myself that I couldn't die, that I couldn't die on you."

"And you didn't."

"I didn't." I pressed my lips together and looked around the park before I continued. "Why didn't we know how sick Dad was?"

"Sick?"

"Heartbroken, crazy, depressed . . . whatever he was. Why didn't we know?"

"We hide the parts that hurt the most."

13

"Fuck me runnin' backward." I sucked my finger into my mouth and glared at the pot of boiling spaghetti.

"I wouldn't know how to start, but I would love to try."

I glanced over my shoulder and glared at Mathias. "It was an expression, not a suggestion."

"Too bad." He came fully into the kitchen and slid up behind me.

"I burned my finger." I turned as he pulled me into his arms, and I looked over his face. "You look . . . irritated."

"Yeah." He sighed. "Your *friend* Charlie is sitting across the street in his car."

Oh for the love of all things holy. "You're shittin' me, right?"

Mathias laughed and shook his head. "I wouldn't joke about something like this. Did you know that you drop your *g's* when you're irritated?"

"I'm southern. That's what we do. Are you sure it's him?"

"Yes, quite sure."

"Well, goddamn it! What am I going to do about him?" I left his embrace, growling, and went into the living room. At the window, I had a clear view of the street and of Charlie in his stupid little red sports car. "Okay, he's either waiting for me to come out or working up the nerve to come knock on my door."

Mathias walked to stand beside me and looked down to the street. "He's waiting for you to come out."

"How do you know?"

"He has the car running, for one. I expect if you came out and got in your car he'd follow you." He wrapped one arm around me and pulled me away from the window. "There are a few options. One, I can call over a couple of guys to warn him off. Two, we can call the police and you can report him for harassment. What do you know about the stalking laws in the area?"

"Not much. Never needed them." I crossed my arms over my breasts and went back into the kitchen. "If I call the cops my brothers will find out."

"How?"

"The cops will run my name, and my brother has my records flagged. He called me about the thing out at Lisa's."

"I don't blame them for watching out for you, even in such a limited way."

"Yeah." I lifted the lid on the sauce and stirred it. "Get the strainer out of the cabinet."

"I thought you didn't cook."

I laughed softly. "I don't normally have stuff around to cook. I eat out a lot or have sandwiches. After our mother left us, I did all the cooking at home. Dad and my brothers were all thumbs in the kitchen. When Wes moved out into his own apartment, Stan and I were afraid he'd starve."

"Jane."

"I know." I took the strainer from him and placed it in the sink. "I'm thinkin'."

Charlie Wallace was a pain in the ass. A huge pain in the ass, but he'd already demonstrated to me that he was more. I poured the water off the pasta carefully and then dumped the pasta into the strainer. The activity wasn't proving to be any kind of distraction. I knew enough about this behavior to understand that it really wasn't my fault, but I felt guilty anyway.

Maybe somewhere along the way I'd done something to make him think that there was more between us than there really was, at least on my end of things.

"If I told you I didn't want to see you anymore, what would you do?" I looked toward him and found him frowning. "Hypothetically speaking, of course."

"Of course," he repeated, and sat down at the kitchen table. "I'd go get some beer, go to my brother's place, and spend the remainder of the evening complaining to him about you."

"And tomorrow?"

"I'd be hung over."

"Okay, so on Friday?" I glared at him.

"I'd send you flowers and try to get you to meet me for lunch. Thinking maybe that I could talk you out of it."

"And if I refused?"

"I'd delete your phone number from my cell phone, pick up a fine-ass woman in a bar, and spend the weekend fucking her."

He had reduced me to an entry in his cell phone. "You jerk."

"Hey, you hypothetically dumped me."

"So why isn't Charlie drinking with one of his friends or finding some woman to bone?"

"Because Charles Wallace is the kind of man who doesn't like to be told no. His parents have given him everything he's ever asked for. Women don't normally tell him no, and those who have, in his mind, just don't understand how perfect he is."

"Oh that's crap . . . he wasn't *that* good in bed."

"But he thinks it. Trust me, he thinks it. And he also thinks that you don't know what's good for you."

"Are you trying to make me homicidal?" I dumped the

pasta into a serving bowl and went back to the sauce on the stove.

"No. I'm giving you the information you asked for."

"I've got another alternative." I grabbed the bottle of wine from the counter and offered it to him. "Tomorrow, I'm calling his mother."

He took the bottle and cleared his throat. "Jane, that's just not right. Why don't you just call the police?"

"What? Are you saying his mother is worse than the police?"

"Let me just say this . . . if I ever make you so mad that you want to call someone to come take care of it . . . I prefer the police to my mother."

"So, what's so scary about your mom?"

"Nothing. She's an amazing and beautiful woman." Mathias tossed my bath poofy to me and reached for the soap I was motioning to. "I'd just rather go to jail than have her give me that 'I'm so disappointed in you' look. Most men would."

I took the soap and lounged back in the tub. "I see my mom a couple of times a year. Usually on my birthday or Mother's Day."

"Do you wish you had a better relationship with her?"

I shook my head. "I used to. I mean, there were certainly moments in my life when I desperately wanted her to be there for me and she wasn't. Now I just wish I understood what was so horrible about life with her family that she had to run away from it."

"And if you knew? Would it make her leaving okay?"

"No." I shook my head. "She broke too many promises that night for it to ever be okay."

"Did your dad ever talk about it?"

"No. But her leaving ruined him. She broke his heart and it never mended. It was like an open wound in him every day until the day he ate his own gun." I massaged soap into the poofy and put the soap bottle aside. "I don't really want to talk about this."

"You have the bolt locks on, right?"

"Yeah, why?"

He laughed softly. "I'd rather not have to deal with your psycho ex bareassed."

"I guess we should check to see if he's still out there."

"I'll do it when we're done." He lifted my foot up onto his chest and used his thumbs to rub my instep. "No more looking out windows for you tonight."

"No?"

"No."

"Why is that?"

"Because when we get out of this tub, I plan to lay you out on the bed and make a meal of you. I won't have you being distracted."

I swallowed hard. "Well, I certainly wouldn't want to be distracted."

My bedroom was pitch dark when Mathias came back in. He pulled the towel from his waist and tossed it aside, and I relaxed. Obviously Charlie had given up and gone home. I watched silently as he moved to the end of the bed.

"Lay down and spread your legs."

I did as he instructed, spreading my legs wide and lifting my hands above my head. His hands grasped my ankles, spread my legs farther, and held them there. Cool air drifted over the exposed and heated flesh of my pussy, and I moved against the pleasure of it briefly before I stilled. If he'd wanted my full attention, he certainly had it.

He moved fully onto the bed and knelt between my legs. "There is something so honest and bare about you. I don't know exactly what it is, but I love it."

Mathias released my ankles, and I resisted the urge to move from the position he'd placed me in. His hands ran upward over my legs and then down my thighs. I was soaking wet and he'd barely touched me.

"You don't play games. There is nothing coy about your passion."

My hips jerked upward as he pushed two fingers, with no warning, into me. Gasping at the hot, vivid invasion, I closed my eyes and began to rock against it.

"Yes, just like that. You don't hide your pleasure or deny yourself."

He leaned down then and slipped his tongue between my labia to tease at my clit. I jerked against each flick of his tongue, my hands fisting in the pillow above me on the bed. His fingers pulled free of my clenching entrance and he slid both of his hands under my ass.

I started to move against his mouth, taking the thrusting of his tongue while his name poured from my mouth like a prayer. He lifted his head abruptly, pulled me forward, and buried his cock in me hard.

An orgasm rushed through me, and I came in a blind moment of pleasure and pain that left me breathing raggedly and clutching at his thrusting body. I wrapped my legs around his waist and held on tight.

Mathias slowed his pace and began to stroke into me leisurely, allowing the orgasm that he'd given me to ebb away. I moaned against his mouth and shuddered when he slipped his tongue into my mouth. Tasting myself on his lips and tongue turned me inside out for a few seconds. My eyes watered, and I dug my hands into his back. My fingers slipped on his sweat-dampened flesh as I lifted myself up off the bed to meet the thrust of his body.

He lifted his head and met my gaze. "More?"

"Yes." I nodded and arched under him. "More."

He lifted off of me and pulled his cock free. "Get on your knees."

Doing as he requested, I couldn't help but smile the moment he grasped my hips and urged my thighs farther apart. I moved back against him and laughed when he forced me to remain still. Mathias pushed his cock into me and held me there for a few unbearable seconds.

Then, when I thought I couldn't take any more, he started to move. And God, could he move. Fisting my hands into the blankets, I held on for dear life and took each pounding thrust with pleasure.

"Yes." I arched under his hands and sucked in air as he dug his nails down my oversensitive back.

His hand slid under me, and he pressed two fingers to my throbbing clit. "How's this?"

"Perfect." I lowered my face to the mattress as he began to stroke my clit in unison with the thrust of his cock into me. "Just perfect."

I came in a sweet rush, and if he hadn't wrapped his arm around my waist, I would have fallen. He moaned as my pussy clenched around his invading cock and jerked against me hard as he came.

"Okay, so Mrs. Wallace agreed to meet you for lunch at Lillian's Café at noon. You aren't to be one minute late."

I glanced up from my handheld and looked over at Casey's face. "He's stalking me of all things."

"Oh good lord."

"So I'm going to have a little talk with his mother."

"He's a mama's boy, so it might work." She dropped her gaze to the notebook in her hand. "Lisa Millhouse called and wants to see you and Mercy out at her place at 4:00 this afternoon, if you are available."

"Confirm that with Mercy and tell Lisa yes for my part in it."

She nodded and jotted down a note. "Mr. Montgomery asked me to remind you that you would like to sit in on interviews for permanent security personnel."

"When?"

"He has two this morning starting in twenty minutes and four tomorrow."

"Get the times situated and rearrange my calendar as needed." I swished my chair around, looked at the glass wall briefly, and then refocused on her. "The blinds look good."

She tucked a strand of blond hair behind her ear and cleared her throat. "I'm going to have to take a leave of absence soon."

"Oh yeah?"

"Yeah. I'm going to need intensive counseling to nurse the unrequited interest lurking in my heart."

"Connor is playing hard to get?"

"Connor is playing deaf and mute." She pursed her lips and then sighed. "I dropped half a box of stupid files in front of him yesterday. He helped me pick up the mess and all but patted me on the head. I spent the rest of the freaking afternoon putting all that paperwork to rights for nothing."

"Maybe you should try indifferent and cold?"

"That's my plan for next week."

"Or you could just walk right up to him and tell him you'd like to use him sexually for several hours."

"Several days," she corrected.

"Honesty can't hurt."

"Sure it can. Honesty can hurt a *lot*." She frowned as she said it and then nodded as if she was agreeing with herself.

"But how much anticipation can you take before it's more frustrating than fun?"

"Good thought." She stood and clicked her pen. "I'll work

on this and remind you before your lunch. I did some of your e-mail this morning, but then it got a little crazy so I didn't get to much of it. I've marked all the items that require a personal response from you."

"Thanks."

"That's why I get paid the big bucks." She offered me a little salute and closed the door behind her.

Could honesty hurt? Yes, maybe it could. There was a very selfish part of me that wished my mother had continued to live the life she had with our family rather than walking out and leaving us all. She wasn't happy in the home she'd made for my family. Maybe she never was. In today's age, she never would've gotten married at all.

It's amazing how a few decades could change the way people view the world and their place in it. There were women all around me who would never marry, never have children, and not live to regret it at all, but I knew I wasn't among them. My biological clock wasn't hammering on me, but there were times when I could feel it start to tick a little faster.

I had a great life already. Even if I counted my pansy, mama's boy stalker, things weren't all that bad. I had a great apartment, an excellent job that I loved, and a man who thoroughly filled my every need. Never before had I allowed myself to fall so deeply and so fast into a relationship. Sex was great, and I've certainly never denied myself in that arena, but maybe that was mostly because I got something of a late start.

Shaking myself loose from those thoughts, I stood and went to join Mathias in the large conference room. He was there, staring intently at his laptop when I entered. I poured myself some coffee, topped his off, and then took a place across the table from him.

"So you've already vetted these guys?"

"Yes." He slid two files across the table. "They all have military or law enforcement backgrounds and no criminal records. Financials, personal life, and the like check out."

"Okay."

I opened up the first file and checked out the photo paper clipped to the inside. "He's pretty."

Mathias snorted. "If you are going to base your recommendations on their appearance you can just go back to your office."

Laughing, I flipped past the cover letter and looked over the resume. "His computer skills are good; the BA in communications is a plus." I cleared my throat and lifted my gaze. "But he's spent nearly ten years in the marines."

"And?"

"The last ten years haven't been the best on a military level. How much combat do you suppose he's seen?"

"The marines do see a lot of combat. I fail to see how that has any bearing on the man's ability to perform security tasks in the building."

"Combat makes men rough, even hard."

"I was in Afghanistan for two years before I joined the FBI. Then I was 'borrowed' by another government agency. During that time I was sent places that I cannot discuss and I did things I can't even let myself think about. Do you think I'm rough and hard?"

"No." I wet my lips. "I'm just concerned."

"And I understand your concern. Remember, I promised you no blunt force on the team. I didn't promise to hire a bunch of pansies who can't even pick up a weapon."

"Understood." I sat back from the table as I picked up the other file. "A woman."

"Yeah, she's had several years of experience in the private sector as a bodyguard but is looking for something a little different."

"It irks you that I wanted to sit in on these interviews." I tilted my head slightly as I looked over his face. "Doesn't it?"

"There is an implication there that you don't trust me to do my job."

It had nothing to do with that. I frowned and considered my response. The fact was that it was my job to hire and fire in the building. It was the one duty that Mercy had placed in my lap the day she'd moved into the director's office.

"I have a job to do at Holman that goes far beyond the security personnel."

"True."

"I'm also ultimately responsible for the people that work in this building. While they may answer directly to the head of security in this building, and in turn your company, they are required to follow my direction, and I want that to be clear from the very beginning. This has nothing to do with you and everything to do with me."

"So you're here to establish the pecking order." He summed up, amused.

"Something like that."

If only I could establish a pecking order with Charlie and his mother. She was fairly easy to spot, since the current bane of my existence was sitting right beside her. Obviously Casey had not made it clear that I had asked for a lunch to explain the problems I was having with her son.

I stopped just short of the third and only empty chair at the table and glared briefly at Charlie before focusing on his mother. "I asked to meet with you, Mrs. Wallace. I should've made it clear that I wanted to meet you alone."

"Anything you have to say to me, young lady, you can say in front of my son." She glared at me pointedly. "Take a seat."

I sat down, which pissed me off. "Fine. If that's the way you want to play it."

"So give me three good reasons why I should allow your relationship with my son to continue."

Wow, maybe the whole family is crazy.

I picked up a water glass near my place setting and drank from it as I considered how I should phrase the unpleasant thoughts running through my head. "I dumped your son, Mrs. Wallace. I'm done with him and have no interest whatsoever in getting in your good graces. I asked you here to discuss the fact that your son has stolen a key to my apartment, which he used to enter my residence uninvited so that he could sit in a chair and watch me sleep. As if that was not enough, last night he parked himself outside my apartment building for several hours, to what end I'm not sure. Since your family is well respected in Boston, I'm doing you this favor."

"Charles?" She turned and glared at him. "Is this true?"

"Mother, I'm in love with this woman. I want to spend the rest of my life with her."

Oh for the love of everything on Earth. "The next time he shows up at my door or approaches me, Mrs. Wallace, I will be calling the police."

"Janie, you don't mean it." He reached out and grabbed my hand.

I shook my head and pulled my hand free. "I never made you any promises, Charlie. Whatever fictional relationship you've created between us is not my problem."

"You love me."

"No, I don't. I don't even like you right now." Standing from the table, I looked around the crowded café and then settled my gaze on his mother. "I find this whole thing distasteful and uncomfortable, a feeling I'm sure you share. It's in the best interest of your family's reputation that this situation vanish. I'm not sure if he's stupid or insane, but I expect you to resolve this matter for me. You won't like it if I have to."

Shaking loose the guilt that I felt for hurting Charlie, I

walked away from the table and out of the building. I didn't realize he'd followed me until I was opening my car door. He shoved it shut and whipped me around.

"We aren't done until I say we are."

"The night you were in my apartment . . . what did you really come there to do?" I pulled free of his hands. "Did you come there to hurt me?"

"Of course not."

"I don't believe you."

"Jane. You're very important to me."

"I told you that there is nothing more between us. If you don't leave me alone, Charlie, I'm going to be forced to do something neither one of us will like. We had a good time, but that is all it was and now it's over."

"I deserve better than this from you." His eyes darkened and his hands tightened into fists. For just a few seconds, I thought he might hit me, and then he took a few steps back. "This isn't over, Jane."

"It's over, or I will report you to the police for stalking. How would all those people at your job feel when they find out you've been charged with a crime? Is that included in your five-year plan to make partner?"

"You owe me."

I frowned and glared at him. "Owe you for what?"

"Do you think you would have landed that job at Holman's without me? I called James Brooks personally and asked him to give you the assistant director job. Just like I called when you wanted to leave the sales staff and go to the administration level. So you owe me." He moved toward me but paused when I backed up and hit my car. "I've done all I can to remake you into a woman my mother would approve of, and you come here and tell her this bullshit?"

"My life is my own, and I don't owe you a damn thing." I pulled open the car door, never letting my gaze leave him, and tossed my purse in. "Don't make this situation worse, Charlie. I've killed one man, and I know I could do it again if I was placed in the situation of defending myself."

He paled a little and stepped back.

I slid into the car, locked the doors, and dug through my purse for my keys with shaking hands. His words were whipping around in my head. It couldn't be true. Mercy had told me that was her decision. She'd wanted me in the assistant director position. I could still remember how she'd smiled and waved the salary offer package she'd prepared and motioned me into her office. I considered it one of the best days of my life, and Charlie had tainted it.

I engaged the engine and shot into traffic without looking back. Picking up my cell phone, I called Casey and told her to cancel my appointments for the rest of the day. I needed time to collect myself before I returned to the gallery. It couldn't be true, but if I asked her and there was even a hint that it might be true, I'd probably cry like a baby.

At home, I shrugged off my work clothes, wrapped myself up in my favorite flannel granny nightgown, and turned on the television. It rankled that he'd upset me with his absurd declaration. But his family did have a lot of connections, and James Brooks socialized in those same circles.

The former director, Milton Storey, had never liked me, so I'd been surprised when he'd offered me a job in the admin area. I went from the lead on the sales team to the senior buyer, over the heads of several people that had been there longer.

Would Mercy tell me if James had pressured her into making me assistant director? If Charlie had influenced that, I would never feel right about the gallery again.

14

I raised my head from the pillow on the couch and watched Mathias come in. He pulled off his jacket and walked to the couch.

"Hey."

"Hey yourself." He squatted down in front of me and touched my cheek. "What's up with you?"

"Just had a headache after lunch."

"I know you spent your lunchtime with Charlie's mother. Did she upset you?"

"I ought to fire that girl." I punched my pillow and pulled my blanket up to my shoulder. "She's lucky I couldn't live without her."

"She confessed the truth under duress. Mercy can be intimidating when she wants to be."

"It isn't a big deal; I can take the afternoon off if I want to."

"Sure you can, it's just that you never have. Not once. No sick days, no half days, and as few vacation days as you can get by with. I've been through your personnel records, you know."

"Yeah, I know." I closed my eyes briefly and then sat up. "Charlie was at the lunch with his mother."

"Did he get rough with you?"

"Since you didn't get a call from me asking you to post bail, the answer to that would be no."

He sat down on the couch and pulled me up into his lap. "Then tell me what's wrong."

"No."

"Why not?"

"Because men suck at this stuff. I'll tell you and then you'll want to fix it. All I really want is someone to bitch with and for him to agree with me. But you can't do that because men are 'fixers.'" I leaned against him. "I'm just a little upset."

"You're a lot upset. I've seen you a little upset, and this is not it." He hugged me tight and sighed. "And yes, I want to fix this. If need be I can go find him and kick his ass."

"He didn't hurt me." My fingers curled into his shirt and fisted briefly before I could help it. I released the cloth quickly and tucked my face into the side of his neck. "He just told me something that he did. I don't know if I believe him or not, but it bothers me."

"What was it?"

I frowned. Suddenly it was entirely too horrible to repeat. "It's about the gallery."

"He has no power in the gallery. How could he do anything to affect your job?"

"Well, his family gives generously to the Holman Foundation every year. But he wasn't threatening me. Charlie told me that he asked James Brooks to give me the job I have now, that I would still be a commissioned sales clerk otherwise."

"And how did that make you feel?"

"Like all the work I'd done had been for nothing. It made everything I've done at Holman feel empty and stupid."

"Jane, I don't believe Mercy would have you be the assistant director of the gallery if she didn't believe you could do it."

"And if you found out that Shamus had influenced James's decision about hiring you?"

He stiffened briefly and then relaxed. "Okay, that would be unsettling and I would be angry. But I also wouldn't just blindly believe it. I'd go to Shamus and ask him."

"So I should ask James Brooks if he allowed a social acquaintance to sway his judgment in the placement of administrative staff in the crown jewel of the Holman Foundation's holdings?"

"Put that way, it seems ridiculous that Brooks would do something like that."

"Smart-ass." I slid off his lap and stood. "I need some food."

"So what happened at the lunch meeting with his mother?"

"Well I got there and found that Charlie accompanied her." I glanced over my shoulder as I opened the refrigerator to look at him. He looked ready to pounce on someone and kick the shit out of him. "And he'd told her that I'd arranged the meeting with her to convince her that I was worthy of being romantically involved with her son."

"Great." He laughed, pulled out a kitchen chair, and sat.

"I corrected his and her assumption, made it clear that I would involve the police if he didn't leave me alone, and left. He followed me out to my car and told me he'd influenced both of my last promotions at the gallery." I pulled out some deli meat and cheese. "I left and came home."

"And he hasn't shown up here?"

"Not yet." I shut the frig with my hip and shrugged. "But that could be because I threatened to kill him."

"Good."

"Not good. I shouldn't do that to people. I did it to that scumbag ex-husband of Lisa's too. People are going to start reporting me to the police for menacing." I snagged the loaf of bread from the counter and went to the table. "You didn't want to eat out, did you?"

"I grabbed a pizza with the guys after the last interview. I would've been here sooner, but I haven't spent a lot of time with the team lately."

"How did the interviews go?"

"The woman is a yes, the rest are a no."

That was a relief; I hadn't been pleased with the candidates I'd met. "When is the next round?"

"Next week. I have a few guys coming in from New York and Atlanta to interview. I knew a few of them when I was with the Bureau. I have five positions left to fill."

"Is the face guy here yet?"

"Actually, he arrives tomorrow. He's promised to bring all of his new little toys for us to play with. We should have that system up and running well before the Castlemen show. I want a few days to test it. I've contacted Interpol, and they'll be sending me files on the people they are watching. The high-dollar thieves from the Bureau list are mostly involved with the fencing of jewelry."

"Do you honestly think that someone would break into the gallery?"

"Yes. Castlemen's collection rarely travels and is practically priceless; the black market would soak it up like a fine wine. The pieces wouldn't surface for years."

"So, this face guy? He just travels around the world setting up face-recognition software?"

"Casinos were his main line of business until 9/11. Since then he's done a great deal of government work on and off the radar. I was lucky to catch him at a point where he's not working for them."

"And how does it work?"

"You'll have to ask him the specifics, but the software is designed to take apart each face it scans and categorize it into sections. Some sections of the face are very difficult to alter without major reconstruction."

"Okay. So what happens if we spot someone in the gallery who is suspect?"

"We put a name to his face. Security will monitor his or her movements around the gallery. Depending on the person's background and if there are outstanding arrest warrants, they will be authorized to notify the authorities of the person's presence in the gallery. If instructed by law enforcement to hold the person, they will make every effort to secure him without causing a scene in the gallery."

"That's reasonable." I picked up my sandwich with both hands and eyed it with some satisfaction. Not eating lunch and sleeping through dinner had me starving.

I took a big bite and the doorbell rang. I glared in the direction of the door and nodded when Mathias rose to answer it. After wiping my mouth, I barely had time to stand as Mercy came into the kitchen and looked at me, hard.

"Hey, what's up?" I asked softly.

"What's up with you?" She glanced back over her shoulder as Mathias came to the kitchen doorway pulling on his jacket. "I didn't mean to run you off."

"I'll be back." He came around her and kissed me right on the lips and left.

I stared after him, dumbfounded and slightly amused. He'd been so careful before about not even touching me in front of Mercy.

"And here I thought the two of you were just getting it on." She shrugged off her coat, went to the door, flipped the bolt lock, and came back into the kitchen. "Now, what's wrong?"

"Nothing is wrong."

"You called in sick. I don't remember you ever calling in sick, not ever. Something happened with that asshole's mother, and I want to know what it is." She sat down and crossed her arms over her breasts. "Come on, fess up."

"Mercy." I looked down at my sandwich mournfully. I was really hungry. I picked it up and took another bite. She would just have to wait.

"You'd best eat that sandwich fast."

I grinned and swallowed. "Are you here as my boss or friend?"

"Friend."

"Okay." I put down the sandwich and got up. I pulled a beer out of the frig and popped the cap on it. "Want one?"

"No. I'm driving."

"Okay." I sat back down and snagged the bag of chips on the table. "Charlie was there with his mother when I arrived. He'd convinced her that I'd asked to meet with her in order to gain her goodwill so that I could continue to date him."

"I hope you informed her otherwise." Mercy wrinkled her nose in distaste. "He's a total troll."

"And growing more so by the minute." I dumped some chips on the napkin next to my sandwich and set the bag aside. "I explained my purpose for the meeting, informed her that if Charlie's stalking behavior didn't end immediately I would call the cops and file charges, and then I left."

"There's more."

I nodded. There is no way to measure how much I did not want to tell her the rest. Or maybe I just feared Charlie hadn't been lying about it.

"He followed me out to my car, angry. After a few veiled threats on my part and whining on his, he said that I owed him because he'd helped me get the promotions at Holman. First from the sales floor and then into the assistant director position. He told me he'd called James Brooks personally and asked for the favor."

Mercy reached out, grabbed my beer, and took a big healthy swig. She set it down carefully and cleared her throat. "Now, give me a second to calm down."

"Okay."

She took a few breaths. "I can't believe you bought that bullshit!"

I jumped a little and then shook my head. "Milton Storey hated me, Mercy. He was never satisfied with my sales record despite the fact I outsold everyone else. I didn't ask for the senior buyer position because I figured he wouldn't even let me interview for it. He also found me stuck up and insufferable because I refused to date his troglodyte son. So, yes, I do believe that Milton might have been influenced by James to elevate my position in the gallery."

"And me?" she asked pointedly.

"The first day you walked into the gallery, you came into the administrative wing like a raptor looking for prey. You cut a path a mile wide through most of the support personnel in a matter of weeks. Yes, I did worry that my education or my work wouldn't meet your standards."

"Did you just call me a bird?"

"I was thinking more along the lines of that little dinosaur in that movie that ran around killing everyone."

"You suck." She sighed. "And you haven't answered the question."

"No. You told me that you chose me, and I believe you." I sighed. "But it doesn't change the fact that Charlie very likely influenced the course of my career."

"That's crap. He might have sped it up a little, but he didn't do anything significant." Mercy waved her hand when I started to protest. "You impressed me before I met you, Jane. I received detailed reports on every person in the gallery. If you hadn't already been the senior buyer, you would've been within six months of my arrival."

"You mean that?"

"I wouldn't say it if I didn't. Now, let's also remember this. James Brooks doesn't do a damn thing unless he wants to, and I doubt seriously he paid one bit of attention to Charlie. For all we know, Milton moved you up to administrative staff so he could look at you all day."

"Gross." I took my beer back and finished it off. "You'd better not have any cooties."

"None that I'm aware of," she said, amused. "And don't let him drag you down over this. You've worked very hard to get where you are."

"Yes." I nodded and then shook my head. "What if someone came along and took all the credit for your success and you couldn't prove him wrong? How much would your place in the world mean to you after that?"

She paused and seemed to consider my question. "Okay, maybe for a few minutes I would be pissed and self-righteous about it. I admit to being pretty angry when Jeff King insinuated that I slept my way into every decent job I've ever had."

"Was that when you beat him up?"

"Yeah." She smiled pleasantly. "It was."

"And now?"

"I know the truth. I know I did the work, made the effort, and received what I deserved. I'm the director of one of the best galleries in Boston because I worked damn hard to make it so."

"So I should forget about Milton?"

"I hope one day we can all forget about Milton."

"James never mentioned me to you in reference to the assistant director job?"

"Not until the day my recommendation hit his desk. He nodded, said 'good,' and signed the paperwork on the job offer. That was it, Jane. I promise."

Relieved that she'd said it and more relieved that I believed it, I stood up and went for another beer. "Charlie sucks a lot."

"Do you think he'll make a pest of himself after today?"

"No, he wouldn't dare risk embarrassing his mother, and now that she knows about it . . . she'll hammer home the fragile condition of their family tree, his place on the inheritance scale, and of course the state of his trust fund, which she still administers."

"And if he does?"

"I'll follow through and file charges."

"Good." She eyed my beer as she spoke.

I snatched my fresh beer up off the table and glared at her. "Get your own."

Laughing, she stood. "No, I'm driving. One sip is more than enough at this point."

"Thanks for coming over."

"You should have come back to the gallery and asked me. Then you wouldn't have spent all of this time in your granny nightgown." She glanced me over. "I'm sure Mathias was just overcome with lust at the sight of you in it."

"Some friend you are."

"Hey, a friend tells a friend when she is dressed poorly. Put on a decent nightie before he comes back."

"He prefers me naked."

"Then get naked; anything would be an improvement."

I followed her to the door and watched her pull her coat on. "I'm probably in over my head with him."

"Yeah, that's the fun part."

I was sitting on the bed toweling my hair dry when Mathias returned. "Hey."

"Did you guys get all the girl stuff out of the way?"

I laughed. "Something like that. You were right, of course; she wasn't influenced into giving me that promotion."

"And if she had been?"

"I don't think I could have stayed there." Even saying that

hurt a little more than I thought it would. "It's important that I make it on my own."

"What about Milton Storey?"

"I've decided he doesn't exist in Jane-land."

Laughing softly, he walked over to me, leaned down, and kissed me. I sighed when he lifted his head.

"I need you to promise me something."

"Okay." I raised one eyebrow.

"That I will always exist in Jane-land."

"Yeah," I whispered against his mouth as he kissed me again. "You might even achieve landmark status."

"Is there an application to fill out?"

"No, but there is a field test." I curled my hand into the front of his jeans and pulled him closer. "Take off your clothes and hold on tight. Things could get a little rough."

"I'm loving this already."

And I was very close to loving him. Had I really only known him a handful of days? The short amount of time really didn't matter. I think the first time I lay naked with him on my bed, I knew that he was the one for me. His honesty, thoughtfulness, and effortless ability to be so intimate with me had stripped me bare, and I reveled in it.

I always will.

Turn the page for a sneak peek at
SEXUALLY SATISFIED.
On sale from Aphrodisia!

"Thank you all for coming," said the casting director, clutching his binder to his chest. "You were all terrific, and we'll be in touch soon." He gave the six-foot blonde with the huge fake boobs a wide grin, which she returned with a flick of her long bleached hair. *If this bimbo can convince the balding old fart that she finds him absolutely devastating, then she's an Oscar-caliber actress who deserves the job,* I thought caustically.

I sighed, picked up my tote bag and trudged to the door with the other rejects. Another bomb of an audition. I couldn't even get hired for a tampon commercial. It had been two . . . no, three months since my last job. If I didn't land a role soon, I'd have to go back to the grind of office temping.

As soon as I opened the door and stepped outside, the heat hit me like a blast furnace. I immediately felt sweat beading on my upper lip and trickling between my breasts. Oh, the joy of New York City in August. And now I had to take the subway, the stickiest, stinkiest sauna in the world.

I staggered up to my third-floor apartment, pushed my way in and kicked off my shoes. "Apartment" was a bit of an exaggeration. The ad had described it as a "charming, cozy studio" but "tiny rat hole" was really more accurate. I turned the ancient air conditioner to high; it immediately coughed, sputtered and died. "Goddamnit!" I shouted. I hauled out the floor fan, feeling tears of frustration pricking at my eyes.

Five minutes later I was sitting half naked in front of the fan, sipping iced tea. I tried to remind myself of all the good things in my life. My boyfriend of three months, Steve, was the sweetest guy I'd ever met—and extremely cute in the bargain. I was beginning to wonder if he was The One. Anita, my best friend since sixth grade, was supportive and fun and loyal. Even on a sweltering summer day, New York was infinitely preferable to boring Hanover, New Hampshire. And I'd had some success with my acting career; if I could just hold on until the big break came . . .

My cell phone rang, and before I even flipped it open, my telephonic telepathy set in. I just knew it was Steve. We'd talked about getting together tonight, and now I really needed his company.

"Hey, Gillian," he said. "Have you melted yet in this heat?"

"No, but I wish I could. I had a thoroughly shitty day." I proceeded to moan and groan and complain, knowing Steve would be sympathetic. He'd been through enough lousy auditions before landing the plum role of Winston on the long-running soap *Nights of Passion*.

I finally ran out of complaints. "So, what would you like to do tonight?"

Steve was strangely silent. Usually he was an expert at pulling me out of a bad mood.

"Is something wrong, Steve?"

He hesitated. "No. . . . Well, yes. I don't know how to say this, Gillian. . . . I planned to get together with you tonight to discuss it. But I think it's better to do it over the phone."

I never understood the phrase "my heart sank" until that moment. "You want to break up with me," I said woodenly.

He heaved a long sigh. "I'm sorry, really I am. I like you so much, Gillian, and we had some great times together. But I don't think we're compatible."

My throat tightened. "I don't understand. We're interested in the same things, we're in the same business, we enjoy doing the same things—"

"It's not that. I just think we're not compatible . . . sexually. In bed. It's never been very good for either of us."

I was stunned. True, Steve and I didn't have the best sex life, but, god, I had tried to spice things up. He had never seemed interested in trying anything new. It was the same routine every time.

"Look, Steve, I understand what you're saying, but we could work on it—"

"No . . . Gillian, I'm really sorry. The truth is that I've met someone else."

My shock deepened. I couldn't speak. I just sat there as Steve rambled on, apologizing, swearing it wasn't my fault. . . .

I finally interrupted him. "Okay, Steve, good luck." I hung up abruptly and burst into tears.

Once the worst had subsided, I called Anita's cell. Voice mail, damnit. "Hi, Anita, please call me back as soon as you can. . . . Steve just broke up with me." I hiccupped. "It came out of the blue. I'm feeling lousy right now. . . . Thanks."

I washed my face with cold water, praying Anita would call back soon. *I hope she's not having one of her party-hearty club nights*, I thought. When Anita was in that mood, she made Samantha from *Sex and the City* look like a shrinking violet. But Anita was so honest and grounded, the only person I could really talk to about deep emotional stuff. We'd met when we were both twelve and dreaming of fame and fortune in New

York. A few months after high school graduation, we moved together to the city. My success had been modest, but Anita's modeling career had taken off. She hadn't reached single-moniker supermodel status, but she was well on her way.

My cell rang, and I snatched it up. "Anita?"

"Gillian, are you okay? I got your message. . . . God, I'm so sorry. What happened?"

"I don't know. He just said we weren't compatible in bed. Then he said he'd met 'someone else.' That was it. The end."

"Well, it's his loss." Anita was indignant. "I'll bet this 'someone else' won't last more than a few weeks."

"Doesn't matter." I sighed. "It's true that our sex life was pretty mediocre. Not horrible, just not all that good. I had to fake it several times."

"Girl, you should never have to fake it! Find some guy who knows what the hell he's doing. Why don't we hit some clubs this weekend?"

"Sorry, I can't. I'm spending this weekend in Easthampton with Aunt Mary. Steve was supposed to come, too. I guess that's why he broke up with me tonight—he couldn't bear the thought of an entire weekend with me."

She snorted. "Screw Steve. There are some great clubs out in the Hamptons. . . ."

"Oh, Anita, I'm not up for that yet. I'll just spend a quiet weekend with Aunt Mary. I need to get out of this inferno of a city for a few days and relax."

"Okay, but call me anytime if you want to talk."

"Thanks, Anita, you really are the best. I feel a little better already. Let's get together for coffee on Monday."

The train ride to Easthampton seemed endless. I sniveled most of the way. I felt like the world's ultimate loser—I'd win a reality show based on that concept with no effort at all. I was a mediocre actress who could barely make a living in TV commercials. And apparently I was lousy in bed—couldn't even keep Steve's interest for more than three months.

Aunt Mary met me at the station, and just the sight of her silver hair, bright blue eyes and broad smile was enough to cheer me up. I had told her on the phone that Steve and I had broken up; she was tactful enough not to press for details. Aunt Mary and I had always enjoyed a close relationship; she was more like a much older sister than an aunt. She had retired from acting a few years earlier and had always been my mentor and most enthusiastic cheerleader. Mary had never been a hugely successful actress, but she had been well known in New York as a talented and hard-working professional.

I was sprawled on a chaise longue with her cat, Jasmine, purring on my lap when she came out to the patio with two glasses of iced tea. "Gillian, Jackie and Ken Williams are coming over for cocktails. Ken is bringing his golf partner, some guy named David. Sorry . . . I know you're not in a sociable mood."

Damn! Jackie and Ken Williams were the most boring people on the planet. But they had always been good neighbors to Mary, and she was careful to keep their relationship cordial.

I smiled briefly at Mary. "No problem. Company might be a good distraction for me. I feel pretty skanky; I think I'll have a shower and change." I dumped Jasmine to the ground, ignoring her yowl of annoyance.

I felt almost human again after taking a long, hot shower and changing into a pale blue sundress. I looked at myself critically in a full-length mirror. God, I really had to drop ten pounds . . . maybe fifteen. But my skin looked good, tanned to a honey shade, and the strong sun had brought out golden highlights in my wavy brown hair. Perhaps one day, after I got over the humiliation of Steve dumping me, another man might find me attractive and even enjoy me in bed.

The guests had arrived by the time I stepped out to the patio. Mary made the introductions. "Gillian, you remember Jackie and Ken . . . and this is their friend David Wentworth."

"Hi, Gillian." He smiled and reached out a hand. I gave it a limp shake, trying hard not to gawk. He wasn't conventionally handsome, but he was striking. Somewhere in his early forties. About six feet tall, with the lean, hard physique of a marine, this man clearly had discipline. Light brown hair just starting to go gray. Full lips, ordinary nose. His eyes were his most stunning feature—glacial blue and penetrating. I felt mesmerized. *Powerful* was the word he brought to mind.

I had a sudden attack of shyness. I dropped my eyes from his face and found myself staring at his crotch. I burned with my easily aroused blush as I looked away, praying he hadn't noticed.

The four of us exchanged the usual pleasantries. I sat on the wicker sofa to alleviate the weak feeling in my knees. David handed me a glass of white wine and sat next to me. Mary, Jackie and Ken huddled on the other side of the patio, complaining about the hideous new McMansion under construction down the street.

"I understand you're an actress, Gillian." David's voice made me think of brandy—smooth and mellow but potent.

"Yes." Why did my voice sound so squeaky? I cleared my throat. "Although, struggling actress is more accurate. I've performed in a few off–Broadway plays, starred in a couple of commercials . . . nothing really major. And nothing at all recently."

"It's a very tough and frustrating business. But I'm sure you'll make it. You're very pretty and obviously very bright."

It was a superficial and conventional compliment, but it seemed authentic to me when he unleashed his brilliant smile. Perfect teeth, of course.

"Thanks." My voice had spiraled into Minnie Mouse range

again. His thigh seemed much too close to mine; I was sure I could feel his body heat through the thin cotton of my dress. "So what do you do?"

"Real estate. My parents owned a firm in Denver, so I grew up in the business. I came to New York for college, decided to stay after graduation and work in the industry here. It took a while, but eventually I started my own company."

"Impressive."

"Well, it took a lot of work. I have to admit I'm a bit of a workaholic . . . but I also take playtime very seriously." His eyes locked onto mine, and my mouth went dry.

At that point Mary, Jackie and Ken joined the conversation, which promptly turned dull—the weather, golf, politics . . . It was hard not to squirm like a fidgety five-year-old. I was still hugely aware of David sitting so close to me, frequently catching my eyes with his and sending me small, secret smiles. The pheromones were flying.

Finally Jackie and Ken rose to say their good-byes; David stood as well. I felt a wave of disappointment. How could this devastating man disappear from my life so quickly?

David saved the day. "I'm driving back to New York tonight. I'm parked at the end of Jackie and Ken's driveway." He turned his intense gaze on me. "Gillian, would you walk me to my car?"

"Sure, I'd love to." Damnit—squeaky voice again, plus I sounded way too eager. "I'll be back in a little while, Mary."

Mary raised one eyebrow and gave us a brief, enigmatic smile. "Sure, that's fine. Dinner can wait a little bit longer."

Jackie and Ken decided to walk the beach back to their house, thank God. I couldn't have endured their incessant chatter bursting the bubble of attraction that surrounded me and David. We walked slowly down Mary's driveway and even more slowly down the road to Jackie and Ken's driveway and his car. A midnight-blue BMW convertible.

"Nice car." *Great, I sound as inane as Jackie and Ken.*

"Glad you like it. We should go for a drive sometime."

"I'd love to." My confidence was rising; this amazing guy really seemed to like me.

"I enjoyed meeting you, Gillian. I'm just sorry I have to leave so soon."

"Business in the city?"

"Yeah, I have to prepare for an early breakfast meeting on Monday. But I'd love to take you out for dinner sometime. Could I have your number?"

I rattled it off as he wrote it down—with a gold pen on a leather-covered notebook. Apparently his real-estate business was doing pretty well.

"Great, I'll call you soon." He tucked the pen and notebook into his jacket pocket. Then he reached out and touched my hair . . . skimmed his fingers along the curve of my cheek. I thought I'd swoon.

"You're such a pretty little thing," he whispered. "I wish I could take you home with me." Then he was leaning down, pressing his warm, full lips against mine. The kiss was gentle but firm, practiced but somehow surprising. I wrapped my arms around his neck, caressed the taut muscles of his back and his chest. He smelled wonderful—a spicy-sweet scent I couldn't quite identify.

He kissed me harder, more urgently. I felt lost. . . .

I'm kissing a stranger in the middle of the street! I dropped my arms and pulled away.

David wasn't fazed; he just gave me a lazy, sexy smile. "I'll call you soon," he said again and brushed his fingertips lightly against my breasts. My hard nipples were clearly visible through the sheer cotton of my sundress. I felt a slow burn rise in my face.

He quickly got into his car, started it up and put it into gear. "Bye, Gillian."

"Bye, David." I watched his blue convertible turn the corner and drive out of sight.

Over dinner, Mary studied me carefully. "David is certainly an attractive man . . . and he was certainly attracted to you. Are you going to go out with him?"

I shrugged, pretending nonchalance. "I gave him my phone number, but I doubt he'll call. He's a flirt—probably just likes to collect digits."

"Oh, I think he'll call," replied Mary. "And if you do go out with him, be very careful. You're in a vulnerable position right now, and David has a reputation."

"Reputation? What do you mean?"

Mary took a sip of her wine and fiddled with the glass stem. "I've heard gossip, and I see his name sometimes in the tabloids. After all, Wentworth Properties has made him very, very rich. He must be worth tens of millions."

I nearly dropped my fork. "Oh, my god, he's *that* David Wentworth? I never made the connection."

"Yes, he's *that* Wentworth. People say he's ruthless, used to getting what he wants by any means. And I heard that his divorce—I think it was about three years ago—was pretty messy."

"Well, thanks for the warning, Mary. I will be careful. I doubt anything will happen with this guy anyway. He must be used to having gorgeous women throw themselves at him."

"You're not the type to throw yourself at anyone, Gillian. I'm sure that's very appealing to David."

I thought of our passionate kiss in Ken and Jackie's driveway and fought hard to keep an embarrassed blush at bay. Thank God Mary hadn't witnessed that little scene.

That night I lay in bed, unable to sleep, my mind whirling. I thought about calling Anita—meeting David definitely fell into the "major news" category—but it was very late. And for some reason I wanted to keep this stunningly wonderful development to myself for a while.

I tossed and turned in bed for hours. I kept reliving every moment of our meeting—his electric-blue eyes and lazy smile, that unbelievable kiss. My heart was pounding. *Please, God, let him call me. . . . I have to see him again.*

Suddenly Miss Prudence and Miss Hornypants popped into my head. These two voices had first appeared during my adolescence, when my hormones and my good sense were constantly engaged in battle.

"You acted like a complete slut," said Miss Prudence. *"Letting a stranger kiss you and touch your breasts—in public! What were you thinking?"*

"He wasn't a complete stranger," Miss Hornypants pointed out. *"She'd known him a few hours."*

"A few hours!" Miss Prudence was outraged.

"It was just a kiss and a little fondling. It's not like she dropped to her knees and gave him a blow job."

"It was bad enough! He probably thinks she's an easy piece of ass."

"No, he doesn't. He was very attracted to her, and she felt the same way. Why pretend otherwise? They simply acted on their feelings."

"She's going to regret—"

"Oh, both of you leave now!" I demanded.

Once they had disappeared from my mind, I turned my thoughts back to David. What would he be like in bed? I immediately knew the answer: amazing.

I pulled my nightshirt all the way up to my neck. I closed my eyes and massaged my hard nipples, remembering David's fingers brushing gently against them. I imagined his lips and tongue on my breasts, kissing and licking, sucking and teasing . . . and then slowly making a wet trail down my stomach. . . . I imagined the roughness of his cheek against the soft skin of my thighs as he slowly parted them and lapped hungrily at my pussy . . . teasing my clit with the tip of his warm tongue. . . .

I felt an insistent ache growing between my thighs. My breathing quickened. I spread my legs and slowly rubbed my pussy lips together. I was very wet. I slid two fingers inside, imagining David's hard cock pumping into me, and rubbed my clit with my other hand. Within minutes I came intensely, convulsing and stifling a scream.

I didn't know it then, but it was the first of many incredible orgasms David would give me.

GREAT BOOKS,
GREAT SAVINGS!

When You Visit Our Website:
www.kensingtonbooks.com
You Can Save Money Off The Retail Price
Of Any Book You Purchase!

- **All Your Favorite Kensington Authors**
- **New Releases & Timeless Classics**
- **Overnight Shipping Available**
- **eBooks Available For Many Titles**
- **All Major Credit Cards Accepted**

Visit Us Today To Start Saving!
www.kensingtonbooks.com

All Orders Are Subject To Availability.
Shipping and Handling Charges Apply.
Offers and Prices Subject To Change Without Notice